PAUL CONNOLLY's debut novel, *The Fifth Voice*, received glowing reviews, reached the top 10 on Amazon's literary fiction (humour) bestsellers l   dent Book of the Year by   *uring Influence of Ken Potts* is 1

Paul was born in I   larly escapes to his writing   nber of award-winning a ca   and he supports Everton FC.

Find out more at www.paulconnollyauthor.com.

G000088126

Acclaim for *The Fifth Voice*

"A funny, touching and charming tale."
DAVID NOBBS – Bestselling author of *The Fall and Rise of Reginald Perrin*

"I got caught up in the lives of the characters…the more I think about it, the more I want to read it again!"
TIM BROOKE-TAYLOR – *The Goodies, I'm Sorry I Haven't A Clue*

"A charming story, full of memorable characters…a cappella as a metaphor for life!"
DEKE SHARON – *Pitch Perfect, The Sing Off, The House Jacks*

"Debut novelist finds his voice."
LIVERPOOL ECHO

"A poignant and funny novel full of great characters. Connolly tells the story with insight and authority."
BRISTOL POST

"A charming summer novel. Deserves to be a film. It's ready to go."
MALCOLM BRABANT – Special Correspondent, BBC, PBS NewsHour

"Intriguing. I love the idea of The Fifth Voice…a marvellous metaphor for love, something hard to grasp and hang on to, but always worth pursuing."
CHRIS BUDD – Author of *A Bridge of Straw, Manners from Heaven*

"A funny, poignant and thoroughly enjoyable book that I will certainly be recommending. Top stuff."
AUSTEN HUMPHRIES – Film director

"A masterpiece with all the necessary ingredients...a cast of wonderful characters, love and loss, suspense and pure joy."
MICHELE KALLIO – Historical novelist

"An enchanting human study, a compelling musical story."
JOHN PALMER – Musical director

"Connolly certainly knows about music and singing. He also knows how to write a thoroughly entertaining novel."
HELEN HOLLICK – Award-winning historical novelist

"A wonderful comic novel...the writing style is pitch perfect. *The Fifth Voice* is a funny and uplifting book and would make a great mini-series or feel-good film."
MARGARITA MORRIS – Author of *Oranges for Christmas*

The Enduring Influence of Ken Potts

PAUL CONNOLLY

SilverWood

Published in 2019 by SilverWood Books
SilverWood Books Ltd

14 Small Street, Bristol, BS1 1DE, United Kingdom
www.silverwoodbooks.co.uk

ISBN 978-1-78132-867-5 (paperback)
ISBN 978-1-78132-868-2 (ebook)

British Library Cataloguing in Publication Data
A CIP catalogue record for this book is available from the British Library

Page design and typesetting by SilverWood Books
Printed on responsibly sourced paper

Dedicated to The Royal Harmonics

Acknowledgements

Big thanks to Paul Jones for applying his rule of plausibility, to Ceri Stafford for his keen eye, to Sara Taylor for her female perspective, to John Brown for his memories of Pinewood Studios, to friends at home and on Lundy Island for their interest and encouragement, and to my daughter Georgina for her love.

Part One

On The Road Again

One

Old Trouble, New Trouble

A mild wave of nausea rose from the pit of Vince's stomach as he gazed vacantly at the television screen. From his slumped position, he sat upright in his armchair and took a series of deep breaths, and as he did so he noticed something move in his peripheral vision. Glancing downwards, and to his surprise, he saw an ant carrying something across the polished wooden surface of the living room floor – something he instantly recognised as a piece of his own dead skin.

He watched the tiny, shiny black insect holding the blood-spotted flake aloft like one of its rainforest cousins carrying a giant leaf segment back to its subterranean nest. And as the ant made for a gap in the floorboards, Vince flicked it with his slippered foot to prevent it from disappearing out of sight, but that was enough to kill the creature.

He sighed and sank back into the armchair, his dressing gown falling open to reveal two feeble legs, the muscles of the left calf and thigh badly atrophied, the right with only slightly more definition. Vince dragged the edge of the gown to cover his lower half, and wondered since when domestic ants had started behaving like the jungle variety. Or perhaps it was a migrant ant that had arrived from South America in a consignment of bananas and had been forced to improvise its feeding habits? Whatever the explanation, it was weird.

Idly, he scratched a patch of dry skin on his right elbow and felt several scales fall away to reveal a smoother surface beneath. He looked at the floor again and noticed that a pile of skin had collected near the leg of the armchair. 'Oh God,' he said.

Just then he heard the sound of the letterbox opening and closing in the hall and he placed both hands on the arms of the chair, allowing his upper body to take the strain as he hoisted himself to his feet. Taking two steps forward, he stumbled and fell in a heap on the floor.

Angie appeared at the doorway of the living room. 'Forgot your crutches again?'

'Yup. Mind over matter doesn't seem to be working any more, Ange. Give us a hand, will you?'

Angie helped Vince to his feet and fetched the crutches. 'All right, love?'

'A bit pissed off as it goes. Not fair is it? I mean, here I am, East Berkshire's answer to George Clooney, every woman's dream in any other circumstances, and yet my legs behave like a new-born foal's, and ants are beginning to eat me alive.'

'What do you mean, ants eating you alive? Have you been on that stupid Xbox again?'

'No, nothing…doesn't matter,' said Vince.

'Mmm. Anyway, lover boy, you can't use that line any more. It turns out that East Berkshire's answer to George Clooney is actually George Clooney. I read in the Advertiser that he's bought a place in Sonning. And he was spotted in a restaurant in Marlow the other night, so I hear,' said Angie.

'Marlow's Bucks, not Berks. Doesn't count. But it's still very inconsiderate of him, turning up on my manor, don't you think? Sod him, he'll just have to live with the competition.' Vince was now standing with the crutches, looking at his reflection in the mirror above the mantelpiece. He turned his head from side to side, scrutinising the line of his jaw.

'No contest,' said Angie. 'Now get dressed and go and do your leg exercises – and put some cream on that elbow. My shift starts at one. What are you going to do with the rest of the day?

When was the last time you had a quartet rehearsal?'

'A few months, I guess, but it's just not the same without Ken,' said Vince, turning on his crutches to face his fiancée.

'But you all agreed you had to carry on, even without Ken. If anything, *because* of Ken. Wasn't that it?'

'Yes, yes we did. But we've all got stuff to deal with. Danny's got a new nipper, Henry's always off visiting his mystery woman on the island, and Neil's still got his head down with the film stuff. And as you can see, I'm completely fucked. So it doesn't make it easy.'

'But you were all so positive, so excited, winning silver at the British championships, and you were so determined to carry on regardless.'

'*Carry On Up The Khyber*, more like. Or in Neil's case, *Carry On Camping*.'

'Or in your case, *Carry On Matron*,' said Angie, pushing her folded arms up against her ample bosom.

'Ooh-er,' said Vince. 'But listen, we *were* excited and passionate and determined to continue, but without Ken—'

'Stop! What was the last thing Ken told you all?' said Angie, suddenly animated to a degree that took Vince by surprise. He dropped his gaze slightly and allowed Angie to continue.

'He said he knew you'd succeed. Not just as a quartet, but in life…because you found The Fifth Voice,' said Angie. 'The holy grail.'

'*Ken* was our Fifth Voice,' said Vince.

'And that's a beautiful sentiment, a lovely tribute. But you all know it's much more than that. And what would Ken think if you gave up now? Gave up on each other? What sort of a tribute would that be?'

Vince threw one of his crutches onto the sofa and pulled Angie close to him, pressing her face into his chest and breathing in the scent of her freshly washed hair. 'I miss him,' he whispered in her ear.

*

Danny pinched his nose as he flipped open the lid of the pedal bin with his right foot and dropped the dirty nappy. He'd never liked changing Ben's nappies, but he didn't remember them being quite so gruesome to deal with. Ellie lay on the plastic changing mat, arms and legs flailing, bright blue eyes looking intently at the soft toy mobile above her head, a smile of relief breaking out across her soft round face. No, this wasn't Danny's favourite chore, but it was all about sharing the burden wasn't it? In which case, why had he changed every nappy for about a week now?

It was just before noon, the late winter sun was bright and the sky cloudless for once, and the day cried out to be seen at close quarters. And yet Hannah was lying down again, and Ben was playing on his iPad, not a care between them that the first fine day for weeks was calling for their attention. Danny pressed together the fasteners on Ellie's bright pink babygrow and admired his handiwork. The face of Peppa Pig stared sideways at him with grudging approval.

Danny carried Ellie to the living room and lowered her gently into a bouncing baby contraption, from where she could observe her brother tapping and swiping at the tablet that seemed to occupy most of his time these days. 'Ben, keep an eye on her, will you? Put your iPad down and play nicely with her while I go talk to Mummy, there's a good lad,' said Danny, checking the straps on the baby bouncer.

Treading softly up the stairs, Danny stopped halfway to listen. Below, Ben was talking to his sister, who was gurgling back. Good lad. Above, a gentle weeping sound was coming from the main bedroom. *Oh God, not again.*

The bedroom door was closed, and Danny eased it open without a sound. 'Love, it's a beautiful day out there,' he whispered. He slid into the darkened room, the only light coming from a gap between curtains that had been dragged together carelessly. A bright beam of light slanted its way across the room, illuminating an expanse of carpet where a dress and shoes had been dropped, cutting a broad diagonal stripe across the bed and across Hannah's bare legs, and casting a small square onto the wall above a bedside table beyond. Dust particles hung in the air, caught in the light's path. The air smelt faintly of milk and alcohol, immediately bringing the Dr. Feelgood song into Danny's head. He approached the bed.

'Love, what's wrong? Come on, stop it now. It's a beautiful day. Let me just open the cur—'

'Leave them!' said Hannah. 'Leave me alone, I'm too tired.' She sniffed, confirming that she had been crying.

Danny sat down softly next to his wife. He moved his right arm towards her instinctively, but held back from touching, his hand hovering over her upper back. 'Don't!' Hannah shouted into the pillow, her voice heavily muffled but clear in its intent. Danny removed his arm and stood up, his eyes following the line of light that traversed the bed and hit the far wall, partially illuminating the small table on his side. He could make out the shapes of a paperback book, a cylindrical glasses case, and a small square of something that hadn't been there earlier. He walked around the side of the bed and picked up a piece of A4 paper that had been folded in half twice. Written in red crayon (or was it lipstick?) were the words WHY ME?

Vince left a voice message.

'Mate, how are you doing? Listen, I know I've been preoccupied with my health recently, but sod all that. I'm totally ready to start singing again. We need to crack on, Danny Boy. Give me a call back when you get a mo.'

Danny played the message and deleted it.

Two days passed. Vince left another message.

'Everything all right, Dan? Or are you ignoring me? I know you've got your hands full with the family, but pick up the phone, mate. We need to get the show on the road again.'

Danny was frozen in a now familiar pattern. Hannah was in bed and the kids were parked in front of the TV for a couple of hours. He couldn't stay away from work for much longer, or he wouldn't have a job for much longer. Bowman-Lamy were good to him, but he sensed they would need to draw a line sometime soon.

He checked on the kids. Ellie had dozed off and Ben had abandoned *Bananas in Pyjamas* in favour of a DVD recording of Everton vs Watford in the 1984 FA Cup Final.

Ascending the stairs two at a time, Danny crossed the narrow landing, opened the bedroom door firmly, kicked several items of discarded clothing to one side, walked to the window and yanked the curtains apart, allowing light to flood the room. He stood calmly at the side of the bed, awaiting his wife's response. It came quickly. Hannah sat upright, pushed the duvet to one side, got to her feet and smacked her husband across the face with a force that took his breath away.

Danny felt the blood drain from his legs and he was suddenly weak with the shock. He stared wide-eyed at his wife as she climbed back under the duvet.

'Ellie will need feeding when she wakes,' Danny said at last, and left the room. He didn't hear Hannah mumble the words 'I'm sorry' and 'I don't know what to do' into the pillow as he made his way downstairs.

Checking on the kids again, he told Ben that he'd take them to the park soon. 'Graeme Sharp just scored, Dad. One-nil Everton. Ellie's still asleep. When's Mummy getting up?' said Ben.

'Soon, son.'

'Lots of soons,' said Ben.

'I know. I'll be in the kitchen.'

Danny mixed up a batch of formula just in case, then unplugged his mobile phone from the charger next to the kettle. The message on the screen told him Vince had called again, but there was no voice message this time. Danny opened the address book, scrolled down to D, and found *Denise Counsellor*.

A secretary answered the phone and, after a little persuading, agreed to put Danny through. 'You're in luck. She's between appointments. Just a moment.'

Denise listened as Danny reminded her that he and Hannah had been to see her previously for relationship counselling, and then he explained about Hannah. 'Can you help us?'

'I see,' said Denise. 'But postnatal depression isn't really my speciality. Have you been to your GP for a referral?'

'She won't listen to me,' said Danny, pressing his free hand against his forehead.

'Is Hannah getting any help from her mother? I seem to recall they're close.'

'Hannah said she doesn't want to see anyone. I've been making excuses when Dorothy calls,' said Danny. 'I know it's crazy, but—'

'I would call her, Danny. Start there. Then see your GP. Listen, I've got to go, but let me know how you get on. I wish you well. Bye now.' And Denise rung off.

Danny put his head around the living room door. 'Just two calls to make, Ben. Then we'll feed Ellie and get moving.'

'Two-nil,' said Ben. 'Andy Gray.'

Danny phoned Dorothy and apologized that he'd put her off from coming to see Hannah and the kids. 'Hannah has been in bed for the best part of a week, Dot. She's not right. I think she needs you.' Dorothy said she'd be there in half an hour.

Danny then phoned Vince, skipping any introductory formalities. 'Sorry, mate. Listen, things have gone pear-shaped here. As soon as I get a chance I'll give you a shout and we'll get together. I haven't heard a pitch pipe, haven't sung a line, in weeks. I really could do with some harmony in my life right now.'

Two

A Teaser or Two

Snowdrops and daffodils were scattered left and right, the sun was bright, the air crisp, and the seventeenth fairway was as smooth as a billiard table. Henry was reflecting on winning a British silver medal and on finding a new woman in his life, but saying nothing. He was one up with two to play.

Henry had known George Taylor for twenty years, and so it seemed like one of life's stranger twists of fate when Henry had discovered that Neil, the baritone in his quartet, was George's son. The two of them went way back, to when Henry was a rookie trader in the City and George was the senior guy who took him under his wing and taught him everything. This was the first time Henry had seen George since the quartet's success some months earlier, and the first time they'd played golf together in – neither of them could remember how long.

George struck his tee shot cleanly enough, then watched as his ball veered left and out of sight. 'Ouch,' he said. 'Swing's letting me down.'

'You're too hard on yourself,' said Henry, placing his ball. 'You've kept pace all the way. Not bad for an old fella, George.' Henry sent his ball on an almost identical trajectory to George's. 'I think the wind's picking up,' he said, and they set off up the fairway.

The conversation of the first sixteen holes had been undemanding, perfunctory stuff. The Rotary Club, the City, and vintage reds all featured. Now Henry wanted to ask George about Neil, but was aware that he might be stepping on thin ice. He wasn't sure if relations between father and son were still strained or if the two had made up once and for all.

'I haven't seen much of Neil lately,' said Henry. An easy opener.

'That makes two of us. Things are hotting up at Yellow Braces, it seems. He's up in town most of the time, meetings with Mr. Burns and the team, putting the finishing touches to what I believe they call *pre-production* before they start filming. It's all a bit beyond me, Henry.'

Henry cleared his throat. 'Last time we spoke at any length – the Rotary it was – you and Neil were, how can I put it…still not seeing eye to eye?'

George approached his ball at the edge of the fairway. 'Not too bad a lie. I thought I was well into the long stuff,' he said, taking a seven iron from his bag and wasting no time in sending the ball heavenwards. 'I don't find it an easy matter to discuss, Henry, but I don't mind admitting I was an obstinate old fool for too many years. Margaret made me see that. Neil's making his way now. Working on a big feature film, A-listers and everything. Can you believe it? And when I heard him sing with your quartet, that was a real eye-opener…a bit of a turning point.' George lifted his visor and wiped his brow. 'What can I say? You boys can actually sing. That's what really surprised me!' He gave Henry a sideways glance and just the hint of a smile.

'You're too kind,' said Henry, contorting himself beneath a low oak branch and taking a shallow grip on his pitching wedge. 'Best I can do is hack this one out, I'm afraid. Advantage Taylor.'

'Part of me still wishes he'd find a young lady, mind you,' said George.

'Well, that's not going to happen, is it? I mean—'

'You think I disapprove of Neil's sexuality, don't you?

Believe it or not, I never judged him on that score. People always misunderstood me there. Why do people jump to the wrong conclusions, Henry?'

'Well, you've always given the impression that you disapproved,' said Henry. 'But if you're okay with the way he is, why are you still wishing he'll find a girlfriend? Doesn't make sense.'

'Maybe not,' said George, lofting his ball exquisitely onto the green, landing it within a foot of the pin. 'But can't you see why it plays on my mind a little?'

Henry removed his cap and scratched the shining, chestnut-coloured dome of his head. 'No. Indulge me, George.'

'I've got a better idea. Now, I'm going to level this hole. All square, one to play. If I win the eighteenth, I'll tell you why. If you win, or we level it, you'll have to work it out for yourself. And let's have a tenner on the last hole to add a little more interest.'

Fifteen minutes later, Henry shook George's hand and reluctantly celebrated a one-shot victory. George slid a ten pound note from a money clip and handed it to Henry. 'Well done, and on to the nineteenth. Your round.'

'So, you're not going to tell me, then?'

George gave Henry a wry look. 'Just get the drinks in.'

For some time now, Henry knew that his life was at a crossroads and that he had to pick a direction. When he thought back over the last year or two, the phrase *you couldn't write the script* was the one that came most readily to mind. From a starting point of conventional suburban married life and a top job in the City, here he was, having lost his job and divorced his wife, contemplating a future with the most enigmatic woman he had ever met, who happened to live on a beautiful remote island. And along the way he had somehow managed to win a British silver medal for barbershop singing with his quartet pals Neil, Vince, and Danny, under the guidance of a wonderful, eccentric, and now sadly departed, mentor.

He had not spoken much of what had been happening in his life, especially as it related to Cat and the island. Not even his three singing pals knew much beyond the fact that he had found someone while holidaying on an island in the South West and that he seemed all the happier for it. Henry had imagined that he might confide in George that day on the golf course, but their conversation turned to Neil instead and the relationship between father and son. George was in a much better place now, much more accepting of Neil, and pride in his son's achievements was evident. However, Henry still couldn't work out why George was so hung up on Neil finding a girlfriend, despite his being gay. That was just plain odd.

So, here he was, wondering what next. He knew he needed to plan his next trip to the island. He had only ever visited Cat, never the other way round, and that suited them both. As the island nature warden, Cat found it difficult to get away and openly admitted that the mainland wasn't her thing. But it ran much deeper than that. Cat was *connected* to the island in a very special way. She could touch the granite rock and connect with the past. She could locate ancient artefacts by feeling the energy they emitted, and she was prized for her abilities by naturalists, archaeologists and anthropologists alike. Henry also suspected that Cat's instincts, powers, or whatever it was that she possessed, were of much interest to organisations of a slightly less conventional, more mystical, bent.

For Henry's part, he was more than happy to visit the island as often as possible, having fallen under its spell. He could think of nowhere else like it and revelled in being away from the chaos of the mainland, there being no roads, cars, TV, newspapers or internet on the island. And the generator went off at midnight, so early nights were guaranteed. He immersed himself in the life of the island, and he loved the wide open spaces, the vast starry skies, the relentless force of the sea, and the beauty and diversity of the wildlife.

His and Cat's relationship was an unconventional one.

They followed their own paths, time passed, and then they came together again. They barely communicated in between: the odd text message, the occasional phone call. Texts often arrived a day late, and phone connections were unreliable. It didn't seem important to talk when they weren't together, and that didn't diminish their relationship. If anything, it enhanced it. Each carried a gift as a reminder of the other. Cat had given Henry a small granite stone flecked with grey, white and orange crystalline patterns. It was a part of the island, a talisman. And Henry had given Cat his pitch pipe, which she kept in a secret pocket.

Was he happy? More than he had been for a long time. At the moment all he wanted to do with his life was visit Cat and the island and pursue his singing ambitions with the quartet, but something was bugging him. It was no good. He had to admit it: he was bored.

He looked around his small rented flat with its oddly shaped rooms (the result of a sub-standard conversion), its sparse decoration, and the complete lack of anything that made it feel like home. He couldn't help thinking that barely two miles away Jenny was tucked up in the considerable comfort of the substantial Georgian home they had shared for twelve years. It was about time she sold up and released his share of the equity, he thought, and it crossed his mind that he should raise the matter with his ex-wife as soon as he could muster the energy.

The phone rang. It was Jenny.

'Jenny… I was just—'

'Thinking of me, Henry?'

'Not exactly,' said Henry. 'How may I be of assistance?'

'You sound like a butler, Henry.'

'Not much chance of a finding a butler in this place. Or a cat to swing, come to that. How's life at Warrington Manor?'

'Don't worry, Henry, you'll get your share. It's just taking a little time to go through. We agreed everything, so I don't know why you're—'

'I'm not,' said Henry. 'Are you still seeing Jeffrey Moss?'

'Not that it's any of your business, Henry, but no.'

'Prick.'

'Yes, he did have one, as I recall. Actually, how could I forget?' said Jenny.

'You're well out of it. The last time I saw him he had some other poor cow in tow. That was the day I pushed an ice cream cone into the middle of his obnoxious face.'

'How very mature,' said Jenny.

'Anyway, the purpose of your call is?'

'To remind you that the annual golf club ball is not far off, and to ask if you would consider making a charitable donation. And to see if you'd like to join me and a few of the organisers for drinks. A little soirée here on the second of March.'

'Hang on, let me have a look.' Henry consulted an imaginary diary. 'Ah, no can do, I'm afraid. No problem with a donation though. Remind me nearer the time.'

'Okay. Well, if your plans change, you can always pop round on the night. That's all. Keep well, Henry. Bye for now.'

So much for the blissful recollections of earlier. Trust Jenny to spoil the mood. Henry got up from his chair and accidentally kicked the leg of a small wooden coffee table, causing him to jump in the air and head butt the rim of an aluminium pendant lampshade. He threw himself onto the sofa, clutching his head with one hand, his bare foot with the other, and swearing profusely.

The phone rang again and he grabbed the handset.

'Jenny, what the—'

'I'm sorry, sir, but is this Henry Warrington?'

'Ah, yes, I thought it was...well, yes, speaking.'

'Excellent. I was hoping to catch you. This is Anthony Goulding of Myers-Swann, the executive recruitment firm. Can you speak?'

'No. Well, maybe...I have a few minutes, yes,' said Henry, squeezing his big toe.

'Excellent. I'll keep it brief, Mr. Warrington. I have been engaged by a leading finance house to fill a senior trading position in their Commodities division, and I believe that you may fit the bill exactly. High six-figure basic, a generous bonus package, plus all the usual add-ons. Is that something that could potentially be of interest?'

Oh no. An invitation to rejoin the rat race. The risks, the pressure, the stress.

'Potentially,' said Henry, rubbing his forehead.

'Excellent,' said Anthony Goulding for the third time.

Three

A Cappella Fellas

Newton Burns, entertainer, bon viveur and national treasure, twisted a long strand of white hair around the end of a gold fountain pen as he perused the file in front of him. It made for happy reading. Pre-production for *A Cappella Fellas*, his latest project, and surely the one dearest to his heart, was nearing completion and the signs were good. Financial backing sound, script fine-tuned, score in the bag, casting complete. He couldn't remember a time when his film production company, Yellow Braces, was such a fun ship to steer.

Around the elegant rosewood table were the director, one of the financiers, the screenwriter, the composer, the musical arranger, and the head of casting. 'Looking good, team,' said Newton Burns, removing the lid of his pen and signing his name on several sheets of paper. 'Lorna, let's start with you.'

The head of casting, a slight, sharp-dressed woman in her early thirties, peered through a thick fringe of auburn hair, parted her gloss-red lips, and took a sip of mint tea. 'Frampton's been a royal pain, but we finally pinned him down two days ago. Everything else is in place. Pellegrini, Rossi, Fontaine, Bannerman. Pretty much the A-team.'

'Rossi still doing the prima donna act?' asked Newton Burns.

'Most of her requests have been the usual. She has our assurance that both her limousine and the interior of her trailer will be Barbie pink, for example. But some of her other demands have been, shall we say, slightly more extreme, and I've had to play a little hard ball with her agent. Nothing I can't handle.'

'Good, good. Any other points of interest? Anything Mac should be wary of?'

'Nothing he doesn't already know. Mac, you've worked with them all, haven't you?' said Lorna.

The director, gaunt and grizzled-looking, with a beard that covered over half of his face, removed a piece of nicotine chewing gum from his mouth, and started coughing loudly. 'Excuse me, no smoking Day Three and it's killing me. Well, yes. Rossi can be difficult, as you say, but nothing a bit of flattery and regular late-night visits from the local beefcake won't take care of. Joey Pellegrini will be doing the visits, you understand, not me.'

'You don't say?' said Lorna.

'That's harsh,' said Mac, sandwiching his chewing gum between two Post-It notes. 'Joey's harmless enough. And I've got nothing but admiration for Fontaine and Bannerman. Consummate pros, can't do enough for you. Frampton's still a loose cannon, though. Half a bottle of JD before every session, and that includes the early morning shoots.'

'Total box office, though,' said Newton Burns.

'Total basket case,' said Mac. 'He nearly killed the dolly last time I worked with him. The guy could start a fight in an empty room. Correction…he *did* start a fight in an empty room. I seem to recall him trashing his trailer on the set of *Woebegone* when he couldn't find the JD. Trailer trash, literally. The guy's a liability, but I dare say I can cope.'

'That's why we're paying you the big bucks,' said the financier.

'You're too kind,' said Mac. 'But then four box office number ones in a row, each with a worldwide gross profit of at least three hundred per cent, might have a little to do with it, hey Ed?'

'Actually, we lobbied for Weinstock, but he was booked solid for the next five years. You're certainly a good second to Weinstock, though,' said Ed, with his best poker face.

'Mee-ow,' said Newton Burns. 'So, Ed, anything of a more constructive nature to add?'

'We're happy enough that we'll get the return we're looking for. As we've said from the start, the timing is right for this type of project. Off the back of the *Glee* wave, and with the *Pitch Perfect* vehicle in top gear, not to mention the *Sing-Off* effect and the *X Factor* bandwagon, we're sure we're on safe ground,' said the financier.

'You forgot to mention anything about merry-go-rounds and rollercoasters,' said Mac, smoothing the edge of his beard, just below his eyeline. 'I mean, you barely scratched the surface of the cliché iceberg there.'

'Tsh tsh,' said Newton Burns. 'Let's not go upsetting the moneymen, Mac. The package Ed and his team have put together is first rate, and we're thrilled they're with us on this one. I would just challenge you on one thing, though, Ed.'

The financier, a picture of business-casual perfection in his pale blue Oxford button-down, draped at the shoulders with a tan cashmere sweater, shifted slightly in his seat. 'Yes, Newt, what's that?'

'Well, it's just that you make *A Cappella Fellas* sound a bit *me-too*, and I don't see it that way. From the moment I picked up Eric's initial script, I knew we had a winner on our hands, but not for the reasons you suggest. I agree that the timing's spot on, but we're not just tapping into some sort of zeitgeist here. I think we have something very special indeed...one of those once in a decade projects.'

'I sure hope you're right,' said Ed, allowing his sweater to fall from his shoulders as he reached to pour himself a glass of water. 'I was simply ballparking why I think we have a banker here, but if you're confident we're on our way to *Kerching!* City, Arizona, then who am I to argue? Out of interest, though, what gives you such confidence?'

'Did he say "*Kerching!* City, Arizona?"' said Mac, shaking his head.

'Two things,' said Newt. 'Gut feeling. And Ken Potts.'

'Gut feeling is good but, for the purposes of financial forecasting, we have to overlook your gut,' said Ed.

'That's easier said than done,' said Mac, nodding towards Newt. 'Without his gut, he wouldn't need those yellow braces, and without his yellow braces, we wouldn't have Yellow Braces, and none of us would be here.'

'You scoundrel, Mac,' said Newt, patting his over-sized midriff. 'All bought and paid for, I think you'll find.'

Ed frowned. 'Look, all I was trying to say is that the industry's littered with the remains of projects that started out as someone's gut feeling and ended up as turkey entrails.'

'*Really?*' said Mac.

'Yes, really. But, as I say, we're not relying on Newt's gut feeling. The backers are already confident we have a solid performance platform in place, and I'm sure they'll be delighted to know why Newt thinks we can hit it out of the park with this one. Let's leave Newt's gut for now. What I'd like to know is, what's Harry Potter got to do with it?'

'Ken Potts,' said Newt. 'A dearly departed friend and confidant, someone I sang with and spent many happy hours with. A genius of a man, the most talented musician, the craziest storyteller, a man of instinct and wisdom, someone who called it right every time. And yet a modest and humble man who shunned the limelight. That's why you could trust him.'

'So, how does this dead guy feature in the general scheme of things?' said Ed.

'In three ways,' said Newt. 'First, I consulted him on the project very early on. He gave it his blessing, even suggested improvements to the script.' Newt nodded in Eric's direction. 'Second, he recommended Neil there, and I don't know about you, but I think he's done a magnificent job arranging Joel's songs. Third, I have a feeling he's up there somewhere keeping an eye on things.'

'He is,' said Neil.

An uneasy silence followed. Ed poured another glass of water. Lorna sipped her mint tea. Mac popped a pellet of nicotine gum from its foil sachet.

'That's very touching,' said Ed at last, 'but I can't go back to the team with that story, can I? They'll get the jitters if I start talking about gut feelings and ghosts. C'mon guys, give me a break.'

Newt stood up and snapped his braces with this thumbs. 'Perhaps it would be unwise to report back along those lines, I agree. But I can't deny what I feel. By all means stick to the facts and figures. I would, in your shoes. I'm not asking you to believe in ghosts any more than I would expect you to admire my gut, Ed. I'm simply telling you why I feel especially good about the project.'

'Okay, okay. I'm not going to rock the boat back at base camp,' said Ed. 'I won't mention the ghost of Harry Potter, but if he manages to work some of his magic from the afterlife, then so much the better.'

'*Ken Potts!*' said Neil. 'His name is Ken Potts.'

'Neil is one of Ken's protégés,' said Newton Burns. 'At which point, perhaps we should turn to the music men. Joel? Neil?'

'If I may...' said Neil, removing his glasses and sweeping a hand through his unruly mane of black hair. 'I think there's a lot in what Newt says. Ken's influence shouldn't be dismissed. He was a wonderful coach and mentor to my quartet. He taught us an enormous amount, but he taught us one thing more than any other, and that's the power of belief. And...well, I'm not sure how to say this, but...well, it's just that...'

'Yes?' said Ed.

'Well, you see, I received a letter from him this morning,' said Neil.

Four

The Question of the Letter

After Angie's pep talk, Vince seemed to find a remarkable source of energy from somewhere. He started working on his leg muscles as much as was possible, though he knew he was fighting an uphill battle with his MS now well into the progressive stage. He willed his legs to work to the point where he could again walk moderate distances with the aid of a stick instead of crutches.

The incident with the ant, as bizarre as it was, had shocked him into seeing how he had been allowing himself to fall apart. The act of sweeping away his own dead skin that day seemed to take on a special significance. Never had a dustpan and brush been put to such good use.

So Vince determined to take control of his health again to the extent that he could, and that included not just physical exercise and nourishment, but the kind of sustenance his spirit was crying out for. He hadn't sung for months, and it was crippling him every bit as much as the degenerative illness that was hacking away at his central nervous system.

The quartet, having celebrated their silver medal success, and even having vowed to continue, had entered a state of hibernation, and Vince sensed that the time was close when they would make a decision to wake up or sleep forever.

Danny eventually returned his calls, and he sounded keen, but he seemed trapped by his personal circumstances. Vince never knew what Henry was up to, and Neil had made it clear that his work with Yellow Braces allowed him no time for anything else at the present time.

But then, out of the blue, Neil called.

Hannah was suffering, Danny understood that much. He hated watching his wife descend into regular, dark bouts of depression. When her mood lifted for a while, she was mostly fine with Ben, but less so with Ellie, and it was breaking Danny's heart. He didn't take the slap or the various verbal assaults personally, but he couldn't envisage putting up with much more of it.

His call to Denise felt like a cry in the dark, but it was the right thing to do. Dorothy's arrival improved things, helping break the dreadful pattern of their days. She took control, gently but firmly, and Hannah seemed to respond to her, though the effects dissipated quickly when Dorothy returned home. Hannah glowered at Danny with contempt much of the time, and her attitude towards him was erratic and difficult to predict. But then, just occasionally, her expression softened to a look that sought understanding. At its worst, Hannah's brooding resentment permeated the entire house like a haunting.

For their part, the kids' behaviour ebbed and flowed according to the situation. Was Ellie too young to pick up on what was going on? Though he hoped so, Danny doubted it. Babies are so instinctive. Ben showed a maturity that defied his years. He knew when to speak, when to attend to his sister, when to play up to Hannah, and when to back off. He made Danny proud.

Things gradually got better, Hannah reluctantly agreeing to see her GP and then a specialist in postnatal depression. Then, one Saturday morning, Hannah awoke early, drew back the bedroom curtains, opened the window wide, and went to make breakfast for them all. At the breakfast table, she announced that she was feeling a lot better and suggested a family outing to the river. Ellie giggled instinctively. Ben went in search of his

Everton shirt and his football. Danny couldn't remember when he'd enjoyed eggs and bacon quite so much.

That afternoon Danny received a call from Neil.

Henry had far fewer dilemmas to deal with. He was happy and looking forward to his next adventure with Cat on the island. He was also so bored right now that, to his own amazement, he was contemplating a return to the City.

Neil's call came not a moment too soon.

Neil read aloud:

Gentlemen,

I thought I should speak to you again, contingent upon certain circumstances arising. I hope you don't have to read this, but if, according to the conditions explained to my dear wife, you do, then what follows is my final piece of advice, and my sincerest wish.

It is now some months since you competed at the British quartet championships, and congratulations on your performance. I am proud that together you found The Fifth Voice that helped deliver that success, but as yet you have been unable to harness its real power.

You all have changed lives and new challenges. I can guess at most of what you're experiencing. I knew you well. You know your own priorities, and your own limitations, and you are faced with difficult decisions. Allow me to suggest that not singing together isn't one of them.

How can I dare be so prescriptive with your lives? Because I know the power of The Fifth Voice, and because I know what could lie ahead.

Travel well,

Ken

They were sitting around a restaurant table, and a silence descended on the group. A pale-looking wine waiter with a thin black moustache and a shirt collar at least two sizes too big sensed an opportunity and moved in to refill their glasses. Henry was leaning backwards in his chair stroking his shining head with both hands. Vince and Danny looked at each other with the same quizzical expression.

'What do we think?' asked Neil at last.

'Refreshingly citrus with a tongue-spanking edge,' said Vince, holding his glass aloft.

'Good to see you're back on form,' said Neil.

'Well, okay,' said Henry. 'In summary, Ken wrote us another letter before he died, which Bella was under instruction to send to Neil, but only if certain circumstances came about. He hints at challenges in our personal lives, and seems to be worried that we'll decide to quit as a quartet. And then there's a promise of something if we carry on.'

'In a nutshell,' said Neil. 'That might explain the phone calls from Bella. She calls me every now and then to ask how we're doing, how the singing's coming along. She even called on New Year's Day with best wishes.'

'You think she was checking up on us? Is that what you're saying?' said Danny.

'It's always lovely to hear from her, but it makes you think.'

'I'm struggling to know what to think,' said Danny. 'On one level it sounds mysterious, and yet it's quite straightforward. For some reason he's appealing to us – compelling us, even – to carry on. Why would he do that?'

'Can I just ask?' said Henry, 'Were we planning to carry on, or not? I certainly had no intention of quitting.'

'For a while, I honestly didn't think I could carry on. Physically, I mean,' said Vince. 'And Neil, you've made it clear throughout that you're just too busy with work. And Danny, well, you said you were up to your ears with family…well, family matters. As I see it, none of us had any intention of quitting, but three of us just haven't been able to find the time, or energy, or whatever. Life getting in the way, simple as that.'

'Quite, but do you think Ken had something else planned for us before he died? And if so, why wouldn't his letter just tell us directly what it was?' said Neil.

'I don't think that's what I ordered,' said Vince, as a small plate appeared in front of him. 'It's barely a mouthful.'

'That's exactly what it is,' said Neil. *'Amuse-bouche.* A little something extra from the chef.'

'All this fancy dining in London is turning you into a man of some sophistication,' said Vince, prodding the contents of the plate into his mouth and continuing to talk.

'Incomprehensible. All I can hear are food noises,' said Neil. 'Would you care to repeat that last bit?'

Vince swallowed and took a glug of wine. 'Well, I was just wondering if Ken might have, well, you know…lost his marbles… towards the end.'

'No, I think we can dismiss that thought,' said Neil. 'That's a very lucid message. There's a keen mind at work there. He chose his words carefully. It's the bit about The Fifth Voice that's intriguing.'

'Well, it's always been a bit of a puzzle, hasn't it?' said Henry. 'Cracking the vocal technique and being able to ring chords properly was a fantastic breakthrough. But when Ken told us that we'd found The Fifth Voice at last, we all knew he meant something a lot more than that.'

'Ken was definitely helping us to achieve something a lot bigger than just the vocal stuff,' said Neil. 'I took it to mean that we became like brothers. And we are – albeit slightly distant brothers recently. And now, Ken's telling us there's still more to come.'

'A riddle, wrapped in a mystery, inside an enigma,' said Henry, his voice more hushed, as though for dramatic effect.

'October 1939, on the question of Russia. Very good. I've missed your Churchill quotes,' said Vince. 'But I need some food if we're going to start stretching the little grey cells. Something like a sausage, wrapped in bacon, inside some pastry would do the trick. It's about time the starters arrived, isn't it?'

No-one could deny Vince's quick-wittedness, and there were laughs all round. And the meal progressed along similar lines, the four friends trading quips and anecdotes as they enjoyed the splendid food and wine. The conversation also ranged across a wide span of musical trivia – from the best way to remember the circle of fifths, courtesy of Neil, to the circumference of Beyoncé's backside, courtesy of Vince.

At last, over the cheeseboard, it was Danny who brought the subject back to Ken and the letter. 'We didn't really come to any conclusions, did we?' he said. 'Can we really know what Ken meant by it? The business of wanting us to carry on as a quartet is easy enough, but why the power of The Fifth Voice stuff? Neil, can you shed any more light on it?'

'Well, I don't know any more than you guys,' he said, pointing to the letter, which was still lying in the middle of the table. 'But you might find this interesting…we're not the only ones contemplating Ken's ability to exert his influence from beyond the grave.'

'Meaning?'

'Well, it turns out that Ken had something to do with the film I'm working on. Newt consulted him on the script early on and, now that the project's going so well, Newt is convinced that Ken's up there somewhere, keeping an eye on things. Coincidentally, he said so on the same day I received the letter.'

'*Really?*' said Henry.

'Bloody Nora,' said Vince.

'Okay, that clinches it,' said Danny. 'We don't know exactly what Ken meant, but does it matter? Surely the only thing we need to decide is what happens next. Are we starting up as a quartet again or not? If not, then it's all a bit academic, but if we take Ken's advice, then at least we'll stand a chance of finding out what he meant. Of course we've got other things going on in our lives that would be easy to use as an excuse, but that's always going to be the case. Family, health, work, love life – it's all still going to be there whatever happens. But if we ditch the one special thing we all share, we'll be copping out.'

'Perfect,' said Henry, sniffing at a glass of late-bottled vintage port. 'Are we all agreed that the team's back together then?'

Neil extended his arm into the middle of the table and their glasses chimed in four-part harmony.

Five

Ever So Slightly Taken for Granted

Angie was bottling up behind the bar at The Ship. Tuesday morning, the quietest shift of the week. Even Mondays, after the chaos of the weekend, were busier, with the drays delivering and the 'sick notes' arriving – the handful of locals for whom the only cure for two days of alcoholic excess was a further day of slightly more measured intake. It was eleven-twenty. She had already cleaned the brasses, filled the optics, set out the lunch menus, cutlery and napkins, and changed the blue roller hand towels in both the Ladies and the Gents. And still not a customer in sight. Except for old Eddie in the corner, but that didn't count.

At eleven-thirty, the barroom door swung open and Vince walked in on his stick.

'What the hell are you doing here?' said Angie from across the bar.

Vince was stumped. 'Ah. Hello, love,' he said at last.

'Carry on,' said Angie, her arms now folded across her chest.

'Well, I was on my way to the chemist. Thought I'd try the scenic route as part of stepping up the exercise, and it seemed rude not to stop by and say hello...'

'Bullshit,' said Angie. 'You thought I was at the care home this morning, didn't you? Same as last week? Well my shift patterns have changed. Sorry, forgot to mention. Oh, and the taxi that dropped you off has just left the car park. Stepping up the exercise are we?'

Vince looked momentarily abashed, but then flashed one of his cheekiest grins. 'Just the one, Ange,' he said. 'I'll have just the one pint and I'll keep you company.'

'So, that's about three minutes' worth of company, then.'

'Harsh.'

'Fair. It's Tuesday bloody morning, Vince.'

'You're right. Okay, fair enough. I'll be off to the chemist then.' And with that, Vince went on his way.

Angie returned to bottling up.

Since moving in together, she and Vince had settled into a happy enough co-existence, something she had once believed would never happen. For years they lived in separate flats, each doing their own thing, then coming together as it suited them, or more usually as it suited Vince. Not on the same scale as Henry and his long-distance love on the remote island that Vince had mentioned, but far from the kind of commitment Angie thought was only reasonable to expect.

It was at the time of Vince's last but one health setback, when he discovered that his MS was progressive, that the seriousness of his situation had really hit home, and one of the outcomes was that he relented over sharing a place. And on that fateful Sunday afternoon in Ward 12 of St. Luke's, after his collapse, he first said the words *I love you*, and she knew that he was both genuine and afraid.

To most observers, they were devoted to each other. And yet Vince still managed to maintain something of a playboy image, his undoubted good looks still capable of drawing the attention of women of all ages. People often remarked on his similarity to George Clooney, though no-one more often than Vince himself.

And boy, did he like a drink. That didn't help matters, health or otherwise. To be fair to him, he did rein it back when he decided to make a major effort, which is why she was disappointed to see him pop his head round the pub door just now. His most recent setback, quite possibly the worst so far, had hit him like a wrecking ball. Both legs went this time, and he feared the worst. She did all she could to support him and encourage him to pick himself up. And how often had she literally picked him up over the last few weeks?

He'd ended up feeling pretty sorry for himself for a while, but he'd come back fighting. That was the thing about Vince: he wouldn't let life drag him down for long. And in a way, his turning up at the pub just now was one of the signs that his spirits were close to being fully restored. The old devil.

No, Vince wasn't perfect, but how hard would it be to find another guy quite as good? He was good at his job, when health allowed, and always good with people. He could charm the birds from the trees. And he could sing. Yes, he could sing all right. It was his singing that wooed her in the first place, back in her glamour model days, back when her boobs were all over the tabloids and paid the bills nicely. But while Vince had been impressed by Angie's popularity at the time, not to mention her ample assets, he had looked beyond all of that from the start. He had a way of making her feel good about herself, and that was worth a lot.

When she gave up the glamour game a few years back, it came as a relief. Not only had she grown tired of being seen as little more than a pair of breasts, she also felt the need to do something more rewarding, which was caring for people. And with part-time jobs as a nursery assistant, a carer in an old folk's home, and barmaid at The Ship, she wasn't short of experience. Add to that looking after Vince, and it was safe to say that she couldn't care more. There weren't that many hours left in the day. All of which left her with a sense of fulfilment, but she was knackered most of the time, and she couldn't help feeling ever so slightly taken for granted.

Angie finished bottling up, checked again for any customers, and caught old Eddie's eye over in the corner. A slight lift of his head meant he was ready for a refill, and she took him over a pint of mild. *Ever so slightly taken for granted.*

Back behind the bar, she reached into a pocket and took out

an unopened letter. She had fished it out from amongst the bills, flyers and charity appeals on the doormat as she'd left the house, and was intrigued by its form of address: *Ms. Angela Long.*

She ripped open the envelope and took out the letter. It was an invitation to a charity event at the Dorchester Hotel to mark the tenth anniversary of the closure of *Finesse* glamour magazine, for whom Angie had once modelled – red carpet reception, photo shoot, followed by a gala dinner.

Angie returned the letter to her pocket, and let out a loud and sudden laugh.

'Eh, what?' said old Eddie in the corner. Which was as many words as he had uttered all morning.

Six

A Storm Brewing

Over breakfast that morning, with Hannah back to something approaching normal, Danny had felt like a weight had been lifted not just from his own shoulders but from the whole house, like a ghost had been exorcised. Their outing to the river had proved a success, Ben kicking his football around with unbridled freedom, and Ellie smiling and flapping her arms, lying in the shade of an old oak, while people sauntered by in light-hearted conversation, walking their dogs, or enjoying ice cream. In the background the steady river traffic gently churned the water, which lapped against the riverbank with comforting regularity. It was sunny and warm, with just the slightest breeze to take the edge off.

Danny and Hannah sat with their backs against the oak's stout trunk, neither wanting to break the spell so long as the kids were content. Danny heard Ben, some thirty feet away, asking a boy slightly older than himself which football team he supported, and sensed his son's quiet distaste with the answer, 'Chelsea'. 'At least we both play in blue,' Ben remarked as the two of them started a kickabout, and Danny nodded to the adults in the boy's group, who were settling in the middle of some long grass for a picnic. Ellie made a snuffling noise from the cocoon of her buggy, and a glance was enough to confirm that she had fallen asleep.

After five minutes or so, Danny sensed it was safe to breach the silence. 'How are you feeling?' he asked. He spoke softly, as befitted the scene, but also to remove any possible trace of confrontation from his voice. A duck quacked somewhere on the water behind them, an intrusion that seemed to help the moment.

'I don't know how to explain,' said Hannah.

'Look at the two of them,' said Danny. 'We're so lucky to have such beautiful children. Look how Ben gets on with other kids, how bright he is. And as for that little bundle—'

'Don't. I know,' said Hannah.

And they left it there, Danny venturing only to put an arm around Hannah's shoulder. She didn't shrug him off but he felt her upper body stiffen, bringing back a memory of an awkward teenage moment in the back row of a cinema many years ago.

Things continued in a similar vein, Hannah calmer than she had been for weeks, more attentive to what needed doing, and yet still not quite herself. A dumbed-down version. Danny felt like an idiot when he at last realised that what he was seeing was the effect of medication, not someone on the mend by any natural means.

Dorothy continued to pay regular visits, which helped enormously. The sight of her entering the house, with her kind eyes and quiet determination, always came as a welcome relief. She was able to push Hannah just that little bit further than Danny would dare, coaxing at first, then more demanding, with a keen sense of how far she could go without causing unpleasantness or worse. 'She'll get there,' Dorothy assured him.

Then, one Saturday afternoon, returning home from a local non-league football match with Ben, Danny found Dorothy holding Ellie in what looked like a stand-off with her daughter. Hannah was in tears, the howling kind that follow rage. 'How could you?' was all Danny heard as he entered the living room, and the scene revealed his wife distraught with anguish, incapable of answering her mother's question. Dorothy held the baby close to her, cradling her head in the crook of her neck and rocking gently on her feet as she did so.

Exchanging glances with Dorothy, Danny steered Ben away from the scene, through the house, and out into the back garden.

'What's wrong with Mummy?' asked Ben. 'Is Ellie okay?'

'Mummy's still not well,' said Danny.

'I know,' said Ben.

Ben continued to surprise and delight Danny. Not yet five and so smart, so aware of mood and situation, and the possessor of an already impressive vocabulary. 'Mummy isn't the only mummy who's not well,' he said on one occasion. 'Peter's mummy isn't sad like mine, but she's got a broken arm and can't make sandwiches.' His manner, his choice of words, and his sensitivity, warmed Danny's heart.

But he also worried about him. Is he perhaps too sensitive? Might he be bullied because of it? There were no signs or reports from pre-school of any such thing, and the way he dealt with other kids, with open friendliness and charm, suggested he was unlikely to end up on the wrong side of a bully. But you never knew. Danny remembered being bullied briefly into swearing allegiance to the red of Liverpool for about two weeks at the age of ten. A mild kicking from the twin protagonists was enough to make him go along with the charade until he found a way of getting the bullies collared for pinching sweets from the school tuck shop – after which they had weightier things on their minds than press-ganging classmates into converting from one football team to another.

Conversion. That was a big thing in his childhood now he thought about it. In RE, they learned about Catholic missionaries converting tribes in Africa, and Danny's own father had converted to Catholicism in order to marry his mother. The mother he had for the first two years of his life. The mother he couldn't remember.

And it struck him that attempting to convert people was what a lot of the world's problems came down to. Religion and politics, the two biggies, are mostly about trying to coerce people into one narrow set of beliefs. My God's bigger than your God. My social policy's better than your social policy. Bollocks, the lot of it. The more he thought about it, the more he came to the conclusion that everyone's a victim of some sort of manipulation most of the time, whether they know it or not.

Danny reflected on how he had been manipulated by Hannah. When they first met, Hannah had made all the running. And how could he not fall for a pretty, blonde professional sportswoman, an equestrian at the top of her game, full of zest for life, full of ambition, and seemingly full of interest in him? But after the injury that put paid to her career, everything changed. Her spark was no longer there. Ben came along and all seemed happy enough, until her affair with Ian Grant was discovered and the question over Ben's paternity arose. He nearly left her, but she cleverly manipulated him into staying. Though, as much as she may have manipulated the situation, he could never have left Ben. Never, whatever the biological realities might be.

And then along came beautiful Ellie, at which point a storm started brewing in the shape of Hannah's depression. An illness, a terrible thing, and yet a manipulative thing too. Being constantly on tenterhooks, constantly in fear of the next wave of raw and irrational behaviour. He tried to understand and to help, but there was a barrier he couldn't get past, an invisible force field that kept him out. How he longed for those brief moments, those little flashes of Hannah as she was when they first met, that gave him a glimpse of hope that things might get better.

Seven

Across the Miles, Across the Sea

It had been an especially eventful day, Cat thought. The latest batch of results from the sea bird census were in and ready for examination (with first glance suggesting that puffin numbers were up significantly), she'd been interviewed by a BBC documentary crew making a programme on the protected coastal waters of Britain, and one of the conservation volunteers had celebrated both her 70th birthday and 25th consecutive year of volunteering on the island. And to top it off, the office had received a call from Professor Edmund Whiley, Fellow of the Royal Society, who confirmed his imminent visit to interview Cat for a research paper on the subject of *Divining, Healing & Other Extrasensory Facilities, Mediaeval & Modern*.

A lot to be excited about. If the early signs proved true, the sea bird protection schemes were paying off. Gwen's face at being presented with a birthday cake and an inscribed pottery model of the old lighthouse had been a picture of delight. The documentary crew had been a bit tiresome – perhaps *thorough* was a kinder word – but the news from Professor Whiley had banished any sense of frustration at lost time over the TV interview, and she was sure that the nine retakes would be all worth it in the end.

This thing with Professor Whiley was exciting but she was also a little apprehensive about being the subject of an academic study: this wasn't just about the island, but about Cat herself.

For some time now, the breadth and depth of her knowledge of the island, ranging as it did across natural history, social history, geology, archaeology and beyond, had come to the attention of high-ranking academics, most of whom were fascinated, not so much by what Cat knew, but by her uncanny ability to make discoveries.

Her ability to locate and unearth ancient artefacts was attracting interest from far and wide, and not all of it strictly academic in nature. Just before Henry's last visit she had received a letter from The Holistic Earth Movement (Texas chapter) requesting an audience, and only last week she had a similar request from The West Midlands Natural Healing Collective (Solihull branch). That last one came as a particular surprise, as it seemed to bear no relevance to Cat's sphere of expertise. However, the letter had revealed that one of the collective's members, a Mrs. Doreen Sharp of Dudley, had reported a marked improvement in her hearing (which had been severely restricted from birth due to some congenital condition) during a recent visit to the island. She swore that the island, and quite possibly Cat herself, whom Mrs. Sharp had been very taken by, possessed a kind of healing magic.

Quite how all of this had come to pass Cat was at a loss to know. All she did was carry out her duties as a nature warden, and apply her knowledge of the precious island she was fortunate enough to call home in ways that she felt would be of practical use. That was that. Yes, she was puzzled by the more outlandish attention she was receiving, but she wasn't about to fret about it. Was she?

The day had been long, tiring, but rewarding. And now, sitting on a rock overlooking the Atlantic on a clear, calm evening as the sun descended into the sea and darkness closed in, she was quietly content. Every day on the island was special because just being there was special, but she couldn't help thinking that today had been one of those you wished you could share with someone special. Someone close, someone not hours away by land and sea.

She and Henry were last together a couple of months ago. They hardly communicated by phone in between Henry's visits, as it seemed unnecessary and in some way against the spirit of their relationship, which retained a certain charm for the very reason that it was long-distance. And the heart did grow fonder with absence. She found herself thinking of Henry now, and how nice it would be to share her news with him in person, over a meal and a few drinks in the island pub, or as they strolled under star-strewn skies as the day's light finally vanished and the life of the island came to rest.

It had been an especially eventful day, Henry thought. Inspired by the quartet's recent get-together and their commitment to resume activities, he had sorted out a lot of sheet music, dusted off his MP3 player, and set about reacquainting himself with their repertoire before breakfast. They hadn't yet fixed a date for their first real planning session or rehearsal, but the last thing he wanted was to go in rusty. He also spent an hour after breakfast on specific vocal drills, haunted by the memory of Vince taunting him over an occasional tendency to come in slightly under the note and an old habit of scooping up to notes rather than hitting them dead-on.

He'd had word from Jenny that the sale of the marital home was almost complete, and so spent the rest of the morning perusing the shop fronts of local estate agents. He didn't really go in for internet browsing: where was the fun in that? It also gave him an excuse to get out of his tawdry billet, and while on the hoof it gave him the opportunity to mull over his meeting with the headhunter that afternoon. He still wasn't sure what he was doing entertaining the idea of a return to the daily grind, but Anthony Goulding of Myers-Swann had caught him at a dull moment, had stroked his professional ego with talk of a high six-figure basic with all the trimmings, and well, what had he got to lose? Just a fact-finding mission, that's all. An excuse to shave, put on a shirt and tie – it had been a while – and test the waters to see if anything about his old lifestyle held any lasting appeal.

After a spot of lunch at his favourite Italian, and in the continued spirit of adventure, Henry decided to take the train to his appointment rather than drive. Ascot to Reading wasn't so bad a jaunt, he imagined. The last time he took a train was on the little branch line between Marlow and Maidenhead, the day he'd shoved an ice cream cone into Jeffrey Moss's face. He couldn't remember the last time he took a mainline train – he had always driven in and out of London – but the last one he'd been on was the type with corridors, compartments with sliding doors, and appalling sandwiches. He also fancied there'd been quite a bit of grime, and…steam? No, that must have been before even his time.

As it turned out, the Waterloo mainline train was clean and modern, if a little cramped, and Henry was pleasantly surprised. What came as a bigger surprise was Reading station, now an enormous glass and metal mega-structure with vast concourses, shopping malls, flyovers, underpasses, and almost as many platforms as Grand Central. Last time Henry had been to Reading, there was just a handful of platforms, a footbridge, and a shop selling the usual line in appalling sandwiches.

The commercial area of the town centre held a few surprises, too. Most of the gloomy sixties-built office blocks were gone, and in their place gleaming sci-fi towers had popped up everywhere. Henry referred to the directions he'd scribbled down on a scrap of paper, and had no difficulty finding Myers-Swann on the fourth floor of a gloomy sixties-built office block a quarter of a mile from the station in the direction of Caversham.

The meeting with Anthony Goulding went well. There were a few more details about the firm he was being put up for, and about the remuneration package, all of which seemed in line with Henry's expectations. Anthony Goulding was probably about twenty-five, surely not old enough for a headhunter, and his puppy dog manner made him seem even younger. His suit and shoes were good, though his hair let him down, slicked back tight against his head in the style of Leonardo di Caprio in *The Wolf Of Wall Street* – surely this was trying too hard. Though Henry did find his habit of saying 'Excellent!' at the start of every sentence endearing, reminding him of Tony Webster ('Great!') and David Harris-Jones ('Super!') in David Nobbs's *Reginald Perrin* novels.

Henry threw a few curveballs into the conversation, including a sneaky question about the possibility of working from home, but Anthony Goulding wasn't about to be caught out, and Henry was quietly impressed. As they approached the conclusion of the meeting, Henry decided that he was having fun and, what the hell, why not go for the job interview after all. Anthony Goulding seemed confident that he'd found the right man, and they parted on a general note of professional satisfaction at an hour well spent.

On his return to Ascot, Henry was disinclined to enter the cheerless confines of his flat straight away, and popped into the pub on the corner opposite. Seeing St. Austell bitter on draught always reminded him of the island.

The day had been eventful by his own not-very-eventful standards and now, as he sat sipping his pint, he wished he could share his news with someone special. Someone close, someone not hours away by land and sea. How nice it would be to catch up with Cat over a meal and a few drinks in the island pub, or as they strolled under star-strewn skies as the day's light finally vanished and the life of the island came to rest.

Eight

Reunion, Remembrance

Margaret Taylor felt blessed that her dearest wish, that her son and husband should be reconciled after years of hostility, had come true. This was the essence of a prayer of thanks that Margaret had built into her daily routine. After morning exercises, consisting of stretching and some light yoga, she would sit, usually in the lotus position, eyes closed, and give quiet thanks. It didn't matter to what or to whom she gave thanks – God, planet Earth, the Universe – she just needed to express it, because the more of that kind of energy there was out there, the better the world might be.

And yet, as she reflected once again on this good thing, there was the familiar visceral tug of an underlying sadness, a hollowness that would never go away. Neil and George were back on good terms, praise be, but nothing in the world could bring back Robert.

'I'm off to play golf,' said George, appearing at the open bedroom door. 'It seems disrespectful, somehow.'

'Don't be silly. We said we'd visit the grave, take flowers, this afternoon. You'd only be under my feet all morning. Enjoy your game, and I'll see you at lunchtime.'

'Is Neil…'

'I'm not sure. He's in London, so I don't think…but he'll be here this evening. I booked Villa d'Este, eight o'clock.'

'Fine, see you later.'

Only a few months ago Neil and George were at each other's

throats, and now here we are, all going to dinner together, Margaret thought. Every year they visited Robert's grave on the day of his passing and on his birthday, but this was the first time they had marked either occasion with a family dinner. And it was appropriate, since Neil and George had spent all those years fighting because neither could cope with the loss. How sad, and yet how wonderful that we can look upon this day both in celebration of Robert's life and of a fresh start, she thought.

'Right, up and at 'em, Margaret!' she said aloud as she raised herself elegantly from sitting cross-legged to a standing position. 'Fruit, Greek yoghurt, green tea, and Chapter Twenty-Three, I think.' She made her way to the kitchen, smiling at the unintentional rhyme as she did so.

Keeping busy was what Margaret did best. Her senior citizens' ballet class was now in its sixth year, and very popular with the older ladies of the village. She worked two afternoons a week in a charity shop, was an active member of the WI, did the odd stint at the cricket club, and was a member of the village reading group. And just now she was grappling with a new project: an autobiography.

The idea of writing an autobiography only really took shape when she was asked to give a presentation to the WI on her life as a ballet dancer. She had expanded the brief somewhat, covering not just her years with the Paris Opera Ballet, Royal Ballet and English National Ballet, but also giving a sketch of her life beyond the ballet years: as a wife, mother, and teacher, the whole thing delivered under the title *A Dancer Domesticated*. She'd enjoyed putting it together so much and, spurred on by WI friends and others who found her story fascinating, she decided to write the book.

She had mapped out the storyline quite easily. Not too difficult, it being a chronological progression starting at age five when her mother, having spent the war years watching Sadlers Wells Ballet dance through the Blitz, imbued in her an abiding passion for all things dance. Though not overly pushy, it became clear that by directing her daughter along a very specific course, she was compensating for a dream that she, a large-framed, rather inelegant woman, could never have realised.

And the final draft was going well, midway through editing Chapter Twenty-Three (green tea!). However, this morning she hesitated as she sat down at the computer because she knew there was another strand that needed adding to her life story, something she'd shied away from up to now: how a mother copes with the death of a child.

'I'm sorry I'm a bit late,' said Neil as he arrived at the table in a fluster, with a double-kiss and hug for Margaret, a handshake, and then a reconsidered semi-hug, for George. Still early days, thought Margaret. No sooner had he sat down than a flurry of activity set about in front of him: a glass of unasked-for water poured, a napkin delivered into his lap with an elaborate flourish, a menu the size of a folded Monopoly board presented for his immediate attention, and an enthusiastic if slightly smarmy welcome. 'How lovely to see you, sir!' *Had he ever been here before?*

'You've been here once before,' said Margaret. 'You were twelve I seem to recall.'

'He's got a good memory, then,' said Neil, shifting his chair, moving the water glass, and reaching for a bread stick. 'Sorry I couldn't make it to the… I'm paying a visit tomorrow morning. Did you…?'

'Yes, yes, all fine. A bit of a tidy up, fresh flowers,' said George. 'The headstone's gleaming, like it was just yester…'

Margaret reached forward to touch hands with her husband and son, just for an instant. 'Let's get some drinks, shall we? I fancy some fizz.'

'Champagne? Really?' said George, fumbling for the wine list amongst the stack of Monopoly boards. 'Why so many bloody menus?'

Neil smiled at Margaret. 'Prosecco?' he said. *'De rigueur,* I think.'

'As you like,' said George. 'A bottle of *De Rigueur* it is. Mmm, can't seem to find it here…waiter!'

Margaret and Neil started sniggering, leaving George at a loss to know what had just occurred. 'Something I said?'

'Yes, Pa, something you said.' Neil and Margaret both reached for water. How nice to hear the return of *Pa*, thought Margaret. 'Just prosecco will do,' said Neil. He couldn't remember the last time the three of them were out to dinner together, and certainly not the last time he'd been able to tease his father without causing a major incident.

'*De rigueur*… I see,' said George after his wife and son had calmed down. 'The return of the old fool!'

'Not at all, Pa, you're on good form! Now, tell me what's been going on.'

And they spent the next hour or so catching up over an excellent meal of assorted antipasti, followed by pasta, then grilled fish with tomato salad and green beans. When George mentioned his recent round of golf with Henry, it gave Neil the cue to announce that, since then, the quartet had been together for the first time in a while, and that they were planning to start rehearsing again soon. He didn't mention the letter from Ken, which might have seemed just a little surreal, certainly to his father.

And George, having so often in the past derided Neil over his singing, reiterated what he'd told his son on the night of the quartet's success in Harrogate, that he was delighted for them all, really rather surprised at how good they were, and how proud he was. George, proud of Neil, thought Margaret, still coming to terms with this new world order. Not so long ago, he had spat venom at his son over breakfast one morning, telling him that his chances of earning a living from music were as good as his chances of flying to the moon. And now…

'We're proud of *both* of our sons,' said Margaret, bringing the subject back to Robert, and they raised a glass in his memory.

After a brief pause for thought, George said 'And what about

Yellow Braces and Mr. Burns? What's the latest?'

Neil updated them on developments, how pre-production was now more or less complete, with almost everything in place ready to start filming. He talked with excitement about his various meetings with Newton Burns, with the composer and the director, his arms waving around, painting each scene as he did so. He was very happy with how his arrangements had turned out, but more importantly so was everyone else on the team, and he couldn't wait to see all the hard work come to fruition.

'See, didn't I tell you you'd make your fortune from music one day?' said George with a straight face.

'Better that than fly to the moon,' said Margaret, winking at her son.

Nine

Best-Laid Plans

'Can you remember why we called ourselves From The Edge?' asked Vince. They were gathered in Henry's flat, making the best of the available space.

'It was the answer to one of Ken's crossword clues,' said Danny, squeezing his legs together to allow Vince more room next to him on the two-seater. 'I was the one that solved it, I seem to recall.'

'And it seemed appropriate. You know, *from the edge* meaning from the start of a song,' said Neil, who was standing at a slight forward angle with his back to a sloping wall, his head inches from an exposed beam.

'Mmm. I'm not convinced it's the name to take us forward,' said Vince.

'Whyever not?' said Henry, who was sitting on the floor by the window, his knees under his chin. 'What's in a name anyway? It's just a convention, a form of shorthand for ease of reference.'

'Cobblers!' said Vince. 'What's in a name? Everything's in a name. What if The Beatles had been called The Earwigs? Or The Woodlice? Names matter, and I'm just thinking that we might be better off if we entered the next British championships under a new banner, so to speak. Something cool.'

'Well, we won't be taking part in the next championships, will we? We missed that particular boat, I'm afraid,' said Neil, his hands pressed flat against the beam to remind him that it was there.

'What do you mean, we missed the boat?' said Vince.

'Well, we missed prelims in November, so we didn't qualify to sing at the next British championships in May. It's as simple as that,' said Neil.

'How did we miss that?'

'Surely we don't have to go over all that again, do we?' said Neil, forgetting about the beam and bashing his head. 'Bugger! Well, you were physically incapacitated, Henry was away on Fantasy Island a lot, I was up to my neck with work, and Danny was attending to the small matter of becoming a father for the second time.'

'Ellie was born in early November,' said Danny.

'Yes, well, but still…where did the time go?'

Tempus Fugit and all that,' said Neil.

'So it's time we did a bit of *Carpe Diem*, then, isn't it?' said Henry.

Vince was still shaking his head in disbelief. 'Anyone know any more Latin clichés?'

'Well, it's not a cliché, but the Everton club motto is *Nil Satis Nisi Optimum* – nothing but the best is good enough,' said Danny.

'Not a cliché, and not bloody true either. When was the last time your lot won a trophy?' said Vince.

'Nineteen ninety-five, FA Cup. We beat Man U one-nil, Paul Rideout header—'

'Sorry, Danny, but can we get back to the matter in hand?' said Neil. 'Vince, the fact is that we're going to have to set our sights on next year if we plan to compete at national level again. But there's plenty else we can be doing: other competitions, festivals, private dos…and we'll be all the better for it. We might not have made it through prelims even if we'd been able to pitch up. We had no time to rehearse. At least now we'll have time to plan and build up to it properly. And that means practice, practice and more practice, not fiddling around with the name of the quartet.'

'And if you want another indication of time flying,' said Henry, 'it's the anniversary of Ken's death in two weeks' time. It was while we were at the Holland Harmony Festival in Amsterdam, remember? Last weekend in March.'

'Oh. My. Word,' said Vince.

'Listen, when was the last time we all attended a Maidenhead chorus rehearsal on the same night?' asked Neil. 'I certainly can't remember when. Let's all make the effort to be there a week on Wednesday and we'll remember Ken properly, with the guys.'

'Agreed,' said Henry. 'Now can we please stop talking and do some singing?'

'Are you sure there's enough oxygen in here to sing?' said Vince.

The forty-strong male chorus of Maidenhead A Cappella rehearsed every Wednesday in the function room of a social club that was conveniently located for car parking and public transport, and had the singular advantage that, unlike church halls, so often the venue for choir rehearsals the length and breadth of the land, it had its own well-appointed bar with two real ales on tap.

Not that the availability of a bar held quite the same appeal as it would, say, to a rugby club, but it made a difference after standing and singing for two and a half hours on a mid-week evening. Nor were rugby club levels of consumption encouraged, as it was generally acknowledged that while a pint or two could have a loosening effect on the vocal apparatus, anything more tended to yield diminishing returns. And nowhere was this ethos summed up better than in the club motto, *Superior Singing and Serious Enjoyment*. Here, 'serious' meant 'responsible' rather than the alternative interpretation of 'giving it large'.

The chorus was one of the best in Britain, having won several championship medals under the direction of the charismatic James Pinter, a larger-than-life personality, keen wit, and skilled musician. And down the years it had had several very successful quartet singers in its ranks, including Cliff "Tonsils" Thompson, the only Berkshire-born singer ever to win an international quartet gold medal, and Ken Potts himself who, aside from being an excellent quartet singer, had been known to TV audiences for his many appearances on *The Good Old Days* early in his career.

The fact that it had been some months since Vince, Danny, Henry and Neil had all attended a rehearsal of their parent chorus on the same evening was a cause of some embarrassment. Not so much for Vince, who had taken extended leave of absence, as well as standing down as club chairman, following his last health set-back. For him this was something of a triumphant return. But the others had only attended rehearsals on and off, not often enough to keep up with the repertoire and take part in concerts, and for this reason they returned to the fold with some trepidation. Not least because they knew they could expect a royal ribbing from their musical director.

And so, while Vince returned to cheers and congratulations on his latest recovery, Danny, Henry and Neil each arrived to a series of choice putdowns from James Pinter, egged on by boos and jeers from the chorus, before finally being welcomed back onto the risers to sing.

The evening started with vocal warm-ups, a series of drills that made no sense to the uninitiated but were designed to get the vocal chords moving and the brain engaged, as well as allowing the chorus to start blending the output of forty voices into a sound closely matched in vowel integrity and tonal quality. *Me-o Me-o My, Me-o Me-o My* on a descending run of semi-tones, *We-Sit-Late-Men-Sun, Down-By-Old-Point-Bay*, and similar gibberish phrases carefully chosen to exercise the full gamut of vowel sounds, diphthongs, and consonant shapes.

This was followed by work on several repertoire songs, some familiar, some not so familiar to the returning four. Old favourites such as *Moondance, Kiss From A Rose*, and *Dance The Night Away*, as well as newer arrangements including *Seven Bridges Road* and *Haven't Met You Yet*.

In the interval, James Pinter was on hand with a further supply of jibes for Neil and Henry, who happened to stray within his orbit, all in good humour. Vince made a point of catching up with as many chorus pals as he could, while Danny disappeared to take a phone call.

The second half of the evening resumed with work on a brand-new song, most of the chorus reading from sheet music to aid learning. Henry was familiar with the arrangement and joined in. Vince was now too tired to stand, so decided to sit and watch proceedings, and was joined by Neil, concerned that Vince might have over exerted himself in all the excitement.

The evening concluded with a tribute to Ken Potts, with Vince and Neil rejoining the chorus to sing a selection of Ken's favourite songs. James Pinter also announced that the chorus had received a monetary donation from Ken's wife Bella, to be used as a bursary to support and encourage younger singers in the chorus.

Finally, James Pinter called upon Vince, Danny, Henry and Neil to sing *Irish Blessing*, which they had sung at Ken's funeral a year ago.

Only then did they realise that Danny had not returned after the interval.

Ten

The Storm Breaks

The thing about overdoses is that they can be deliberate or accidental. When Hannah went to bed early that Wednesday evening, leaving Dorothy to mind Ben and Ellie, she was more exhausted than usual. Quite why, she didn't know. It had been a fairly ordinary day, and the kids had been really very good: no tears or tantrums to speak of. But then exhaustion came most days. After Ellie was born, that's what had happened to her. Somewhere in the prefrontal cortex of her brain a switch had been flicked off.

All she wanted was a good, long, dreamless sleep. Not the Big Sleep. No, not that kind of sleep, but the kind that turns you into a new person: a shiny, energetic and optimistic version of yourself, one that can stare life straight in the eyes and not be the first to blink. But once again sleep just wouldn't come. She was sure that no-one would believe that the sleeping pills (not that many), helped down by whisky (not that much), were anything other than an attempt to end things. But that's not what it was. She wanted to sleep, but she wanted to live too. Didn't she?

Lucky then that Dorothy had looked in on her. Finding Hannah asleep, and with the evidence of her consumption on the bedside table, her mum, an ex-nurse, had checked for vital signs and set about rousing her daughter while calling for an ambulance. Hannah came to on the way to the Emergency Unit, surely proof that her self-medication had not been too excessive, but they pumped her stomach as a precaution nonetheless.

And now all eyes were on her. She tried to tell Danny and Dorothy that it was just about sleep, that she was aware of what she'd taken, and that she was okay, really. But she could tell how hollow her words must sound in the light of what had happened, and she could see the disbelief in their faces. Could she blame them? Try as she might to convince them that she would be better balanced from now on, more tolerant with the kids, the reality was that she had no idea how things would turn out.

Lying in the hospital bed, she had thought all of this and was glad of the time to be able to. At home, her obligation to domestic duties meant that she had little time to think things through. Every day was an assault course, asking so much of her. A baby doing the only thing she knows: expecting and demanding to be fed, changed, and amused. Human nature at its most primitive: the raw instinct to survive at any cost. And as for Ben, with his rampant curiosity, his boundless energy, Hannah could see that he was so, so eager to please her. He was clever and charming, but still…if only she could locate that inner switch and flick it back on, she was sure she would bounce back. Who wants to feel this shit, this hopeless? No-one.

She knew that Danny's patience was wearing thin. God knows, she'd put him through enough with the Ian saga and the question of Ben. How the hell had they survived that? She could only admire Danny's fortitude, and he had proved his love for her in ways that made her genuinely humble. And yet she had begun to see something in his demeanour that suggested he was nearing some sort of limit. Was he starting to resent her? Give up on her? Well, maybe that's what she deserved. Not-so-instant karma after everything that had gone before.

Since Ellie was born (and for some months beforehand, now she came to think of it) she had found close physical proximity unpleasant. Lovemaking was a no-go area. And she had shrugged off pretty well every attempt at closeness, to the extent that Danny had almost stopped trying. Again, she could hardly blame him. And yet since that change in his demeanour, since she first sensed that he was beginning to disengage, she had started to find him more attractive. What sort of messed up shit was this?

Now back at home, she was being treated with kid gloves and wariness. Her mum was being her usual calm self, patient beyond what was reasonable to expect. It's at times like this that you realise what the phrase *unconditional love* actually means, Hannah thought. But with that thought came a darker one. Where was her own unconditional love? What had she done the day her mum had taken Ellie from her? She couldn't remember. And what had Ben seen of the incident when he and Danny had entered the room? Her nose and eyes began to tingle, and she reached for a paper tissue.

Just then came a firm but gentle knock at the bedroom door. 'Here we go, Han. Some tea for you,' said Danny entering. *Han?* When was the last time he called me that, she wondered, her nearly tears suddenly back in their box.

Danny handed a mug of tea to his wife, and for once chose not to sit on the edge of the bed, but in an occasional chair off to one side. This wasn't going to be the familiar display of bedside manners.

'You called me Han,' she said.

'Did I? How are you feeling?'

'That's not a question I find easy to answer these days. But still in one piece.'

'About the overdose…' *Straight to the point! The kid gloves must be in the wash.*

'I've already said, I didn't mean to…it was an accident. Can we…'

'And I believe you. I have to believe you, because if I didn't I'd go mad.'

'So that would make two of us.'

'You're not mad.'

'Well, technically I am. Postpartum depression, to give it its proper name, is a form of mental illness.'

'I'm not sure how to behave around you, Hannah.' *Back to my full name.*

'I can understand that, and I can see it in you too,' said Hannah, cupping the piping hot tea in front of her like a Communion chalice. 'How are you going to behave today?'

'Today I thought I'd aim for light-hearted with a dash of serious intent,' said Danny, as though he'd rehearsed his role in the day's drama.

'I'm curious about the serious intent bit. Tell me more.'

'Well, this is all very scary. I'm really worried about you, and the effect on the kids…and on our marriage. And I'm looking around for reassurance, some sort of light at the end of the tunnel. I was thinking…' Danny got up and looked out of the bedroom window. 'Maybe things would be better if you gave up the anti-depressants.'

'Oh. You think so, do you?'

'You're not yourself. There are other things that can help. Cognitive behavioural therapy, group therapy…'

'Nice tea,' said Hannah.

'Okay, how about this then. In Malay culture, they believe that postnatal depression is caused by evil spirits that were present in the placenta, and they bring in a shaman to perform a séance and drive the spirits out. We could give that a go, you lying there like Linda Blair, your head doing a three-sixty and puking green gunge.'

Hannah tried to hide her amusement behind the mug that was still raised to her mouth.

'Aha! Gotcha,' said Danny.

Eleven

Hilda & Stanley

Vince stared at the painting (oil on canvas) entitled *Domestic Scenes: At The Chest Of Drawers* and wondered if this was the way things might end up between him and Angie. He was visiting the Stanley Spencer gallery in the village of Cookham where Neil lived with his parents when he wasn't up in London. Spencer was widely regarded as one of the finest English painters of the twentieth century, and being a keen amateur painter himself, Vince had taken up Neil's invitation with pleasure. There also happened to be a rather fine hostelry of Vince's former acquaintance just a quarter of a mile up the road.

The scene before him was of Spencer himself and his wife Hilda, both reaching into a chest of drawers, apparently to select clothes for a wedding feast (it being one of a series of paintings called *Marriage At Cana*). Two things interested Vince about the painting. First, Spencer appears as a tiny crouched figure, while a much oversized Hilda looms over him, legs astride his puny body, her private parts in close proximity to Spencer's head. Second, according to the information booklet, Spencer painted the scene in 1936, at the very time he and Hilda were heading for divorce.

Seeing that Vince was deep in thought, Neil wandered into another part of the small gallery. Vince mulled things over. A year ago he had his own flat and free rein to do as he pleased, including how often to see Angie. He had no regrets about throwing in his lot with her, and he was grateful for all she did for him, but he couldn't help thinking that he was far less of a free spirit now than then. His illness was unpredictable and when it hit hard he was lucky to have Angie alongside him, but was he becoming too dependent on her? Was she beginning to loom over him like Hilda over Stanley? How he hoped his health would hold out.

Moving on, his attention was caught by a pencil on paper drawing entitled *Life Room, Slade (1943-44)* depicting two students at the Slade art school in the process of sketching a reclining female nude.

This resonated just as much with Vince. On his living room wall was a twenty-four by thirty-inch framed painting (oil on canvas) entitled *Nude Reclining With The Thermostat Turned Up Full*, Vince's very own work, a life study of Angie. It could so easily have been called *At The Point Of Interruption By A Man Bearing Jaffa Cakes*, but he had decided to overlook the unfortunate incident of Danny arriving unexpectedly as he was painting Angie in full naked glory while struggling to hide an erection that had made its own unexpected arrival through the hole in his boxers.

Life Room, Slade reminded him of a carefree time not so long ago. *Domestic Scenes: At The Chest Of Drawers* made him think of his health predicament, his growing dependence on Angie, and his fear for the future. What a difference a year makes, he thought.

The Cookham pub that Vince last visited a dozen or so years ago hadn't changed too much, though unsurprisingly it was under new ownership. Back then, the pub was run by a very tall chap who drank more in a session than most of his customers did in a week, and who had a certain way with the ladies. Stories of his exploits were the stuff of legend in these parts, including the time he witnessed a ghost walk through the pub's walls (The White Lady, of course), and the many times he sat at the bar for early morning rations in his faithful dressing gown, Old Crusty, before flashing whoever happened to be around, including the slow-moving traffic on the road outside.

Vince thought he recognized a couple of faces from all that time ago, including a slight woman in her early forties with short dark hair, olive skin, and a distinctive high-pitched cackle. He looked in her direction.

'I know you,' she said. 'You're that bloke who knocked my pint over, what was it, ten years ago, maybe more?'

'Did I? I can't remem...well, can I get you another?' said Vince, taken aback.

'No, you knobshite, let me get you one. It was a good night that. And I've always had a thing for Mel Gibson.'

'Most people say I look like George Clooney,' said Vince, his ego suddenly inflated.

'Listen to you, cocky git. No, mate. Mel Gibson. Anyway, enjoy your pint.'

His ego deflated again, Vince raised his glass half-heartedly and turned back to Neil.

'Is there any pub in Berkshire where you don't know someone?' said Neil.

'It's all about putting in the hard miles, Neil. It's a tough job, but someone's got to do it. Anyway, that was years ago.'

'This was meant to be a cultural day out, not an excuse for a piss up. Shouldn't you be taking it easy on the lager?'

'I have been, believe me. Ask Ange. I've been a very good boy of late. But I've got to have some fun, even in my perilous state of health. Just a couple, that's all.'

'Well, at least I've got your attention for a little while. That was the other reason for today, really. I know things have been dodgy on the MS front, but just how bad... I mean, you couldn't walk for a while could you? I can't help thinking back to when Robert...how it was the same for him. I just want to know you're doing all the right things. I'm sure there are more effective drugs than when Robert...but are you doing everything the doctors have told you?'

'I am, yes. But it's heavy shit to deal with, and it's hard to predict what's around the corner. So, it's at times like this, over a few beers, that I can forget about all of that. For a while, at least. Now, let's change the subject.'

Neil held both hands aloft. 'Okay, okay. Pardon me for caring.'

'Oh, stop that,' said Vince, picking up his pint. 'Thing is, I've been worried about Danny recently.'

'Why, what's up?'

'Well, you know things haven't been great since the little one was born? Hannah's not been well. She's been in hospital and it's all a bit tense. I think it's serious, but he won't say much about it.'

'I didn't know things were serious, I'm sorry to hear it,' said Neil. 'All we can do is be there if he needs us.'

'You're right,' said Vince, passing an empty pint glass to his friend. 'Now, let's have a couple more and try a bit of two-part harmony.'

'Is that wise...you tenor, me baritone?' said Neil.

'No, let's try something different. You must know the lead line to most of the standards, and I know the bass to quite a few. How about *Sweet And Lovely*?'

'Can do.'

'Okay, get them in and we'll sing it to that woman over there. See if we can embarrass her into accepting a drink. Mel Gibson, my arse.'

'You're drunk.'

'No, no. I've had a couple, that's all. Cultural day out with Neil. We went to a gallery. As an artist, I have to keep my eye in, you know.'

'And you do it so well. You're the best piss artist I know.'

'Ouch, walked into that one. But listen, it's true. Here...' Vince fished the little booklet from a jacket pocket and waved it at Angie. 'Spencer Gallery, Cookham. Very enlightening. Then we retired to an old haunt for a debrief and a little light refreshment. S'all.'

Angie took the dog-eared pamphlet, examined the front cover, then fanned the pages under her nose. 'I believe you, but my point remains: you're drunk, Vince. And that's not what you're meant to be doing these days. Apart from doctors' orders to cut back, it doesn't help with your medication, and what if you fell…what if…'

Vince gave Angie his best Bambi eyes and allowed his bottom lip to protrude ever so slightly.

'Don't try to soft soap me, Vince. It won't work.'

Vince lifted his walking stick and allowed the rubber tip to gently prod Angie's left breast, grinning inanely as he did so.

'You're pushing your luck, Vince. You're an arsehole.'

'And you are the most beautiful woman I know, with indisputably the finest boobs in the world.' The word *indisputably* didn't come out quite right. 'And there's the evidence,' said Vince, suddenly pointing the stick towards the painting on the wall above the sofa. 'And don't for a minute suggest that I only love you for your boobs, because that would be a cal…a cal… a calumny of the worst kind!' The word *calumny* certainly didn't come out right. 'I love you because…because you're…'

'Your nursemaid?'

Vince tottered, then sat down. 'Nursemaid? Is that what you think? Oh fuck, Ange.'

'Well, it feels like it a lot of the time. I feel a bit, well…taken for granted, Vince.'

Vince looked suddenly sober. 'Not by me. Never. You've been wonderful with my MS, I know that, but I don't take anything for granted…not you…not even tomorrow. That's what it does. Cuts your horizons right back. Tomorrow might never happen, but so long as there's today, I don't see why I can't have a few drinks and enjoy myself.'

'But isn't that rather selfish, Vince? If tomorrow doesn't come for you, where does that leave me? At least if you lay off the sauce, you might have a better chance of seeing a lot more tomorrows. Think of things from my side for once.'

Vince narrowed his eyes. 'Are you playing Hilda to my Stanley?'

'Are you referring to Stanley Spencer and his wife? Let me think. Well, from what I can remember from Art A level, there might be some similarities, yes.'

'There was this painting, something to do with a chest of drawers, and Hilda was all over Stanley, sort of dominating him. He looked helpless with her bearing down on him, all big and buxom.'

Angie searched her memory. 'I think I know the one you mean, but that's not the way it was between them. Well, maybe in some corner of Spencer's mind, but the fact is that Hilda was the suppressed one in that relationship. A fine painter in her own right who played second fiddle to her husband. She lost a lot of self-confidence as a painter while she was with Spencer. That's what I meant by similarities.'

Vince frowned. 'So you're saying you've lost self-confidence being with me? How's that then?'

'Nothing you don't already know. Look, I care for people, don't I? Not just you, but the old folks at the home and the toddlers at nursery. And it's great, to an extent. But when people rely on you, sometimes you sort of end up feeling taken for granted. And then you lose the confidence to do other things. It's hard to understand unless you've been in that position, Vince.'

'But you've already done other things. Great things! You were a household name back then...well, a household bosom, anyway. And you gave up the glamour work precisely because you wanted to be in the real world, remember? Dealing with real people instead of the shitty world of hacks and paps, agents, and all the arse-lickers and hangers-on. You'd had enough of all the fakeness, being seen as a sex object, all of that. So, why...?'

'I don't know, Vince. It's just that some days I miss...well, being the centre of attention for a while.' Angie sank onto the sofa opposite Vince and heaved a sigh. 'That's all, Vince, that's all.'

'Well, you've still got it babe – you could make a come-back if you really wanted! Everyone's doing it. There's even a rumour that the classic '70s Quo line-up are getting back together, and I never thought I'd see that.'

Angie leapt up from the sofa. 'Ha! I'd forgotten all about it!' she shouted, remembering the letter. She rushed into the kitchen, and returned with an envelope, which she threw into Vince's lap. 'Have a read of that! I can't believe I'd forgotten…it arrived a few days ago.'

Vince read the letter and allowed a slow smile to creep across his face. 'Bloody hell, Ange. All that business about not being the centre of attention, and you've been sitting on this? Red carpet…reunion photo shoot…gala dinner at the Dorchester… not to mention all that five-star crumpet!'

'You just did,' said Angie.

'What?'

'Mention the five-star crumpet. Is that meant to make me feel good about it?'

'Ah come on, Ange, you know what I mean. And anyway, if we're dishing out crumpet stars, you'd get six every time. No question. It'll be a great day, a great evening. We've got to go.'

'We?'

'It says here, "…*and partner* are invited to a gala dinner"…'

'Well, you'd better shape up then. Otherwise I'm giving the real George Clooney a shout,' said Angie.

Twelve

The Banker & The Professor

On bright, clear days, the towers of Canary Wharf gleam magnificently, light bouncing between mirrored facades, reflections cast on water, steel and glass, magnifying and multiplying everything in sight. Today wasn't one of those days, and as Henry emerged from the Underground, the great towers all around him seemed shrunken by the dull grey sky and threatening low cloud. It was as if they were huddling together conspiratorially, or maybe closing ranks against the constant headwinds that had been battering the financial district since the crash of 2007.

It didn't much bother Henry that he'd spent all of his working life in one of the most despised professions of modern times. The image of the commodities trader had come to symbolise everything that was wanton and corrupt about the modern world. You couldn't switch on the TV news without seeing stock footage of animated young men and women gesticulating across trading desks, shouting into telephone receivers, all the while scanning banks of flickering computer monitors for the vital signs that could make or break a market or, so it seemed, bring down the entire economy and the country with it. Henry didn't care for the sensationalism, the over-simplification, and the incessant witch-hunting that had become the norm these days. By all means find the real crooks and bang them to rights, but don't tar everyone with the same brush. He had spent years on the front line, having learned from George Taylor and other top-notch guys how to play the game and win, not by anything remotely underhand or dishonest, but by the application of intelligence, instinct, and sheer bottle.

When he himself fell victim during the long aftershock that followed the crash, losing his job just under two years ago, his first reaction was just that: shock. He had never put a foot wrong in all his years, and yet everything came tumbling down. His second reaction was to take stock of everything in his life, and it didn't take him long to decide that he was well rid of life in the City and all the hassle and nonsense it had come to represent. Cat, the island, and From The Edge were what he cared about now. *So what the bloody hell am I doing here*, Henry found himself asking, as he strode along the clean, wide concrete walkways that were beginning to fleck with rain. He knew the answer, which was three-fold – boredom, curiosity, and a desire to get the last laugh – but just being back among the monuments to Mammon on a day as dreary as this made him question himself all over again. He didn't really want all this again, *did he?*

The offices of Stourcroft Stone occupied floors sixteen to twenty-three of the fourth largest tower on the wharf. Trading since 1927, they were a name, but never quite in the first tier. They had solid foundations, something of a reputation in the food and agriculture markets, and had flown well under the radar while all the flack was flying over the last few years. Henry signed in at the main reception, then again at the company reception desk on the sixteenth floor, and was then directed to the twenty-second floor where he was met by a slender, impeccably-dressed woman in her twenties, offered refreshments, and ushered into an empty boardroom. 'Mr. Markham will be with you shortly.'

Henry took off his overcoat, placed it with his briefcase on one of the chairs, and wandered over to the vast window, which ran floor-to-ceiling around two of the four walls. He looked down and across the expanse of docklands, tracing the line of the light railway, and picking out City airport, the O2 arena, and other familiar landmarks. In the distance, through the gathering murk, he could make out the outlines of several other icons of the London skyline.

The door opened behind him and, as he turned, Henry got the sense that he was about to be tackled to the ground by the enormous figure approaching with its arm outstretched. 'Mr. Warrington? Freddie Markham. Sorry to keep you waiting.' He was grinning from ear to ear as he took Henry's hand in a predictably vice-like grip, something Henry was prepared for, meeting it with as near equal force as he could muster. The guy must have been six foot four, almost as broad as he was tall, and had the look of a front row forward recently decamped from the field of play and ready to hit the town for a few beers. 'Please, take a seat.'

Henry returned to his pre-selected chair, one from the end of the highly polished dark wood table, his back to the window. That way, his interviewer would be most likely to take the end chair closest to him rather than cross to the opposite side of the table, which he might have preferred, but would now seem awkwardly formal. This way, there was a natural conversational angle between them, and an important psychological barrier had already been removed.

As tea and coffee arrived, the opening exchanges touched on Henry's journey and a brief synopsis of the weather, and then it was down to business. Business that didn't take very long, as it turned out. Given his experience and track record, Henry had expected that the interview would cut to the chase sooner than later, but he hadn't anticipated quite how brief the meeting would be.

Referring to Henry's CV, Markham asked him to elaborate on one or two aspects of his career to date – specific portfolios he'd managed, the money he'd made on this or that deal – and he concluded with what Henry thought were two pretty lame questions: 'What do you think sets the top traders apart from the rest?' and 'Where do you see yourself in five years' time?'

His answer to the first question contained the words *intelligence*, *instinct*, and *bottle*, all of which he knew to be true. His answer to the second question contained the phrases *head of commodities*, *world class portfolio*, and *market leaders*, all of which he knew to be complete bollocks.

After no more than forty minutes, the interview came to a conclusion with Markham coming as close as he could to offering Henry the job there and then. There were other candidates to be seen, and so on, but the effusive way in which Markham summarised their discussion, and the relish with which he shook Henry's hand again, left Henry with more than a hint that things had gone very well. And after the closing exchanges that touched on Henry's journey home and a recap of the prevailing weather conditions, Henry left the room, signed out on the sixteenth floor, again at ground level, and then jumped in a taxi.

Back on the twenty-second floor, Freddie Markham left the boardroom and walked the short distance to his own office where he sat down at the desk and opened a cardboard folder marked 'Candidates'. He removed the top sheet of paper, placed it in front of him, and reached for a pen. Of the four names on the list, the first three had a question mark against them. Reaching for a pen, Freddie Markham crossed through the first three names, then circled the final name and placed a large tick against it.

The carousel of the ancient projector clunked round to deliver the next slide, and the bright blue sea anemone with its myriad fingers suspended in fine clear water was replaced by a close-up of a puffin on the wing, getting set to land, a sheaf of bright silver sprats wedged in its multi-coloured bill.

'And so back to the island's most iconic inhabitant. Or visitor, I should say. And I'm delighted to report that the results from the most recent census have confirmed that the number of breeding pairs is up again for the seventh year in a row, and the signs are good that we'll be seeing a lot more of our little friend *Fratercula arctica* in the years to come. Okay, we'll take a break there, and in ten minutes I'll be talking about the island's archaeology, with an update on some recent finds. See you in ten.'

Cat took a sip of water, flicked the switch on the projector, and opened the lid of her laptop. In the back room of the island pub were around thirty people, mostly holiday-makers, gathered to listen to the warden's regular presentation on the island's natural and social history. This was something she did every month throughout the year, and she loved being able to talk about the island to new visitors each time, though there were always familiar faces who came back for more. There were hundreds of photos she could use for illustration, but she still showed some of the oldest ones using the slide projector. It would be easy enough to replace the slides or transfer them to digital format, but she considered it fitting to use old and new technology side-by-side, which was for her an enjoyable part of the evening's proceedings.

The bulk of Cat's presentation remained the same, but she always found something new to add each time. And this evening, aside from the puffin news, she had something a little bit special to share.

As the audience trickled back to their places, glasses replenished, Cat readied the laptop, syncing it with a more modern desk projector. For perhaps the first time ever on these occasions she felt a pang of nerves as she stood and welcomed everyone back.

With the opening slide reading 'Island Archaeology: Overview & A New Discovery', Cat told the assembly that she would take them on a whistle-stop tour of the island's fascinating archaeology before concluding with an update on her own recent archaeological activities, which had led her to some interesting conclusions.

With reference to an outline map of the island, Cat started by describing the earliest evidence of human occupation, which were flints from the later Mesolithic period. She went on to describe a Bronze Age settlement, comprising a dozen or so huts within a compound near the north-east tip of the island. From there, the tour continued through the Iron Age, and on to the early Christian period, from which time a burial ground containing four engraved memorial stones had been unearthed, dating back to between the fifth and eighth centuries. And onwards, through the Medieval and Post-Medieval periods, with their fortified enclosures, and later the castle, built in 1243 and still standing to this day. Cat's descriptions were laced with absorbing tales of man's struggles throughout the history of the island: to hunt, to farm, and to fight.

Cat made no reference to her own work and findings until the concluding part of the presentation, when she said, somewhat diffidently:

'As nature warden, my main role is to look after the wildlife but, as some of you know, I also dabble quite a bit as an amateur archaeologist. I seem to have a knack for finding quite interesting artefacts, and in my time I've dug up all sorts of bits and bobs, including Neolithic worked flints, Bronze Age pottery, and even human bones that might be evidence of a previously undiscovered early Christian burial site. But in the last month, I think I've discovered something even more exciting.'

Cat paused, took a sip of water, and clicked to the final slide.

'I started by saying that the earliest evidence of human occupation on the island were flints from the later Mesolithic period, dated at between 8,500 BC and 5,000 BC, which were used as spear heads and harpoon barbs by nomadic hunters. But what you see here are worked objects that might pre-date the flints by some considerable time. We're not sure what they are exactly – possibly hand tools of some kind – but they are clearly man-made. I'm waiting for the experts to confirm exactly how old they are, but there's a chance that what you see here is the earliest evidence of human habitation on the island. Thank you for coming along this evening, and I hope you enjoyed the presentation. Any questions?'

A gentle ripple of applause went around the room, with one particularly loud contributor at the back. Cat looked up to see Professor Edmund Whiley, FRS, getting to his feet, raising his hat, and shouting 'Bravo!'

'I had no idea you were in the room, Professor,' said Cat. 'I didn't expect to see you until tomorrow.'

'Edmund, please. Well, I had a meeting in Tiverton cancelled, and I got lucky with transport. An old friend keeps a boat in Ilfracombe and he fancied a sail, so here I am.'

'Very adventurous of you. We've had our fair share of storm force gales recently. Can I get you a drink?'

'Allow me. And if you've got some time now, perhaps we can forego the formalities of our meeting tomorrow and lay some groundwork...over dinner, perhaps? Unless you've already...'

Cat found herself amused at the professor's forwardness, and assessed him for the first time. Short, wiry, with a prominent Roman nose, round horn-rimmed glasses, and a mess of curly dark brown hair. He reminded her of a young Woody Allen, and his eagerness of manner complemented the impression nicely. The only thing that didn't quite fit was the accent, which seemed to hail from somewhere nearer Middlesborough than Manhattan.

'No, dinner would be nice, thank you. There's local Soay lamb on the menu tonight. Do you come from Middlesborough by any chance?'

'Good, good...dinner, good. Middlesborough? Well, that's a very keen ear you have, I must say. Stockton-on-Tees, to be exact! Any particular reason you ask?'

'Not really, I like to place people, and I have a thing about accents. Being here with so many visitors from all over the country – all over the world – I hear hundreds of different accents, and I like to test myself. No points on this occasion, I'm afraid.'

'You're too hard on yourself. Full marks, I'd say. Stockton's only a stone's throw away. But I find that fascinating... "I like to place people" is what you said, which is what archaeology is all about, when you come to think of it: placing people. Shall we find a table?'

Over dinner, the professor complimented Cat on her presentation, then made various references to her work on the island, which he said was stirring considerable interest in academic circles. His own department of archaeology at Bristol University had sent several students to the island on field trips – Cat remembered spending time with them – and had returned full of excitement at what they'd seen. They had explored the established sites such as the early Christian burial ground and the Bronze Age compound and huts, but they had also reported back on how Cat was not only an excellent and highly knowledgeable guide, but on how she seemed to have a 'sixth sense' when it came to making fresh finds. For some time, the professor had been working on a thesis that certain individuals possess the ability to tap into the energy of inanimate objects, specifically human remains and man-made objects, and are able to sense, and hence locate, them without the use of technology. And the thesis went further by suggesting that some of these individuals are able to channel that energy into an instrument of healing.

'That would explain Mrs. Doreen Sharp of Dudley, then,' said Cat.

Cat told the professor of the letters she'd received from dubious-sounding organisations, which she'd dismissed as cranks. The professor, with a straight face, nodded and suggested that they were, if not proof exactly, then a very strong indication that Cat did indeed possess the kind of extrasensory facilities he had just described. This was followed by a question that caused Cat to choke on a mouthful of Soay lamb.

'Would you mind if I ran some tests on you, Cat?'

Cat took a sip of white wine and composed herself. 'You silver-tongued devil.'

'I'm sorry, that wasn't very subtle, was it? Allow me to

explain. I'm so very glad I made the trip over here, and so grateful that you agreed to see me, and so honoured that you're having dinner with me—'

'I think you may be over-compensating a tad,' said Cat. 'What sort of tests?'

The professor explained that he'd devised a series of tests, ranging from a preliminary questionnaire through to brain-wave analysis, that enable him to evaluate where a person sits on the scale.

'Oh, I'm *on the scale* now, am I?' said Cat.

'Sorry, not that scale...the extrasensory scale, if you will. The E-Scale.'

'It sounds like something you'd clean a kettle with.'

'It's not as bad as it sounds, really, and you'd be helping the research enormously. And who knows, medical science may owe you a debt of gratitude one day.'

'Well, when you put it that way, how could I say no?'

'Wonderful!'

'I was being sarcastic.'

'Ah.'

'Okay, what would these tests involve exactly, and what sort of time commitment are we talking about?'

'Well, we can do the preliminary test, the questionnaire, here. No more than an hour of your time. The rest would need to be conducted under controlled conditions at the university in Bristol. A couple of days at most?'

'Sorry, I'm going to have to say no in that case,' said Cat.

'May I ask why?'

'Because I don't leave the island. Haven't done for three years now.'

'May I ask why?'

'Because everything I need and want is right here...' This was followed by a long pause. '...except for one thing.'

That evening Cat phoned Henry.

Thirteen

News from Abroad

Following the pre-production meeting at his London office, Newton Burns flew out to New York for further meetings and site visits ahead of the start of filming, and he was as excited as he could remember in a long time. His forty years in the business had taken him from small-time singer and entertainer to head of his own film production company, and he had hardly been out of the public eye in the last decade, as a presenter, actor, writer, and comedian. And though he didn't read reviews or take much notice of the latest gossip, he was aware that his stock had probably never been higher.

He enjoyed it all, from presenting awards ceremonies and hosting quiz programmes, to being the face of a long-running TV advert for a pre-mixed cocktail drink. But the projects he enjoyed the most were the ones that had a deep personal attachment. He was enormously proud of Yellow Braces, and though he often thought he must be mad to be in such a high-risk, financially precarious business, it was all worth it to see a project such as *A Cappella Fellas* coming to fruition.

From the start, the story had grabbed him. Eric Winstanley, one of the best of the new crop of British screenwriters, had approached him with an idea that was intended to tap into the recent wave of interest around ensemble singing, and he'd pitched it well...four guys caught up in the horror of 9/11, each traumatised in their own way, turn to singing as therapy.

From the rubble of their lives – bereavement, guilt, heartache, depression – they fight to rebuild what they once had, but nothing will be the same again. Only singing gives them hope of a new beginning. They form an a cappella quartet, enter a national TV talent competition, and…

At that point, Newt was sold. He could see the potential, and it was big. He could see the story of the four victims playing out in his mind's eye: the horrific events of that fateful day, the aftermath, the flashbacks, the titanic struggle to survive, and then the glimmers of hope, the slow steps forward, the start of an epic journey, all propelled by the transformative and redemptive powers of music.

It seemed trite to make comparisons with the likes of *Glee* and *Pitch Perfect*, but he could see that tapping into the singing zeitgeist was hot, and with syndicated talent shows like *The Sing-Off* and, of course, *X Factor*, still hugely popular in the U.S. and around the world, this made the project even more appealing. But the most compelling thing about the project was the momentousness of the subject matter. A country coming to terms with unimaginable horror, four individuals fighting to reclaim their lives. A story about hope, about the indefatigable nature of mankind.

More than anything, Newt saw *A Cappella Fellas* as an ideal tribute to Ken Potts, his dearly departed friend. Ken had been in on the project from the start, having made a significant contribution to Eric's early script, and then it was Ken who had introduced him to Neil. It was only because Newt had absolute faith in Ken's judgment that he was prepared to take a risk with an unknown, but how it had paid off! Neil's a cappella arrangements for the film were an absolute tour de force, and Newt couldn't wait to see them brought to life.

Ken was occupying Newt's thoughts a lot recently. From their early days singing together, and throughout their long association, Newt had come to revere Ken for all sorts of reasons. He was his confidante, standing by with quiet advice when

Newt went off the rails, which he did regularly as a young man, usually on some romantic fool's errand or other. Ken was sage and sanguine, the perfect foil. And he was an immensely talented musician, a wonderful storyteller, possessed of such natural gifts. More than anything, however, he was a great teacher, and nothing gave him more pleasure than to pass on what he knew, always encouraging others, always finding ways of getting the best out of people. But then he was the most modest of men. He could have made it to the top in show business, of that Newt was certain, but he never cared too much for the limelight, and had only reluctantly appeared in *The Good Old Days* back in the day. In his eulogy, Newt had referred to Ken as 'the most talented and reluctant superstar I have ever had the privilege to know', and that just about summed him up.

How very inconsiderate of Ken to pop off when he did, Newt thought, though somehow he could still sense his influence. 'I have a feeling he's up there somewhere keeping an eye on things,' he'd told the team. And then Neil had echoed this feeling when he said he'd received a letter from Ken. He didn't elaborate much at the time, and Newt had no time to find out more before he'd left for New York with a hundred things on his mind. But he was curious to hear more about the letter from Neil over lunch – for one particular reason that he might or might not reveal to him.

He glanced around the clubroom of Quaker's, one of the most splendidly notorious and ironically-named private clubs in London. Dating back to 1919, it had been home to all manner of drunken tomfoolery for close on a hundred years and showed no signs of letting up. It was the closest thing to The Drones Club he could think of, and whenever he visited, Newt lived in hope that Bertie Wooster, Gussie Fink-Nottle, and Tuppy Glossop might appear, leading a conga through the library, the dining room, and the clubroom.

Newt checked his wristwatch, and no sooner had he looked up again than Neil appeared at the doorway of the clubroom, glanced around quickly, and then raised a hand in greeting as he spotted Newt sitting in a high-backed leather chair by the fireside. *My word, the boy's good-looking*, Newt thought, remembering the effect Neil had had on him the first time they met. He was also reminded of his early unsuccessful overtures, and Ken's rebuke when he'd found out about them.

Neil was always excited to see the great man, though he was still a little wary of him, not only because Newt had made advances, but because Neil still had to pinch himself whenever they met for fear that the whole thing was the continuation of an elaborate dream. And his sense of excitement now that *A Cappella Fellas* was starting filming was enough to keep him awake at night. He couldn't wait to hear the songs – his own arrangements of those wonderful songs – made real for the first time. Who was going to sing them was still a mystery. Not the actors themselves, he knew that for sure. And he could only imagine the scenes, the settings for the songs. The script, the storyboards, and numerous meetings with the composer, the scriptwriter and others, had given him an impression of how things would be, but who knew how it would all come together when they started shooting, once the director had worked his magic, once the editing guys had done their bit?

Over lunch, Newt shared a few highlights from his New York trip, which included meetings with the U.S. publicity team, the financiers, and one or two of the actors who happened to be in town. Then there was a visit to Ground Zero and a meeting with representatives of two of the 9/11 victim support groups. Most of the filming would take place at Pinewood Studios, but it was essential to make all the right U.S. connections and establish key relationships prior to production. Everything went well, everything was in place.

Neil wasn't that hungry, as excitement seemed to have a ruinous effect on his appetite. However, Newt persuaded him to try the Eggs Arnold Bennett, which he assured him was light and delicious, 'heaven on a plate'. And for dessert, with a nod to Ken, who loved bananas and consumed more of them than anyone they had ever known, they both had Banoffee Pie.

And so the subject turned, inevitably, to Ken.

'What was all that about a letter from Ken at our last meeting? You didn't give too much away at the time. Were you serious, or just winding up our friend Ed?' asked Newt.

'I wouldn't do something like that, Mr. B... Newt. I was serious, a letter from Ken arrived out of the blue. I have it with me,' said Neil.

Neil handed the letter to Newt, who read it and then examined every line closely, as though looking for clues. 'I knew about The Fifth Voice,' he said at last. 'That's what Ken did best: he set people challenges, people whose talent he believed in, and he delighted in seeing them rise to the challenge. He told me that you'd found The Fifth Voice, which to an old barbershop singer like me, means you found how to lock your voices and ring chords with a precision and clarity that makes the hair on the back of your neck stand on end. But judging by this, there's something a bit deeper going on. It sounds like Kenny had a master plan in mind for you boys, and he's not letting something as trivial as his own untimely demise stand in the way of its execution. The old bugger!'

'Well, we've committed to get going again as a quartet, so we'll see where it takes us,' said Neil.

'That reminds me,' said Newt. 'We've got recording sessions penned in for week nine of the production schedule, if memory serves. You and Joel will need to be there, obviously.'

'Sure, of course,' said Neil.

'And another thing. I need you to get more involved with the production. We talked about your role as special advisor, not just arranger, and it's important to get you working with the actors to give them a real sense of what harmony singing is all about. They've hopefully read your backgrounder and listened to the MP3s by now, but I need you to instil in these guys that passion for quartet singing that'll help them be convincing on set.

Whatever you can do to add that extra edge will be invaluable. They may be lip-syncing, but they need to come across like the real article. And that's all in the fine detail,' said Newt.

'When you put it that way, it sounds suddenly very scary.'

'You can do it. You know all about The Fifth Voice. I can't think of a better way to inspire these guys than telling them the story of your own quartet. But coming back to the recording sessions, we're no nearer to knowing who's going to be singing on the soundtrack. We've put feelers out, and we're talking to the Barbershop Harmony Society in Nashville, as well as the Contemporary A Cappella Society of America, so we'll see. But it strikes me that the answer may lie a little closer to home.' Newt waved Ken's letter, which was still in his left hand. At the same time, he placed his right hand on his breast pocket, allowing his thumb to dip inside to feel the torn edge of an envelope containing another letter.

'You mean you'd like us to audition?'

'The least you boys could do is try out for it,' said Newton Burns.

Fourteen

Tea & Sympathy

When Hannah and Danny had come close to splitting up – when Hannah's affair had been uncovered and the question over Ben had arisen – the atmosphere in the house had been as palpably charged as a Van de Graaff generator. Hurt and tension hung in the air like a smoke cloud, suffocating them both, and it became so unbearable that Danny had moved out for a while, staying with Vince at his old flat. And since Ellie was born, there were days when something of that atmosphere returned, hanging heavy as a blanket of fresh snow over everything.

Before the overdose, Hannah could tell from Danny's face, his body language, and his way of speaking when the atmosphere was at its worst, though she was often too mired in her own internal tortures to care. Since the overdose (*the bloody overdose*), the dynamic had changed and the atmosphere was charged in a different way. Now she was the focus of morbid attention from everyone, and she felt like a scientific specimen under constant observation. Before the overdose (*the fucking overdose*), she had been moderate to high on the Edinburgh Postnatal Depression Scale. Now she was probably considered off the scale, but she was defiant in the face of so much scrutiny. The last time she completed the form with her health visitor, she ignored the standard multiple-choice options in favour of the following spontaneous answers:

1. **I have been able to laugh and see the funny side of things**

   Actually, yes. For the first time in ages, yes. Just the once, but that's a start, right?

2. **I have looked forward with enjoyment to things**

   Downton Abbey, not much else

3. **I have blamed myself unnecessarily when things went wrong**

   Every time

4. **I have been anxious or worried for no good reason**

   All day long

5. **I have felt scared or panicky for no very good reason**

   Aaaagh!

6. **Things have been getting on top of me**

   Everything has been getting on top of me, except for Danny

7. **I have been so unhappy that I have had difficulty sleeping**

   Sleep, what's that?

8. **I have felt sad or miserable**

   ☹

9. **I have been so unhappy that I have been crying**

   I get loyalty vouchers from Kleenex

10. **The thought of harming myself has occurred to me**

    Not since the fucking overdose, and even then I didn't mean to harm myself

The health visitor was not impressed with Hannah's flippancy, but she found the answers to the first and last questions interesting. Hannah explained to her how Danny had made her laugh with his suggestion of bringing in a shaman to perform an exorcism, but when asked about her answer to the final question, she frowned. And rather than explain verbally what she had tried to explain repeatedly since that awful night, and finding only deaf ears, Hannah instead turned over the evaluation form and wrote:

> Hard as this may be to believe, I did not intend to kill myself. For months now, I have felt hopeless, helpless and scared. Scared that the world is conspiring to change things for the worse, make everything that should be joyful dreadful. I am often sapped of all energy, to the point where all I want to do is sleep. But sleep won't come, and it makes things even worse. I fear that Ellie will come to harm — not necessarily at my hands, but by any means (fire, flood, terrorist attack, falling tree branches, whatever). Maybe I once came close to hurting Ellie, but I can't remember. If I did, I can't bear the thought. I love that little girl so much it hurts, and the thought of her being harmed is unbearable. However, I'm going to get through this. Now please file this away and stop asking me the same questions over and over again. I AM GOING TO GET THROUGH THIS. THANK YOU.

Brave words, now she thought back on them.

Hannah was out on her own for only the second time since *that* night. Not only had she made her case clear with the health visitor, she had also told Danny and Dorothy that she had no intention of continuing her role as the fragile victim, and that she was fed up of being treated like a laboratory rat. Which meant spending some time alone when she needed space.

Making her way down the High Street in Maidenhead, with its oversupply of phone shops, opticians, and vacant units, she wondered whether her choice of shopping location had been the right one to lift her spirits. But small things helped her mood: seeing the Boy and Boat bronze, buying a loaf and some samosas from a street stall, and dropping some small change into a charity collection box outside Marks & Spencer. Then, as she rounded the corner into Queen Street, she almost collided with someone she was sure she knew, though not all the visual clues seemed right. The handsome face that stared at her was familiar, the eyes bright, the jaw firm, though with less flesh than she remembered. The man's frame was also slighter than she remembered, and the walking stick seemed at odds with her memory altogether.

'Hannah! It's Vince. Great to see you.'

'Vince! Hello! Well, well. How are you?'

'Ah, keeping my spirits up, even if other things are letting me down,' said Vince, with a wave of his stick. 'But how are *you*, more to the point? I heard from Danny that you've been unwell…'

'Getting there…getting there, thanks.' Hannah flicked a thumb towards the door of the coffee shop they were stood outside. 'Fancy a coffee?'

Inside the shop, Vince stared in bewilderment at the drinks menu that ran the length of the wall behind the counter, beneath which a bank of gleaming chrome contraptions were at work percolating, steaming, frothing, and gurgling. 'I'll have a cup of tea,' he said at last.

They took their drinks to a corner table, and Hannah was reminded of the day Vince had visited her at home, during the spell when Danny was staying with him. 'I'd forgotten you prefer tea,' she said.

'Coffee confuses me,' said Vince. 'Too many types and fancy names. And they all leave a nasty taste in your mouth when you're finished. You know where you are with tea – the cup that refreshes, the cup that cheers.'

'I haven't seen you since the quartet championships in Harrogate. You all did brilliantly, and I'm surprised it's taken you so long to get things going again. It's great that you're starting rehearsals.'

'Yup, first one the week after next. Up and running at last.

And it's great to see you up and running, after…after not being too well.' Vince's hand shook as he raised his cup, spilling tea onto the table.

'Thanks.' Hannah sipped her coffee and smiled. 'Do you remember that time you came to see me, when Danny was staying at your place?'

'Of course, how could I forget? Awkward, wasn't it?'

'Brave, I'd say…and very sweet. You came to tell me how Danny was feeling: ripped up inside, his pride wounded, that he wanted to make things right. You asked me not to lose faith in him, and you said it in such a caring way. I could have told you to keep your nose out of my marriage, but you really helped bring us back together, and I'm not sure I ever thanked you for that.'

'I hated seeing him so miserable, that's all. He was a gloomy sod to have around the place.'

'I'd like to say all's well again, but no sooner had we got back to something like normal than everything changed again… when Ellie was—'

'Lovely little thing. Danny showed me a photo. You must be so proud. And Ben too. He's a great lad.'

'Proud of them…yes, I am, of course. It's me I'm not too proud of,' said Hannah, a tear appearing in the corner of her eye.

'Hey, it's okay. Listen, I don't know what you're going through, but…'

'Postnatal depression.'

'Ah, right, I see,' said Vince. 'Well, look…it's not your fault, you can't blame yourself. This stuff happens. Here, take this,' said Vince, handing Hannah a paper serviette damp with tea.

'I've told myself I'm going to get through this one way or another, but I'm not sure where I'll get the strength from.' Hannah held the sodden serviette by one corner, wondering what to do with it.

'You were a professional showjumper, weren't you? How

many times did you fall off your horse, or get thrown over a fence?'

'Lots of times. It's what happens. But the last big fall was the one that put paid to my career, just before they announced the British eventing team for 2012. I haven't been on a horse since, so I'm not sure your analogy is going to work.'

Vince tore open a sachet of sugar and poured it onto the tabletop. 'I wasn't going to tell you to get back in the saddle. I was only going to say that if you've had your face ground into the mud as many times as you have, you must be made of tough stuff.'

'I suppose so, but this is different.'

'Do you remember Ken, our coach?' said Vince, depositing the contents of another sachet onto the table.

'Heard lots about him, of course, but never met him. Sad loss...'

Vince formed the sugar pile into an exact circle. 'He told me something that helps me a lot, and it might help you too. He said don't let your problems define who you are... MS in my case. So I refuse to let it get to me. I treat it like a wasp in a beer garden, buzzing around the top of my glass. I pick my moment and then launch the bastard into the long grass with a well-timed Subbuteo finger flick.'

'Ken said that?'

'Not in so many words, but he made me believe it. So, in your case, you should tell your postnatal depression to fuck right off. Stare it down, make it frightened. Let it know it's not going to get the better of you. And then watch the bully run off home to its mum.'

'Sounds easy when you put it like that, but it's a lonely business trying to beat this thing. Okay, sure, everyone says they're there for you, but no-one quite gets it. So, one way or another, you're on your own.'

Vince tilted his head gently from side to side and leant slightly forward in his seat. 'At the risk of sounding like I'm reading from the gospel according to Saint Ken, that's something else he taught me. The four of us, in fact. When we first got together, we were a ragbag assortment of basket cases – still are, I suppose. Then Ken stepped in, spoke in tongues quite a bit – a lot of it went straight over our heads – and got us thinking differently. And while we were working away on singing technique and vocal unity, guess what? We were supporting each other. Not by talking about each other's problems in any big way, and not by saying "I'm there for you", but by just being together to help take the load off.'

'Which is marvellous, but I don't have anyone that—'

'Give Angie a call.'

'Your fiancée?'

'Yes. You met in Harrogate. Did you get on?'

'Yes, yes we did. And she was great with Ben: bought him an ice cream and talked to him like she'd known him for ages.'

'That sounds about right. Give her a call.'

'Thanks,' said Hannah.

Vince prodded an index finger twice into the circular sugar pile to create a pair of eyes, then swiped an upturned mouth beneath.

Fifteen

Rock 'n' Roll

From The Edge were gathered for their first rehearsal in months, with Neil playing host at his parents' house. He had called them together, saying that if they were serious about carrying on as a quartet it was time to stop prevaricating. Life pressure, diary pressure...no more excuses. The only thing that mattered now was peer pressure, and he was the one applying the tourniquet.

Danny had hardly hesitated when he received Neil's call, which made him realise how much better Hannah was these days. Until recently, leaving her with the kids for an evening when she'd had them for most of the day would have seemed like tempting fate, but he had been a little more at ease this last couple of weeks.

Vince was raring to go. Mildly chastened by Angie's reproach the day he returned home after a few beers with Neil in Cookham, he had been teetotal for a while, and was feeling virtuous. He was also determined, despite his current physical shortcomings, that he would be on his best possible form when he accompanied Angie to the forthcoming *Finesse* gala dinner at the Dorchester. The thought of wall-to-wall glamour, a sea of shapely female flesh, shimmering in all its low-cut, high-heeled, provocative glory, was medicine in itself.

Henry was also ready to rumble. Buoyed by his recent interview, though by no means certain that he would accept the position even if it were offered, his ego had been well and truly stroked. He had also received an unexpected and revealing call from Cat, and he knew he must fit in a visit to the island very soon. But for now, he was excited by the quartet's reunion and was all focus.

'I've been looking at ways we can motivate ourselves,' said Neil, as they got down to business.

There was a sharp intake of breath from Vince.

'I've been looking up the best practice behaviours of the top quartets,' Neil continued. 'What gives them the edge, what sets them apart from the rest.'

Henry was reminded of his recent interview with Freddie Markham.

Vince scowled. 'Is this going to be one of those bloody group therapy sessions?' he said, his mind already drifting back to the sea of shapely female flesh, shimmering in all its low-cut, high-heeled, provocative glory.

'Carry on, Neil,' said Danny, giving Vince a dirty look.

Neil reasoned that without Ken to drive and guide them, they were in danger of becoming rudderless if they weren't careful. They needed fresh focus, and they needed to find self-discipline. He said it made sense to apply the same motivational methods as the very best in the business. 'So, here's one that we can try...think back to childhood and remember the one thing you wanted more than anything. The one thing that you would have done anything to achieve or to possess when you were growing up...'

'Getting off with Brenda Fairclough,' said Vince, quick as a flash.

'Kind of predictable, but I'm glad to see you're getting involved, Vince,' said Neil. 'Danny, what about you?'

'Er...seeing Everton win the league, I suppose. But then they did, when I was ten,' said Danny.

'So think of another one.'

'Seeing Everton win the league ever again?' said Vince.

Danny rubbed the side of his face nearest to Vince with his

middle finger. 'Okay then, I was really into Egyptology when I was a kid, and always wanted to explore the pyramids. I still haven't seen them.'

'Sounds good. So long as it's something you yearned for but didn't get to realise. What about you, Henry?'

'Well, I was desperate for a Raleigh Chopper bike when I was in my early teens. My older sister got one for Christmas, but my parents couldn't see the sense in buying us one each and said we could share. She never did share, of course, and in any case, yellow wasn't my colour. I still dream about that Christmas…' said Henry, his voice fading away, leaving an emotionally charged silence in its wake. The others exchanged surprised looks.

'This *is* one of those bloody group therapy sessions, isn't it?' said Vince. 'Well, I'm not having it. Forget it. I don't care if Henry didn't get a stupid bike for Christmas, and I don't care if Brenda Fairclough made me the emotionally crippled wreck you see before you – which I'm not, by the way. Just where the hell is all this leading?'

Neil raised a hand. 'This has got nothing to do with group therapy, Vince. We won't be hugging each other or handing out tissues, rest assured. It's called *visualisation*. Some of the leading sportsmen and women use it when they set goals, and so do some of the top quartets. I just thought it might be a useful way of getting us focused, a method of self-propulsion, if you like. Visualise the thing you always wanted, then devote all your energy to making it happen.'

'Well that's got to be the biggest load of bollocks I've ever heard,' said Vince. 'Henry'll look pretty fucking daft on a Raleigh Chopper at his age, and I've seen Brenda Fairclough on Facebook, and getting off with her is no longer a pleasant prospect, I can tell you!'

'You're missing the point, Vince – as usual! That was just an exercise, the childhood memory thing. Now think. What do you want more than anything, as it relates to the quartet? What do you want to achieve above all else? Visualise it and—'

'Oh, for fuck's sake! A gold medal, of course. A British quartet championship gold medal!'

'There we are!' said Neil, as though Vince had at last revealed a deeply buried secret.

Vince shook his head. 'So we've spent the last fifteen minutes visualising Henry's Chopper and Danny prizing the lid off a sarcophagus and unwrapping a mummy, or whatever the fuck, just to arrive at the bleedin' obvious?'

'I'd say it was worth it,' said Neil, unabashed. 'Just hearing you say the words, and the passion with which you said them... I'd say that was worth it, Vince.'

'Can we do a bit of singing now?' said Danny.

An hour and a half later, From The Edge were back in the swing of things, having warmed up, had fun with some new vocal exercises, and reacquainted themselves with most of their repertoire. 'Rock 'n' Roll!' said Vince, as he sank into a chair, exhausted, and they all knew what he meant.

Neil brought in cold drinks from the kitchen, they discussed some of the things they needed to work on next time – specific aspects of vowel matching, tuning, and pitch maintenance – and then they settled on their next rehearsal date.

Neil had deliberately saved his news until the end.

'Chaps, before you go, I've got a proposition for you,' he said.

'No more amateur psychology, Neil, please. I'm knackered,' said Vince.

Neil cut to the chase. 'I met up with Newton Burns a few days ago, and he updated me on plans for the film shoot. The soundtrack recording sessions are a way off yet, but they're still looking for the right quartet for the job. He asked me if we'd like to audition.'

'You're joking,' said Henry.

'Are you serious?' said Danny.

'Rock. And. Fucking. Roll,' said Vince.

Part Two

Roads Less Travelled

Sixteen

A Pinewood Man

When news first emerged that Yellow Braces had optioned a script from Eric Winstanley, and that the story was about a vocal harmony group, the industry gave a collective shrug of the shoulders. Newton Burns was known to be a fan of Winstanley, having given him his first break with *Denmark Street*, a modest box office success, but sufficiently well received to put Winstanley on the map. Newton Burns also had a history of making movies about the entertainment business, so no surprise there either.

However, when it came to light that the back story of the principal characters was 9/11, the industry raised a collective eyebrow. Best known for making British feel-good movies with mostly British actors, this was something of a departure for Burns, and there was a sense that he might be stepping outside of his comfort zone. But Burns paid no attention to the industry gossip, and had a clear and unshakeable conviction that this would be his most successful project to date. His Manhattan office, a tiny two-room garret on the Upper East Side, was on the case straight away, making the right calls, seeing the right people, and generally stoking up interest stateside. And having got Joey Pellegrini on board, their first American A-lister, the word spread quickly coast-to-coast, and before long several of the top agents were pitching their clients for what was beginning to be seen as a hot, if not quite the hottest, project in town.

Early on, the expectation was that filming would, at least in part, be on location in Manhattan, but Newton Burns hadn't entertained that idea for a moment. He was a Pinewood man, and there was nothing that couldn't be achieved at the venerable old studios deep in the Buckinghamshire countryside. And when asked about his allegiance to the place, Burns was fond of quoting Pinewood founder J Arthur Rank, who chose the name of the studios as a deliberate swipe at Hollywood, saying 'Unlike holly, which is the bush of a small tree, the pine is big, strong, and magnificent.'

The script called for flashbacks to the 9/11 scene, as seen through the eyes of the principal characters, and Burns had booked Q Stage which, at 30,000 square feet, was the second largest stage on site after the 007 Stage and would be just right for the recreation of what had come to be known as Ground Zero.

Burns had also consulted widely, taking ideas and opinions from a variety of people who had been involved in similar projects. Amongst them was director Matthew Vaughn, whose movie *Kick Ass* was set in New York and filmed entirely at Pinewood. Over lunch they had discussed their mutual affection for the studios. 'For a documentary on Pinewood, I was once asked why I keep coming back to the place,' Vaughn said. 'And my answer was "The British charm of bad food, sound stages which are really cowsheds, and no air conditioning. But apart from that, I love it." And we've got the best film crews in the world. I'm amazed every time I work with a British crew, how much better they are.'

Newton Burns also wasted no time in securing the services of veteran director Miles McAuley. Known to everyone as Mac, he entered the business in the 1970s, when Hollywood was finding itself again after the implosion of the old studio system, and he was one of the new breed of brash young film school types who had the audacity to believe they could reinvent everything, make movies their own way, and on their own terms. Hollywood struggled to adapt to the new era, and having dabbled unsuccessfully with the European arthouse tradition for a while, eventually allowed the likes of McAuley to cut their teeth on their own projects, and with the reborn philosophy that telling good stories and thrilling the hell out of your audience are what really count. Mac made great movies, it was that simple. He came with a distinguished track record and a high sticker price, but Newton Burns knew he had the right man for the job.

Newton Burns sat at the head of the imposing rosewood table in the boardroom of his office in Soho, London, the headquarters of Yellow Braces. Gathered around him were Mac the director, head of casting Lorna Drayton, scriptwriter Eric Winstanley, director of photography Baz Cohen, composer and musical director Joel Hannigan, the production manager Bob Coe, and the first assistant director Mike Hicks. On the wall at the far end of the table, some twelve feet away, was a large projector screen on which the words A CAPPELLA FELLAS: EVE OF PRODUCTION were displayed in giant white letters on a dark blue background.

'So, here we are, ladies and gentlemen,' said Newt. 'Thank you for indulging me in one of my little traditions – or superstitions, if you will – which is to have a kick-off meeting ahead of the big day. Everything's in place, the backroom team have been meticulous in getting everything ready for tomorrow, and I'm extremely excited to get going. This won't be a long meeting, you'll be glad to hear. More of a final flick through the production schedule and a chance to air any issues you may still have lurking, or even better, to share any bright ideas you might have to get us off to the best possible start. All okay with that? Fine.' Newton Burns pressed a button and a partial plan of the studio lot appeared on the far wall.

'The crew will be starting on the Ground Zero construction at Q Stage bright and early and we expect to be able to shoot the first of the flashback scenes in about a week's time. Meanwhile, we start over here at F Stage, shooting Scene Fourteen, the meeting between characters Matt Archer and Muriel Bampton. I've seen Joey already, and he said he'll be at the restaurant later on, but do we know if darling Ms. Rossi is in town yet? Anyone heard anything?'

Lorna Drayton ran an elegant forefinger along the fringe of her immaculate auburn hair and cleared her throat. 'Yes. She arrived yesterday, but she won't be at the restaurant this evening. She'll be making her usual entrance on set tomorrow. I'm told we can expect a pink limousine to arrive at around nine.'

'She has a hair and make-up call for eight,' said Mac. 'Pink limousine my ass. Who the hell does she think she is? Lady Penelope?'

'I'm just saying what I've been told.'

'So we're already behind schedule,' said Mac, smoothing the grizzled hair of the beard that covered half of his face with both hands. 'Impressive.'

Newt turned to the first assistant director. 'Mike, can you get your second AD to call her people and get her there before eight?' he said, getting up from his chair and snapping his braces with both thumbs.

'And then she'll arrive at ten,' said Mac. I've been here before. Let's leave it as it is. Hopefully, she'll fall in line once she's on set and her leading man starts to work his magic.'

'They've got previous, haven't they?' asked Newt.

'Just a bit,' said Mac. 'She's always more than happy to work with Joey. She falls for him every time, and it usually has a calming effect on proceedings.'

'Okay, let's live with Madame's grand entrance for now,' said Newt. 'But if she starts misbehaving and losing us any more time —'

'She'll be fine once she's bedded in, so to speak,' said Lorna, raising her eyebrows at her own inadvertent joke. 'It's Frampton we want to worry about.'

'I heard he's calmed down lately,' said Newt.

'The spell at the Betty Ford in Los Angeles, you mean?' said Mac. 'Forget it. That was a publicity stunt between projects. He's back on the booze, believe me. I have it on good authority. But at least he's in town already, that's a start.'

'So much for getting off to a flyer,' said Newt, playing with a long wisp of his bright white hair. 'Half the cast going off the rails before we've even started. It sounds like our second AD is going to have his work cut out. But Lorna, can you stay close? I hope it doesn't come to it, but just in case we need to…well, explore alternatives. But we need to move on. I want to bring in Joel to talk about the music side of things. Joel?'

Joel Hannigan, a thin, nervous-looking individual of medium height, blinked repeatedly at the sound of his name, then sipped at a glass of water.

'And by the way,' Newt went on, 'I have to say what a fantastic job Joel and his team have done. We all know he's one of the best composers in the business, but my word, the music is just magnificent. I'm not sure we've given you enough credit for that, Joel, but it's the music that's going to make this movie. Any updates?'

Joel looked awkward but managed a half-smile. 'Well, the incidental music has been in progress for a while, and I've been rehearsing the London Phil for the last two weeks. We won't be recording until week twenty-six or so, once everything's in the can, and then we're back for any reworking after the final edits.'

'Great. And the a cappella songs?'

'All done, thanks to Neil. Really great arrangements. I know nothing about arranging in the barbershop style, so that's all down to him. But we're still looking for a quartet to record the songs for the soundtrack. That's taking longer than we imagined.'

'I may have a suggestion there,' said Newt. Do you remember our last meeting here, when Neil was with us, and Ed Pimm from the backers? Well, you may recall that my old friend Ken Potts featured in the conversation quite a bit…'

'How could we forget,' said Mac. 'All that talk of your pal

pulling strings from the afterlife nearly gave Ed a coronary.'

'I seem to recall he was a little sceptical about Ken making me believe in this project, I agree. But I can't help that. It's true,' said Newt. 'And you might recall that Neil mentioned something about receiving a letter from Ken?'

Mac snorted suddenly, which turned into a deep chesty cough that lasted half a minute. Lorna poured him a glass of water, and they waited for him to recover. 'Sorry, I'm still struggling with giving up smoking. Strange really, I never used to cough when I was doing twenty a day.'

'Well, I spoke to Neil about the letter,' Newt continued. 'And it transpires that Ken had written to Neil's quartet before he died, spurring them on to greater things. A rather marvellous letter of encouragement. What I didn't tell Neil – I'm not exactly sure why – is that I also received a letter from Ken around the same time.'

'The plot thickens,' said Mac, who was now chewing nicotine gum. 'It's a good job Ed isn't here to hear this.'

'It's no big deal,' said Newt, pulling a letter from his shirt pocket. 'I won't read it to you, as it's, well, rather private in nature. Something of a fond and prescient farewell. But he finishes with a P.S. wishing me well with *A Cappella Fellas*, and suggesting that it might be an idea to give From The Edge, Neil's quartet, a chance of auditioning for the film recording. And, well, I took the liberty of inviting them to do just that. I hope you don't mind, Joel. I mean, if they're not up to the job, then so be it. But no harm in giving them a chance…what do you think?'

'Fine by me. Let's get them into a studio to do a demo,' said Joel.

'Splendid. Thanks, Joel. Okay, next item: script supervisor. Eric, Mac, are you all right working with Rebecca Wilson? Bit of a late appointment, I know, but she suddenly became available and she's one of the best.'

'Let me think…does Ken have any opinions on the matter?' said Mac.

Seventeen

The Red Carpet

Finesse was one of the leading British men's magazines, a publication that positioned itself alongside *Playboy* at the classy end of the top shelf. Though its heyday was in the 1970s, it had kept going even when the tide had started to turn against men's magazines, due partly to its relatively sophisticated content, to its high-quality production values, and to the substantial backing of a Birmingham-based manufacturing entrepreneur. However, when the owner turned his attention to other ventures in the mid-90s, the title ceased production, though it returned for a limited run a few years later. That lasted just five years before the magazine finally became unsustainable and was forced to close for good. Ten years on, erstwhile owner of *Finesse*, Colin Mills, driven to raise money for a children's charity close to his heart, had the idea of a grand reunion – with models, management, and staff gathering for a one-off glitzy evening fundraiser in London.

Angie was wearing a sparkling gold gown that revealed both the magnificence of her bosom and a smooth, sleek expanse of thigh. She ran her hands down the length of her shapely form and blew Vince a kiss.

'Fuck me!' Vince was propped against the bedroom doorframe, towelling his wet hair, his mouth ajar.

'I take it you approve then, Vincey,' said Angie, improvising a twirl.

'You won't be able to fight the blokes off with a shitty stick,' said Vince.

'How very flattering,' said Angie, who was now staring unblinking into a wall mirror, applying mascara.

Vince approached his fiancée and looked intently at her reflection. Angie switched the gaze of her slate grey eyes to meet Vince's and halted the rhythmic flicking of the mascara wand. 'What?'

'How about a quick one?' said Vince.

'You're joking, aren't you? Get ready, for pity's sake. The taxi's booked for six-thirty. Chop chop!' Angie blew another kiss at Vince's reflection and continued applying her make-up.

Vince returned to the bathroom and stepped under a cold shower for two minutes before getting ready, as instructed, and presented himself to his fiancée some twenty minutes later.

'You look just great, babe!' said Angie as Vince made his way downstairs into the living room. 'Scrubbed up very well indeed.'

'I'm not sure this exactly goes with the look,' said Vince, tapping his stick against the banister rail. 'But thanks all the same.'

'Nonsense, you look a picture of male elegance! You always did look good in a tux. I'm having second thoughts about that quickie.'

'Don't tease, the taxi's outside.'

'Sorry, babe. I couldn't resist. Let's go.'

The elderly Mercedes saloon slowed to a tentative halt behind a gleaming midnight blue Bentley and a white stretch limousine on the approach to the hotel entrance.

'Isn't that Colin Mills in the Bentley, the bloke who used to own *Finesse*?' said Vince. And look at the limo in front of him! They've obviously had a whip-round, filled up with cheap fizz and been twice round the North Circular to get their money's worth. Look at her trying to get out, legs akimbo. Oh dear, and no knickers, either... I think that pap's just got a snap of her snapper. Fuck me, this is going to be some night!'

'Shut up, Vince,' said Angie. 'Driver, don't bother queuing for the entrance. We'll get out here, thanks. Vince, pay the man, please.'

Inside the hotel lobby, Angie and Vince made their way through the throng, Angie looking furtively left and right to see if she recognised anyone, Vince keeping his stick as close to his right leg as possible so as not to trip anyone or give the impression that a war hero had entered the building.

'Let's get through this mob and find the bar,' said Vince just as Angie felt a hand on her elbow. Turning around, she gave out a squeal.

'Trish! Bloody hell, great to see you!'

Trish, well over six feet tall in her heels, stooped to hug her old friend, though Vince noticed that very little contact actually took place, no doubt in fear of spoiling the make-up or hairdo of either party. 'My God, how long has it been?' said Trish, catching Vince's eye.

'Well, ten years, I guess,' said Angie, catching the eye of someone standing next to Trish, who reminded her of Daniel Craig.

'Sorry,' said Trish, twisting suddenly. 'This is Timothy. Timothy, this is Angie, a darling old friend.' Timothy nodded, smiled politely, and shook Angie's hand without a word.

'Oh, and this is Vince,' said Angie. Vince quickly passed his stick behind his back, switching it to his left hand, and extended his right.

'Delightful to meet you,' said Trish. 'Have we met before? You remind me of someone…' Vince stopped short of offering a suggestion as to who that might be and stretched out a hand to Timothy to complete the greetings.

'Where are we meant to be?' asked Trish. 'Isn't there meant to be a red carpet somewhere?' At which point, Vince spotted a sign which read 'Finesse Red Carpet Reception' and they headed off in that direction.

The red carpet was in most regards faithful to its billing, in that it was definitely a carpet, the colour of which was unquestionably red. But in other ways it defied the usual expectation of red carpets as seen at the Oscars or the BAFTAs. For one thing, it measured no more than ten feet long, at the end of which was a slightly unstable advertising board displaying the old *Finesse* logo surrounded by several other logos: one of the current crop of glamour magazines, a cable TV channel, and a high street restaurant chain.

There seemed to be no organisation, just a scrum of designer dresses milling around at random. Now and then a model in a glittering ball gown or some elaborate chiffon creation would appear in front of the advertising board, pouting, looking over both shoulders, presenting both fulsome front and pert posterior to a gaggle of photographers.

'So this is the red carpet,' said Vince. 'Where's the bar?'

'Wait,' said Angie. 'I think there's some sort of system. Isn't someone calling names over there?'

'Looks like a free-for-all to me, darling,' said Trish. 'Let's push to the front, get the tits 'n' teeth bit out of the way, then we can relax.'

'She's a bit of a girl,' said Vince.

'You don't know the half,' said Angie. 'And her fella's a bit of a dish, isn't he?'

'Is he? Looks like a bit of a twat to me.'

'Reminds me of Daniel Craig.'

'What, the James Bond actor? The one that makes George Lazenby's Bond seem charismatic? Nah, don't think so,' said Vince.

Trish took Angie by the hand, and the pair shimmied towards the advertising board, cracking huge grins for one and all. As they stepped in front of the cameras, Angie was surprised to hear their names being shouted. 'Trish, this way... Angie, looking wonderful, over here...let's have one of you together...'

As the girls posed to order, Vince surveyed Timothy, wondering about his initial assessment of him. Up to now, he hadn't said a word. 'Fancy a pint, Timothy?'

'I could murder one,' came the surprise reply. 'Let's grab the girls and get going.'

As they entered the bar, Angie and Trish were confronted with a sea of faces and figures from yesteryear, the room full of people being reacquainted for the first time in years. The air was thick with the sickly scent of insincerity as bodies collided, air kisses exchanged, and platitudes dished out like so much confetti.

Vince and Timothy side-stepped the crowd and made for the corner of the bar marked 'No serving here. Glass collection only', and Vince's new acquaintance barked an order for two pints of lager at a timid-looking bartender with an ill-advised side parting and an Adam's apple the size of a golf ball.

'Cheers, Timothy,' said Vince, relieved to have a glass in hand at last.

'Tim, mate. It's Tim. She likes to call me Timothy, some sort of image thing, but I can't stand all that bullshit. Cheers, anyway. What's the stick all about, then?'

After about fifteen minutes of getting along like an unexpected house on fire, they were again joined by the girls. 'Champagne!' announced Trish, and Tim barked the order at the timid bartender. 'Bottle of Bollinger, two glasses, please. Wait, make that two bottles of Bolly and four glasses.'

After an initial 'Cheers!' all round, the girls continued chatting, and Vince and Tim settled in at the corner of the bar.

'Has anyone ever said you look like Daniel Craig?' asked Vince.

'What, the R&B bloke… *Bo Selecta*…that bloke?'

'No, no, that's Craig David,' said Vince. 'I mean the actor who plays James Bond.'

'No, can't say it's ever been mentioned,' said Tim. 'Has anyone ever said you look like Mel Gibson?'

'Mel Gibson? Here we go. Yes, they have.' Vince took a swig

of lager followed by a slug of champagne. 'But most people think I look like George Clooney.'

'Can't see it myself,' said Tim. 'There's a rumour he might be here tonight, as it happens. Though why he could be arsed to turn up at this bash, God only knows.'

Overhearing her partner, Trish interjected. 'It's true. He's a good friend of Colin Mills, and he's in England at the moment, staying at his place in Sonning. Colin asked him to do a PA.'

'What, do a *secretary*?' said Vince.

'Personal Appearance!' said Trish with a squawk that threatened to shatter glass.

'More champagne?' said Vince, raising his lager glass.

'Another bottle of Bolly!' barked Tim.

The gala dinner was a mostly fine affair, the food was decent quality, and the wine flowed. The atmosphere was over-excited in the way that reunions tend to be. Angie gave Vince the occasional look to check his drinking, but he seemed surprisingly sober, and even a little thoughtful.

Vince looked around the room, which was alive with carefree jollity, as old acquaintances mingled, almost certain in the knowledge that this would be the last time any of them would see each other again. Glancing at the menu, which doubled as a programme for the evening, Vince saw that there would be a charity auction with special guest appearance after the dessert course. Waiting staff were now serving coffee, and there were signs of activity at the top table: space being cleared, a microphone being adjusted, organisers shuffling here and there.

He didn't want to miss any of the action, but Vince felt the call of nature, and so excused himself and headed for the bathroom as quickly as he could. As he washed his hands, he became aware of a familiar figure standing over a washbasin at the end of the row. The two men moved towards the hand dryers at the same time and stood side by side.

'Good evening,' said the familiar figure.

'Good evening, Mr. Clooney,' said Vince. 'We meet at last.'

The familiar figure looked at Vince with a curious smile, checked his reflection in the washbasin mirror, double-checking Vince as he did so, and left the bathroom.

Eighteen

Island Resolutions

Henry was seasick for the first time ever. On previous occasions he'd taken the boat to the island the crossing had been easy, the Bristol Channel like a millpond. It hadn't occurred to him that the same stretch of water could just as easily turn into a scene from *Moby Dick*.

The ex-German railway ferry lurched through the heaving swell of the sea, bouncing unpredictably, sending Henry's innards up into his throat with a nauseous thump. The crew weaved expertly around the upper and lower decks, collecting filled sick bags and handing out fresh ones. Henry could resist no longer and held out his hand to accept a bag from a passing crew member, for whom vomit duty was a routine part of the job.

In better conditions, the two-hour journey flew by. Scanning the waters for dolphin pods, watching seabirds swoop and soar in the boat's wake, and having a drink or two in the cosy cabin bar were all part of the fun that made the time fly by. But not today. Having relieved himself of the last of his breakfast, Henry stood with both hands gripped to the rail of the starboard side of the lower deck, feet wide apart, his sight fixed firmly on the horizon. He breathed slowly and deeply and marvelled at how the hands of his wristwatch were barely moving.

At last the dark outline of the island appeared, partly swathed in mist, and Henry had to crane his neck to take in the full view as the three-mile stretch of rock, the final resting ground for many an unfortunate and misguided vessel down the centuries, edged nearer. Eventually, Henry could make out the now familiar shapes of the castle and the square church tower, and a sense of joyful anticipation swept through him, clearing away the last remnants of sickness.

Cat watched through binoculars as the ferry made its final steady approach, slowing as it manoeuvred alongside the jetty. On boat days, the focus of activity was getting people and cargo on and off the island as efficiently as possible, and today Cat was helping by driving the Land Rover, transporting new arrivals who were too elderly or infirm to walk the steep beach road to the top of the island, some four hundred feet above sea level. She hopped into the vehicle and made her way along the steep, winding dirt track down to the landing bay, then turned around so that the Land Rover was facing back up the beach road, with the full eastern face of the island in plain view. She got out and looked around at the sudden burst of activity. The boat was tethered and secured against the jetty, and various members of crew and island staff were on hand to oversee disembarking, unload supplies, and generally ensure that the changeover went as smoothly as possible.

Henry was one of the first passengers to disembark, and Cat waved excitedly, like someone trying to warn an approaching train of a fallen tree on the line. Henry waved back and jogged along the wooden boards of the jetty to where Cat stood, arms now outstretched. They embraced without saying a word.

'I didn't expect chauffeur service,' Henry said at last.

'You're joking,' said Cat. 'This isn't for you, music man. I've got real VIPs to collect – very infirm people. Now get up that hill and I'll see you later.'

Having booked at relatively late notice, Henry's accommodation was a small one-room granite building within a courtyard at the rear of the pub and island office. Originally a storeroom, it had also once housed a small electric generator before becoming home to the island's radio transmitter in the 1950s. Long since defunct, the old Naval transmitter, which was used for many years to communicate twice daily to the mainland coastguards, was still in place in a corner of the room. While Henry expected to stay most nights at Cat's more comfortable cottage, it seemed right to have his own bolthole on the island.

Knowing that Cat would be busy until late afternoon, and with little to entertain him in his radio room, Henry set off on a walk around the island. The sky was overcast and a sharp south-westerly wind greeted him as he walked through the tiny village, across a camping field, and up towards the old lighthouse. This was the landmark that fascinated him on his very first visit, a magnificent granite tower topped with a glass lantern room with outside balcony. It always seemed strange that the lighthouse stood some way inland, having been built on the highest point of land. Up to now he hadn't been to the top of the lighthouse, and this was something he intended to put right.

Henry climbed the one hundred and forty seven narrow steps that spiralled tightly up to the top of the tower, and stepped into the small lantern room, at the centre of which no longer stood a lantern but two striped deckchairs.

Just then, the balcony door opened and a very tall man holding his hat to his head stooped to climb back into the lantern room. 'Good afternoon,' he said. 'Very breezy out there, but what a view!'

'I'm surprised they allow visitors out there. Health and safety and all that,' said Henry.

'They let you have the key if you sign an insurance waiver. I take it you haven't, then?'

'Er, no. But never mind. The view's good enough from in here,' said Henry.

'Well, if you really want to step outside, I'll sit here for a while. You don't look like a jumper!'

Henry stepped through the low metal door onto the narrow

balcony that ran the circumference of the lantern room, with just a thin cast iron handrail separating him from a hundred foot drop. He braced himself, his back against the lantern room windows, and looked straight ahead for a minute or so before allowing his gaze to shift left and right. He avoided looking straight down.

Clouds scudded by on the breeze, and patches of blue sky started to appear like fine tears in the blanket of grey. Summoning courage, Henry edged his way around the balcony, gradually taking in stunning views right around the island. He looked across the southern fields and beyond to the murky expanse of the Bristol Channel, its deep green canvas spiked with white-peaked waves driven by the relentless wind. In the distance, the mainland was just visible as a smudge of blue running along the horizon.

Moving carefully anti-clockwise, Henry now looked right across the village, a tight huddle of granite buildings sheltering from the elements. Revolving further, he could now see the full length of the island in all its magnificence. One more turn, and Henry was now looking straight across the Atlantic, with nothing between the island and the New World. Now mid-afternoon, the sun was high above the sea on its westward arc and, as if to order, the tears in the grey clouds suddenly opened wide to reveal a beautiful expanse of pure bright blue that put a huge smile on Henry's face.

He had been wondering as he traversed the balcony what his answer would be to the job offer he received yesterday. Now he was in no doubt.

'I found them just there,' said Cat, pointing to a mound of earth surrounded by a timber frame and covered with a light tarpaulin. 'I knew it was a decent find, and at first I reckoned they were late Mesolithic. But then they looked and felt different from the other flints from that period. So I wondered if they might be older.'

'And are they?' asked Henry.

'We don't know yet. Waiting to hear back from the experts at Bristol Uni any time now. But part of me hopes they're nothing special, to be honest.'

'Why? You could make a name for yourself.'

'That's the problem. It seems that no matter what I do, I end up drawing attention. Like the professor who wants to put me in a laboratory and wire me up to some hideous brainwave machine. And the loonies who keep sending me letters about my so-called special powers. There's a woman in Dudley who reckons I cured her hearing problem. How can that be?'

Henry ran a hand across his mouth.

'It's not funny,' said Cat. 'All I do is dig around with a trowel and, agreed, I seem to have a knack for unearthing interesting stuff. And it's great fun, but this other nonsense is beginning to wear me down, I can tell you. According to Prof. Whiley, I'm some sort of human divining rod. Apparently I can tap into the energy of man-made objects and, if I play my cards right, I can use that energy to heal people. How do you think that makes me feel?'

'Special? Honoured?'

'No, it makes me feel like flinging my trowel, packing in the amateur archaeology, and sticking to what I'm paid to do. I realise that I'm better off just being a nature warden.'

'Do what feels right for you,' said Henry. 'I've had a bit of a realisation as well, today. You know that job I interviewed for? Well, I got it. And standing at the top of the old lighthouse earlier, I decided to turn it down. They can stick it. I don't know why I even entertained the idea in the first place.'

'Excellent!' said Cat, inadvertently channelling Henry's headhunter. Just then, her walkie-talkie sparked into life.

'Cat, you there? Over.'

Cat took her walkie-talkie from the case on her hip. 'Excuse me, Henry. I'm here, Vicky. Over.'

'The email from Bristol has arrived. The carbon dating results. Over.'

'And?'

'Not late Mesolithic…pre-dating anything previously found on the island…potentially highly significant find…'

'Oh, I see,' said Cat, suddenly holding the walkie-talkie at arm's length. 'Thanks, Vicky. Over.'

Nineteen

Abbey Road

'You know Abbey Road?' said Neil.

'What, we're recording at Abbey Road?' said Vince.

'No, I'm just giving you directions. Get to Abbey Road and it's three streets along on the left.'

'You bastard. You did that deliberately, didn't you?'

Neil sat back, enjoying the look on Vince's face.

'Anyway, Danny's the big Beatles fan,' Vince continued. 'But if we're in the area, we should definitely have our picture taken on the zebra crossing. I'll be John Lennon, obviously.'

'You sad individual,' said Neil.

'You can be Paul, Danny can be George, and Henry will have to be Ringo. He'll need a wig, though.'

'Just tell us where, when and what we'll be singing,' said Henry, lazily rubbing the top of his bronzed pate.

'You look well relaxed, Henry,' said Danny. 'The island work its magic again?'

'Yes, indeed,' said Henry. 'It was wonderful, thanks.'

Whenever Henry returned from the island, he rarely spoke about his visit, and the others knew that this was about as much as they were going to hear about it.

At Deanfield Studios (near Abbey Road, but not immortalised by The Beatles), From The Edge gathered early one Saturday morning. The day was clear and dry, and they were standing around on the pavement waiting for the studio to open.

'Okay, *Sweet Roses of Morn*,' said Neil, Henry blew pitch, and they began.

'Woah!' said Vince. 'You're not coming in a semitone under are you, Henry?'

'No, of course not,' said Henry.

'But you just did. Neil?'

'Well, a quarter of a tone would be nearer the mark, I think. But give us a chance, Vince. We're just getting started.'

They started again, and Vince stopped them again, the signal being an index finger inserted into his right ear, the one nearest Henry.

'We've been here before, Vince,' said Henry. 'Why is it always me?'

'That's a question you should ask yourself,' said Vince. 'I'm sorry, but it's the flatting and scooping again.'

'Right, stop there,' said Neil. 'You've got a point, Vince, but it's not going to help if you keep giving Henry a hard time. Give us a chance to warm up, at least. And while we're being picky, you're far too loud. Try using head voice, and be a bit more sensitive to the song.'

An elderly man with a Jack Russell on a lead had been watching developments. 'Il Divo haven't got much to worry about, then,' he suggested, and the Jack Russell agreed by way of a sharp yelp.

'Thank you, sir,' said Neil, and he signalled for Henry to blow pitch again.

This time they sang the song through to the end, despite a wince and two raised eyebrows from Vince. 'Blow pitch, please, Henry,' said Neil. 'Thank you, that was perfectly in pitch, gentlemen.'

'Better,' said the man with the Jack Russell. 'But you're no Il Divo. Skip here loves Il Divo, don't you, Skip? Give us another one.' Skip wasn't so sure. He gave a low growl and stopped wagging his rear end.

After a rendition of *Kiss From A Rose*, Skip seemed pleased with the way things were going and gave a couple of leaps in the air, while his owner was now inviting passers-by to witness the new Il Divo. Soon a small crowd had gathered and, three songs later, the quartet were accepting generous applause. The old man passed around his baseball cap and handed over one pound and sixteen pence, which he seemed to think would help see them on their way to greatness. 'You'll be sharing a bill with the Il Divo boys before you know it,' he declared, before toddling off with Skip, content in the knowledge that he'd done his Simon Cowell bit for the day.

In the studio, the quartet were joined by Joel Hannigan and a recording engineer called Stuart.

'We've never been in a recording studio before,' said Neil. 'The only time we've ever recorded anything was a CD with our chorus. Forty guys in a church with a single boom microphone.'

'That must have been an interesting experience,' said Joel. 'How did it turn out?'

'The production quality wasn't great,' said Henry.

'Really?' said Joel. 'Well, this is all state-of-the-art equipment, and you're in good hands with Stuart. Now, we can do this one of two ways. Either we can try to record you together for a live take, or we can record each of you separately, singing to a click track, and we can mix you together at the end.'

'Shouldn't we go for a live take?' said Neil. 'I mean, that's what a cappella singing is all about.'

'I know what you're saying,' said Joel, 'but we'll almost certainly be mixing individual vocal tracks when it comes to the soundtrack recording.'

'Well, I think we should do a live take,' said Danny. 'That's what we're used to. Singing in isolation just wouldn't feel right to me.'

'That clinches it for me,' said Vince. 'Let's do it.'

*

After the recording, Vince led the group towards the famous zebra crossing close to Abbey Road Studios, having persuaded Stuart the recording engineer to accompany them as volunteer cameraman. It shouldn't have been a surprise to find that they weren't the only group of friends intent on walking in the Fab Four's footsteps that day, in recreation of their iconic album cover. A group of Japanese teenage girls, four drunken Glaswegian fifty-somethings, and a handful of Eastern European metal heads dressed in full-length leather coats, were ahead of them in the queue.

The Japanese girls, in colour-coordinated ra-ra skirts, knee-length socks, and Burberry accessories, giggled their way across the hallowed stretch of black and white, each holding aloft a selfie-stick.

'Lennon will be turning in his grave,' said Vince.

'I seem to recall he had a bit of a thing for Japanese women,' said Neil.

'Fair point,' said Vince.

Next to go were the Glaswegians. No selfie sticks to be seen, and though their clothing didn't suggest that colour coordination was high on their list of priorities, each one was carrying a can of Tennent's Super in identical metallic blue. Their crossing was more problematic than the Japanese girls', with two of their number tripping over each other, one thumping the bonnet of a car that dared to sound its horn, and the fourth member lifting his kilt to present a full frontal to anyone who cared to take notice.

'McCartney wouldn't approve,' said Vince.

'I don't see the connection,' said Danny.

'Mull of Kintyre. That's in Scotland, isn't it?' said Vince.

No sooner had the Glaswegians cleared the crossing than the East Europeans lined up like Western gunslingers about to stroll into town. With a casual air they marched in perfect time, each with devil-horn hands held aloft in a perfectly synchronised display. The Japanese girls squealed their approval and took photos. The Glaswegians gave a fine display of flying Vs, and their kilted brother threw in a full moon for good measure.

Now it was their turn. Vince lined them up in album cover order, made sure his walking stick was on the opposite side to the camera, and gave the order to walk. As they reached the opposite pavement, a small dog ran towards Vince, sank his teeth into his stick, and shook it from his grasp.

'Stop it, Skip,' said the old man. 'Il Divo would be ashamed of you!'

Twenty

A Plan Comes Together

Margaret had been on quite a journey coming to terms with the death of her elder son. The hardest part had been watching the relationship between her husband and youngest son deteriorate severely as they both struggled with their own grief. George had somehow blamed Neil for still being alive, instead of being thankful, and Neil had challenged everything George stood for, and rebelled against every wish his father had for him. That was now in the past, and their reconciliation was a daily source of joy. It also helped Margaret connect more directly with the sadness that would never leave her, and clarify her own feelings at long last.

Celebrating Robert's life over dinner with George and Neil had made Margaret realise that the story of her own life would be hopelessly incomplete without telling Robert's story. And it was this that made her also realise that writing an autobiography, albeit of likely interest to ballet aficionados, would be little more than a vanity project unless it sought to do more than simply record the facts of one more life on planet Earth. There were moments when she felt like a fraud, sitting down to write the next chapter of her life story. But then if pop starlets and Premiership footballers barely into their twenties could get away with publishing autobiographies, surely there was merit after all in documenting the much richer human story of a life spanning several decades more. And at least, whenever she did feel mildly fraudulent about the book, she could console herself in the knowledge that people seemed to want to hear her story: to her own surprise, she had secured both a literary agent and a publishing deal.

Margaret was never in any doubt that she would dedicate the book to Robert's memory. That was an easy and obvious gesture. But if she was to open her heart in print, she knew there had to be a bigger purpose behind the enterprise.

Robert's MS had taken a meandering course at first, as the illness established itself and then appeared to come and go over four years or so. The relapsing-remitting phase then gave way to the progressive phase which, though largely predictable in its eventual outcome, swept Robert away far more quickly than even the consultants had expected, and he was gone within a year. Describing the facts was painful enough, writing about the emotion was almost impossible, and yet Margaret persisted. What spurred her on was the decision to dedicate all proceeds from the book to a Multiple Sclerosis charity to help further research into the illness. Much had been done to improve the lot of MS sufferers, even since Robert's passing, but still much more needed to be done.

Plans for the charity remained sketchy at first, until one evening Neil mentioned Vince. How had she not known that her son's quartet friend was also a sufferer? Either she had not paid close enough attention to her son's life, which shamed her to think of, or more likely, Neil hadn't opened up too much about his quartet friends – which, given the contempt with which George had treated Neil's singing and musical ambitions, was understandable. She had a memory of one of Neil's quartet being ill not long before their appearance at the British championships in Harrogate, but she had no idea Vince had MS.

This gave much more immediacy to Margaret's quest and she started to picture how, with luck, things might work out. Whichever MS charity she chose to benefit from her autobiography, the key to raising as much money as possible would be publicity. Not the kind of publicity that a handful of Sunday supplement reviews and a five-minute spot on breakfast TV news could deliver, but something a lot bigger. The launch itself had to be special, had to draw public interest in a way that regular book launches seldom do. That meant getting substantial media attention, and that meant celebrity endorsement. She would invite leading lights from the ballet world, many of whom she still knew. And surely she could prevail upon Newton Burns to persuade a handful of show biz types to throw their weight behind the cause?

It felt like a plan was coming together.

Twenty-One

No Strings Attached

Following the eve of production meeting, Newton Burns and a gathering of senior production personnel and cast members were making small talk on the rooftop of a fashionable restaurant in Belgravia. Ricky Gervais's latest broadside at the Hollywood glitterati at the Golden Globes, opinion on whether a black actor might play the next James Bond, and the British weather all featured. And the latter featured even more as a light spattering of rain started, as if from nowhere.

'You gotta love the U.K. weather,' said Joey Pellegrini, sliding his Ray-Bans up over the top of his blonde head, his electric blue eyes squinting at the sky. 'Two minutes ago there wasn't even a cloud up there. Why's the weather so crazy here, man?'

Joel Hannigan, dwarfed by the muscular bulk of his companion, scratched at the thin fledgling growth of his sandy-coloured goatee. 'Well, we're an island sitting between the Atlantic Ocean and the large land mass of continental Europe, in an area where five large bodies of air meet.'

'So, a bit like Newt Burns and his four pals over there?' said Joey.

'Very droll,' said Joel. 'You might not understand the British weather, but you've got the hang of the humour. Anyway, the air masses sort of fight it out and the one that wins determines what the weather will be like.'

'So, cloudy with a chance of meatballs is a real possibility, kinda thing?'

'Kind of thing. Oh, and then there's the jet stream, but that complicates matters even more.'

'Then let's not. So tell me, as the composer of all these great songs, what advice can you give me when it comes to singing them? Okay, lip-syncing them. What do I need to know as an actor? What's the method?' said Joey, his eyes glinting and set more intently on Joel.

Joel looked away momentarily, scratching again at his goatee. 'Well, thank you for your kind words about the songs, but when it comes to playing your part as a harmony singer, that's really Neil's department,' said Joel. 'I believe you guys are scheduled to meet with him some time soon. He'll explain the arrangements to the four of you in detail, and also what you need to do to come across convincingly as a quartet.'

'I look forward to it, but I'd like to see Neil one-on-one, get a head start if I can. Do you know if he's around, how I can get hold of him?'

'Sure. Let me...' As Joel reached for his phone, Mac McAuley, who had been hovering midway between Newt's group and Joel and Joey, approached, revolving an empty foil sachet in his fingers as he did so.

'You practising a bit of close magic there, Mac?' said Joey.

'Well, if I could conjure up some fresh nicotine gum, that would be magic enough for me. Know anywhere I can get some around here?'

'I dare say we can send out for some,' said Joel. 'Did you want a word?'

'Actually, I do – with Joey. Do you mind?'

'Not at all. Let me see if I can get that gum for you.'

'Thanks, Joel. So, Joey. How's it hangin'?'

'Pretty well, Mac. All's cool. Looking forward to working with you again. When was the last time?'

'*Bad Behavior Borg*, six years ago. You died four scenes from the end.'

'That's right. And I thought the movie was going to die too. Who knew that the story of a cyborg with ADHD would be the biggest box office hit of the year?' said Joey.

'Well, I had a pretty good idea. But, hey… I have something to ask you,' said Mac.

'Sure, shoot.'

'Well, the word is that Madame Rossi is planning a late arrival tomorrow, and I'm not going to put up with that crap, not on day one. Do me a favour and pay her a visit this evening. She's in town, at the Connaught, I believe. Just go over there and work your charm. You both have a call for eight in the morning. Get Lady Penelope up bright and early, get her damn pink limo to the hotel by seven, and see she gets to the lot on time.'

'Kinda like Parker the chauffeur?'

'The limo comes with its own Parker. I was thinking of you more in the Jeff Tracy role. Y'know, I always suspected there was something going on between those two.'

Joey took a step backwards and dangled his arms in mid-air like a marionette. 'But you know me, Mac. I prefer no strings attached.'

'Ain't you the cute one. Bang on form, Joey. Look, just do me this favour. I know you. You'll hook up with her at some point during the shoot. You always do. Just get started a little early, that's all.'

'Well, if you insist, Mac. But what's in it for me?'

'Aside from the obvious? Well, what if I promised not to do more than three takes on any scene you're in?'

'You'd do that for me?'

'Of course not, I'm yanking your chain. But just do me this one thing and life on set will be a whole lot easier for everyone.'

At 7.40am, a pink Lincoln non-stretch limousine entered the main entrance to Pinewood Studios, stopped at Reception for the briefest of security checks, and made its way to the hair and make-up block, as designated on the call sheet that Veronica

Rossi held, folded in her right hand. Her left hand rested lightly on the solid expanse of Joey Pellegrini's lower right thigh.

'I don't know why I get such a bad reputation, Joey. All I was doing was making a little statement. They refused me some perfectly reasonable requests, so being a little late lets them know I won't be messed with. Is that so bad?'

'Well yes, V, it is,' said Joey, winding down his window to breathe in the studio air.

'Pah! I only do this for you, Joey. You know how to treat me right. I like that,' said Rossi, tapping Joey's right arm with the edge of the call sheet. The car slowed to a halt, her door opened, and she slid out, Joey following behind her.

An hour in make-up. Together. And both had reasons to dread the thought.

'Darling, I hate for you to see me stripped bare,' said Veronica, as she took her place in the make-up seat. She stared at the pallor of her complexion in the dazzling, unforgiving light that shone from the perimeter bulbs of the large wall mirror in front of her.

'It's a bit late for that, don't you think?' said Joey. 'By about ten hours, I'd say.'

'You know what I mean, Joey. My *face* stripped bare, reduced to the blank canvas I'd rather you didn't see.'

'I've seen you without make-up hundreds of times. What's the problem? You're an actor, for Pete's sake.'

'Last evening we had shadows. I like shadows. And look now. I don't recognise myself. How cruel is this light?'

Joey had been here before, and he was starting to regret being so compliant to Mac McCauley's request. He enjoyed Rossi's company, but in small doses, at intervals of his own choosing, whereas she became clingy and liked making a drama out of everything. 'Not so cruel as you think,' he said with genuine affection in his voice, while in his mind's eye he could see exactly how this would play out, at every step between now and the wrap party.

Newton Burns was renowned for being hands-on with all his productions. Though he had co-producers, he was never far away from the action, particularly at the start of production. And with news from Mac that the anticipated early spanner in the works – Veronica Rossi's promised late arrival – had been averted, there was an extra spring in his step as he patrolled the backlots, stages, and offices of the vast studio site that had been allocated for the production of *A Cappella Fellas.*

But then he also knew that in this complicated and often tenuous business, when one problem gets solved there's usually another one waiting in the wings. And the matter of Brad Frampton looked like making its entrance any time soon.

Brad Frampton, Joey Pellegrini, John Fontaine, and Todd Bannerman were cast as the quartet at the centre of the story. And of the four, Brad was the weak link. While he was an undoubted talent and right for the part, he was nonetheless a firebrand of considerable repute. Tales of his drinking, fighting, and general unruliness were the stuff of movie-making cliché. What if Mac was wrong about Brad's recent stay at the Betty Ford Clinic being a publicity stunt? What if he really was mending his ways?

Newt's phone rang. It was the first assistant director. 'Newt speaking. Hi, Mike. What? He's been arrested, you say?'

On a hastily convened conference call, first assistant director Mike Hicks explained what he knew about Brad Frampton's first night in London while Newton Burns and Mac McCauley listened and tried to work out the impact of what had happened.

'He'd been everywhere. We believe he started off pub crawling in Soho, was spotted at Langan's, briefly called in at Tiger Tiger, then on to Mahiki and Libertine, and finally he was picked up on Argyll Street with a kebab in one hand and his cock almost in the other. Quite a night.'

'Almost?' said Mac.

'Yeah, he was about to relieve himself on the pavement outside the London Palladium when a kindly young police officer suggested that it wouldn't be in his or the public's best interest if he proceeded any further,' said Mike. 'The fortunate thing is, there were barely any paps kicking around. There was a strong rumour of a Spice Girls reunion dinner last night, Kanye West was on the town, and apparently Liam and Noel were spotted at the same restaurant without either of them knowing the other was there. With that lot going on, Brad's cock 'n' kebab incident was hardly going to make a splash.'

'Hardly make a splash. I see what you did there,' said Newt.

'He got away with a caution and a night in Paddington Green nick. Could have been a lot worse,' Mike concluded.

'Thank the Lord for that,' said Newt.

'What a fucking liability,' said Mac.

Twenty-Two

A New Friendship

It took Hannah a while to summon the courage to call Angie, as she couldn't quite work out what to say by way of motive. 'We met in Harrogate, months ago. Do you fancy meeting up?' seemed implausible, and 'I'm depressed and in need of a friend. Do you fancy meeting up?' was nothing if not desperate.

After much deliberation, she settled on a variant of the truth, which was that, having bumped into Vince while shopping, she had enquired after Angie and mentioned how much Ben had taken a shine to her when she'd bought him ice cream in Harrogate. She wanted to return the favour.

Angie had sounded surprised on the phone. 'Buy me an ice cream? Sure, why not? And it'll be nice to see you again,' was her reply, which made Hannah squirm at the crassness of her approach, but at least she'd made the call. Angie suggested a stroll in the park with the kids which, while not what Hannah had in mind, seemed the most natural thing to do.

As Hannah waited by the old bandstand in the park, Ben practised kicking his football vertically into the air as high as he could before catching it, a game Danny had played with him many a time. Ellie seemed entertained from the comfort of her buggy, squealing appreciatively each time Ben booted the ball skywards. The air was fresh, and the early summer sun breaking through gave a hint of warmer weather to come.

Hannah scanned the landscape to see if she could spot

Angie's approach and realised that her memory of Angie's appearance was incomplete. She remembered her effortless smile and something special about her eyes, and of course her enviable figure, but when she appeared suddenly in front of her, Hannah was taken aback. She hadn't realised just how beautiful Angie was, with her sculptured features and feline eyes, her elegant curves, and her poise. How could she have forgotten that she had been a glamour model?

But what struck Hannah even more was Angie's sense of ease, the impression she gave that she would be comfortable in any situation, that nothing would faze her. In any case, that *had* to be true, as here was a woman who had given up the glamour business and was now a professional carer, looking after both children and old people. This was someone of substance, Hannah thought.

On that first outing, it was evident that Ben really had taken a shine to Angie. And she seemed delighted to see him again, reminding him of the conversation they'd had in Harrogate about Everton, and about Ben's best friend, Peter. She spoke to him naturally, with no hint of condescension. And rather than gratuitously praise him, as so many adults do with children these days, she asked questions that solicited smart answers, and that was when she would make a telling comment that made Ben feel good.

And Angie was great with Ellie, too. She involved her in small ways while she was talking to Ben, so that the little one felt included. And really, watching Angie with all of her grace and genuine benevolence ought to have made Hannah feel inadequate by comparison. But somehow it didn't.

After that first meeting, Hannah wanted to know more about Angie, her background, what made her tick, and how she became the person she is. They met again for a quiet drink at a newly opened wine bar in Windsor, and while being on their own made it easier to talk and get to know each other, Hannah held her curiosity in check as the conversation turned first, not surprisingly, to Vince and Danny and their singing exploits.

'When I found out that Danny had started singing, you could have knocked me down with a feather,' said Hannah. 'For years I'd been telling him how good a voice he had and that he should be doing something about it, but he never could get over his shyness. I mean, he's no shrinking violet, but he couldn't ever imagine singing in front of an audience.'

'Ha! So different from Vince,' said Angie, throwing her head back, her loose dark brown hair falling in disarray around her face and shoulders. 'The first time I heard Vince singing was when I was working in a gentleman's club, not far from here actually. Anyway, in between routines, the girls sometimes served drinks topless – strictly no touching allowed – and as I was delivering a tray of drinks to a table, one of the guys stood up, looked straight into my eyes, and started singing *Without You*, just like Harry Nilsson. The table and half the room fell silent as Vince sang his heart out, never once taking his eyes off mine. And that was that.'

'Bloody hell, unbelievable!' said Hannah.

'He's always been a big show off. But it's great that Vince persuaded Danny to start singing. You must be proud that he finally took the leap.'

'I am. And I can't imagine anyone other than Vince being able to do that. When they first met at work I know they spent all their time talking about music and their favourite bands, and so on. But getting Danny to actually sing in public is, well, amazing. His therapist could hardly get him to speak when he was a kid…'

Hannah took three sips of white wine in quick succession and allowed her eyes to flit around the room. 'I love the way they've done this place. Sort of shabby chic. It works really well…'

'Yes, it's lovely. Another?' said Angie, rising from her seat.

Angie returned with the drinks and a bowl of olives on a tray. 'And years later, here I am with a tray of drinks again, only fully dressed this time. But less about the blokes, I want to hear all about you. Your horse riding career and everything. All sounds very exciting.'

Hannah shook her head slightly. 'Not as exciting as your past! But I suppose I had a decent career as an eventer, made the British team. It was great while it lasted.'

'What made you give it up? You're still young.'

'Not that young, but I had to retire due to injury. It was the last thing I thought would happen. Just as I was reaching the peak of my career... Boom! Over.'

'Sorry, that's a real sod. You must miss it.'

'I do, but that was then. It messed me up quite a bit at the time, but you have to move on somehow. Why did you leave modelling?'

'Honestly, it was never really me. I mean, I had the necessary equipment, and I enjoyed it for a while – not least because the money was good – but in the end I got fed up being known just for getting my boobs out. Imagine your kids asking you what you did when you were younger? You can tell them "I was a famous horsewoman"'. Angie picked up two olives from the bowl and presented them, one in each hand, in front of her breasts. 'Sounds a lot classier than "I was famous for getting my tits out."'

'You're a scream, honestly,' said Hannah. 'But you're doing yourself down. You're incredible, what with working at the nursery *and* at the old folks' home. You should be proud to tell your kids what a wonderful caring person you are. And talking of which, are you and Vince planning on having kids?'

'Ah well, that's the thing,' said Angie. 'I'm unable to have children.'

Twenty-Three

The Second Letter & The Blonde Beast

In a small office at Pinewood Studios, a week into the production of *A Cappella Fellas*, Newton Burns, Joel Hannigan and Neil Taylor were meeting to discuss progress on the soundtrack of the movie, and the next subject for discussion was the business of which quartet would be hired to sing the nine original songs written by Joel for the screenplay.

Newt addressed Neil directly. 'Do you want the good news or the bad news first?'

Neil ran a hand through his mess of hair. 'Get the bad news out of the way first?'

'Okay,' said Newt. 'As you know, we auditioned several quartets, mostly in the U.S., with the help of the Barbershop Harmony Society and the Contemporary A Cappella Society of America. And we made a decision...we chose a quartet called Top Four, from Cincinnati. They came fifth at international a few years back.'

'I see, well, makes sense. It's only what I expected. An American quartet was the obvious choice. What's the good news?' said Neil.

'Well, their baritone has become quite ill in the last few days, and he'll be sidelined for weeks.'

'That's good news? Poor bloke,' said Neil. 'Can't they get a stand-in bari?'

'They could in theory, but it seems that the other three are reluctant to do that, so we need a replacement quartet. Which is where the good news comes in. When Top Four dropped out, it got us thinking. Using a top American quartet isn't really what we need after all, is it?'

'Isn't it?' said Neil.

'Well, no. Using a top quartet with a highly polished sound isn't the point here. The guys in the story turn to harmony singing as a release from the pain and suffering they're going through, so they're finding their way, searching for their own sound. They're not the finished article, just like...'

'From The Edge,' said Neil. 'You're right, we're not the finished article at all. But we're also not American. Don't you need...'

'Oh, you guys have got the mid-Atlantic barbershop sound down to a tee. That's not an issue. No, it's more a case of you being at the right stage in your development. Your sound isn't squeaky clean, at least not yet, and I think it's a great fit for what we need.' Newt paused and ran a thumb down the underside of one of his braces. 'And Ken...'

'Yes?' said Neil, sitting forward in his chair.

'Well, I'm sure it's what he wanted for you. Think of the letter he sent you. *You've found The Fifth Voice, but there's more to come...*'

'Yes, but surely he didn't mean this specifically?' said Neil.

'We agree that Ken had a journey mapped out for you guys, yes? Well... I think he knew all the steps along the way too,' said Newt, reaching into the breast pocket of the jacket that hung on the back of his chair. 'This is slightly awkward, and I don't know why I didn't show you this before – probably because of the very private nature of the main message – but have a look at the P.S. at the end.'

Neil took the letter from Newt, recognising the handwriting straight away, and felt a warm glow as he read the postscript.

When Joey Pellegrini called him to ask for a meeting, Neil was nonplussed. He knew he would be meeting the famous American actor and his equally famous cast members soon enough. That date was marked in his diary in bold red lettering and made him nervous enough as it was. But to receive a personal call from the actor who was variously referred to as Thor, The Viking, and the Blonde Beast, was unsettling to say the least.

The call came as Neil was walking up the steep hill from his parents' house to Cookham Dean. The hedgerows that lined the quiet road were full with verdant growth, as were the tree branches that stretched out above them from within the gardens of lavish houses hidden from view. Road traffic was infrequent, and the only noise was the faint chug of a far-away tractor engine, the gentle trickling of water (natural or man-made, it was hard to know) and the regular shrill cascade of notes from songbirds, abundant overhead.

On reflection, it was unwise to take the call halfway up the steepest hill in the area. If he wasn't breathless enough already, hearing Joey Pellegrini introduce himself in the over-familiar tone of an old pal was enough to take away what little breath he had left. Neil found himself uttering a series of monosyllables interlaced with huge, desperate gasps, as he struggled to gain some sort of composure. The result was that, with barely a chance to say a coherent word, Neil found himself agreeing to meet Joey Pellegrini in the gymnasium at Pinewood Studios, the actor having concluded that he'd caught Neil mid-workout. 'We can do a few circuits together, and I'd like to ask you a few singing questions as we go,' Joey suggested before ending the call with 'Ciao, man'.

And so here he was, utterly self-conscious, clutching a canvas hold-all containing gym kit that last saw the light of day several years ago when he'd dabbled unsuccessfully with badminton at university.

Neil hated gyms. The whole business of getting changed with other people, demonstrating your inadequate fitness and physique to other people, and then showering with other people, was anathema to him. Why was he even doing this? Joey was the one who requested a meeting with him, not the other way round. Couldn't he have spat out some alternative suggestion for a meeting place as he struggled for breath that day? Why didn't he call him back when he'd recovered his breath and calmly negotiate a Plan B? Sod it. He knew exactly why. The idea of meeting the actor variously referred to as Thor, The Viking, and the Blonde Beast *at the gym* was just about the most leg-wobblingly homoerotic thing he could imagine.

Thankfully the place was empty, but Neil still chose a discreet corner of the changing room. He arrived half an hour ahead of the agreed meeting time to make sure he was ready well in advance of Joey's arrival. And rather than wait for him in the changing room, he decided to have a look at the gym equipment to see if there was anything he could use without appearing like a complete work-out novice. Which, of course, he was. There were lots of impressive-looking machines made up largely of levers, chains, pulleys, and padding, and for the most part their function was obvious, being for the development of chest, arm, stomach, or leg muscles. However, there was one machine that failed to reveal its purpose and reminded Neil of a prototype death device from the *Saw* film series. Which, given that the gym was located on a film studio lot, it could well be.

This thought was amusing Neil when the door from the changing room swung open, and Joey Pellegrini walked in. 'You must be Neil,' he said, striding towards him sporting the biggest of Hollywood grins and the skimpiest of gym wear. A singlet showed off implausibly bulked and honed shoulders, chest, and arms, while the shortest of shorts revealed legs that looked like they'd been chiselled from trunks of Canadian Redwood by Michael Angelo. The overall impact was even more leg-wobbling than Neil had anticipated.

They shook hands, Joey's engulfing Neil's, and the actor thanked Neil for his time, which Neil reciprocated.

'Mister Pellegrini...' Neil began.

'Shit, man. Call me Joey!'

'Sure, Joey. The thing is, well, actually I'm not a work-out kind of guy really,' said Neil, miming the action of an overhead shoulder press as he did so.

'You don't say,' said Joey, taking in his companion's physique. 'But you were sure giving it some the other day when I called. You must be more of an aerobic guy than a muscle guy.'

'Yes, well. I was walking up a very steep hill at the time, and I was a little breathless. It was probably made worse by hay fever.' Neil felt his face redden at the ridiculousness of the situation he now found himself in – standing opposite a near-naked Hollywood hunk, complaining of breathlessness brought on by a brisk walk and an imaginary summer malady.

Joey grinned another of his ultra-brights, with a kindly look in his eyes. 'Jeez, man. No big deal. We can skip the gym and go get a drink somewhere. I can work out tomorrow.'

Neil didn't want to let Joey down, but he could see a compromise. 'No, no. Look, you do your...circuits? ...and I'll use the tread mill. Then maybe we can go for a drink later. How's that sound?'

'Just great,' said Joey, offering Neil a high-five, which he accepted with surprising athleticism.

Twenty-Four

The Return of The Professor

Cat watched the latest batch of young families, young lovers, lost souls, twitchers, bell-ringers, rock climbers, bucket list tickers, and common or garden day trippers as they disembarked from the ferry and trekked up the steep beach road cut into the side of the cliff, like lemmings performing a reverse manoeuvre. She was beginning to feel cynical, and she didn't like it.

The day had begun, as so many did on the island, with a covering of mist that might instil a sense of gloom in the uninitiated but which was almost certain to clear by late morning. Sure enough, the haze cleared, burnt back by the strengthening sun and a light south-westerly breeze, the last traces disappearing in time for the arrival of the noon ferry.

In the week ahead, Cat planned to do some of the things that gave her most satisfaction in her role as island warden: continuing the current sea life survey, counting the wild deer, goat and sheep populations ahead of the next cull, leading nature walks, and generally being on hand to help visitors with any questions they might have about the island wildlife and ecology. And if she found any spare time, she planned to go canoeing, and maybe even do a spot of late evening fishing off the jetty.

And the plan for today was to join a group of bird watchers to engage in one of her favourite activities of all. When Cat first visited the island many years ago as a biology student specialising in ornithology, she spent a month catching and ringing birds in Heligoland traps, and mapping the movement of numerous species as part of her thesis on avian migration patterns. She kept up bird watching as a hobby, and prior to coming to the island to live and work she was an assistant keeper at a bird sanctuary in south Wales. And while it was one of her duties to contribute to a bird survey overseen by the island field society, thereby keeping her hand in, it was always a particular pleasure to join a new group of twitchers to compare experiences and indulge in a bit of friendly competition.

What Cat had no intention of doing in the week ahead was thinking, or making any decisions, about her amateur archaeology activities. All of which was fine in theory, until she spotted the short, shuffling figure of Professor Edmund Whiley, FRS, emerge from the ferry and become increasingly animated upon discovering that his intended quarry was seemingly waiting for him just a hundred metres from the end of the jetty. Cat's heart sank. She had no idea that the prof was visiting the island quite so soon after their last encounter, and certainly not today. *Why the hell has he turned up unannounced, and what does he want from me now?*

Cat's first instinct was to make a dash for it, but then she had a flashback to Henry's recent visit when he announced he'd turned down a lucrative job offer. His advice to 'do what you feel's right for you' rang in her ears and, suddenly emboldened, she stood firm as the prof approached, his hand held out in greeting.

'My dear Cat, so good of you to meet me upon my arrival,' said the prof.

'Professor! I had no idea you were coming,' said Cat. 'I can only imagine you're here for pleasure, not business. Taking a break from the laboratory, are you? Bit of rest and relaxation?'

The prof looked momentarily confused, and he pushed his round horn-rimmed glasses back up the considerable protuberance of his nose as he searched for a reply. 'Yes, yes. Quite,' he said. 'But I am also the bearer of news from the university. I was hoping I might take a little of your time when—'

'When I'm less busy,' Cat interjected. 'Yes, sure. How long are you here for?'

'Just an overnight stay. Perhaps—'

'Then I'll join you for breakfast tomorrow in the pub. We can grab half an hour then. How does eight-thirty sound?'

'Thank you, yes. That would be…thank you,' said the prof, pushing his glasses back up his nose again.

Having dispensed with the prof – firmly but politely she thought – or at least having delayed the inevitable exchange of views on matters pertaining to the confluence of archaeology and the paranormal by just under twenty-four hours, Cat joined up with the recently arrived bird watchers, a group from Cheshire, for an afternoon of avian antics. This involved wandering around the best birding spots – including the high Atlantic-facing cliffs of the west coast for seabirds, and the vegetated combes of the east coast for terrestrial species – noting down everything identified over a period of four hours, and then assembling back at the island pub to compare and tally up sightings, enter them in the field society log book, and exchange war stories over a few beers. And at no point in the proceedings did anyone utter the phrase 'Cat among the pigeons', which, if a pound were on offer every time she had heard it, would surely have made her rich by now. A fine day was had by all.

That evening, Cat found herself in more thoughtful mood. After dinner she walked to her favourite place for watching the sunset and, perched on a rock looking out across the shimmering Atlantic, she organised her thoughts. First of all she was fit, healthy and fundamentally happy. She always started here, because it provided a sound basis for everything that followed: any problems or anxieties could be put squarely into perspective by simply referring back to the things that mattered most.

And so, to the point. Her amateur archaeology – something she had always enjoyed because she loved discovering things from the past, and because it so obviously complemented her love of nature – was beginning to put demands on her that she found scary. She enjoyed being recognised for her finds purely from a scientific standpoint, and that was a big part of the fun, but it was the unwanted attention that resulted from that recognition she had a problem with: a professor who wants to read her brainwaves to test a theory that she possesses extrasensory powers, and a group of crackpots in the West Midlands who believe that she cured someone's deafness, to name but two.

Cat thought she had the tiniest of glimpses into what public figures have to put up with. It's never enough to know that an actor is mesmerising in their latest role, or that a Premiership footballer played a blinder in Saturday's match. The world needs to know their inside leg measurement, and details of every skeleton in every closet they ever owned. Cat could see that she was extrapolating wildly here, but she could also see that where she was at the moment could be just the thin end of a rather fat wedge.

'Do what you feel's right for you,' was the simple, unadorned advice Henry had given her, and that's what she was going to do.

Having brought Henry to mind, Cat wondered what he was doing right now. She took out his pitch pipe from a secret pocket, revolved it in her fingers, and blew a note at random. Only then did she look at the pitch pipe to check the note. C-sharp. She liked that.

Cat found the professor seated at one of the pub's window tables, looking out across a grassland slope and the Bristol Channel beyond. She was relaxed and well rested and gave the prof her warmest greeting as she slid into the bench seat opposite him. 'Good morning, Edmund! How are you enjoying the island?'

'Ah, Cat. So glad you could join me. I'm enjoying the island very much indeed, thank you. I visited the old lighthouse and the graveyard next door, the castle with its cave below, the Saxon burial mound, of course, and then I took a long walk to the top of the island and back, stopping for a picnic. I saw the wild ponies, the little brown sheep, the big billy goats, and more rabbits than I've ever seen in my life! All rather wonderful. And did I see you out and about? Bird-watching, I believe.'

'Yes, I was. You should have said hello!'

'No, no. I was happy to leave you in peace. I realise that you may think I came here to persuade you to change your mind about coming to Bristol for the brainwave analysis, but I can assure you that's not the case. You made your position on that subject very clear, and I'm *not* a man who doesn't take no for an answer.'

Cat lifted her shoulders, then let them drop. 'Thank you for that, Edmund. And I'm sorry if I was rather blunt about the tests. It's just not for me, that's all.'

'Let's order breakfast,' said the professor. 'I fancy the full English.'

Over breakfast, Cat explained her position regarding the unexpected attention her archaeological discoveries had attracted. 'I don't want all this peripheral stuff getting in the way of the science, or spoiling my life on the island,' she said.

'Quite, quite,' said the professor, attempting to spear a particularly slippery mushroom. 'Nothing should get in the way of the science.'

'So if the flints I found are indeed a significant find, then that's fantastic,' Cat continued. 'But let's leave it there. Let's just say I'm good at digging around and finding interesting things from the past. I don't want to be labelled as some weirdo with super powers. Does that make sense?'

'It makes perfect sense, Cat. It doesn't help me with my research paper on *Divining, Healing & Other Extrasensory Facilities, Mediaeval & Modern*, but I fully understand,' said the professor, forking a sausage with determination. 'Believe it or not, I did come here for a little relaxation, though I also said I have some news from the university. You see, the email sent to you from the department said that the artefacts were earlier than late

Mesolithic, and that they predated anything previously found on the island. What we now know to be true is that they also predate anything previously found anywhere in the south of England, which makes it a pretty big deal indeed. Pass the brown sauce, would you?'

'Wow, are you serious?' said Cat, forking a sausage of her own. 'Well, that's amazing, I'm really…happy. What can I say?'

'To the science!' said Professor Whiley, FRS, raising his sausage in salute.

'To the island!' said Cat, raising her own sausage with a flourish.

Twenty-Five

The Campaign Begins

When Neil was first hired as an arranger by Newton Burns at Yellow Braces all those months ago he kept it secret from his parents. He certainly never intended to tell his father, with whom he was engaged in open warfare at the time, but nor did he tell his mother, to prevent the news from getting to his father. But it wasn't long before the secret was out.

Margaret found Newton Burns's calling card in Neil's bedroom, which came as a shock for two reasons. First, because Newton Burns had been the lover of her gay best friend when she moved to London from Paris over forty years ago. Second, because having witnessed many an attractive young man fall for his persuasive charms, she feared that her son's association with the great man might be of an intimate nature, and that could only lead to no good. She doubted that Fruity Newty had changed his modus operandi in the years since she'd last seen him in person, and she suspected he would think nothing of hitting on Neil, even though he was more than old enough to be his father. However, after a little light investigative work, Margaret discovered that her son had been hired by Newt's film production company on the recommendation of Ken Potts, and so the pieces of the puzzle fell into place.

Margaret reflected on this as she drove the few miles from Cookham to Marlow, where she was meeting Newton Burns for dinner at a pub restaurant which, based on the recent rise to

TV fame of its chef owner and the award of two Michelin stars, took the liberty of charging close to twenty pounds for fish and chips. Margaret wondered how Newt could go anywhere these days without being harangued by selfie-seekers, so well-known had he become in the last ten years or so. Maybe because he was such a larger than life character, people kept their distance. She would soon find out.

Margaret turned into the restaurant car park and found the last remaining space, alongside what looked like an old classic Jaguar with its engine still running. She opened the car door as the Jaguar engine turned off, and the driver started to remove himself, with what looked like considerable effort, from the vehicle. A flat cap appeared first, atop a large thickset head with flowing strands of white hair on each side, after which, unwinding slowly, the unmistakable bulk of Newton Burns revealed itself. He closed and locked the car door carefully, then turned around to find Margaret looking across the roof of her car, smiling at the sight of her old acquaintance, one of the most famous men in Britain.

'My God, Mags!'

'Newt. It's been a while.'

They embraced, then Newt held Margaret at arms length as he looked her up and down. 'My word, it's true what they say about dancers, isn't it? They never age. Look at you – as beautiful and willowy as you ever were! And I bet your arabesque is just as divine as it was forty years ago. My, my.'

'You flatterer.'

'Not at all. I meant every word. Alas, the sad wreckage you see before you, the consequence of decades of hedonism, bears so little resemblance to the Greek God of my youth,' said Newt, raising the back of a hand to his forehead before removing his cap.

'Well, you're being a bit harsh on yourself,' said Margaret. 'I've watched your…development…over the years, and what can I say? You've blossomed!'

'Ha! Same old diplomatic Mags! Let's go eat.'

Entering the restaurant, it was clear that everyone recognised Newt, and heads were turning everywhere. Aside from the unmistakable physique, the flowing white hair and the trademark yellow braces were a sure giveaway. But Newt seemed oblivious to the wave of barely stifled excitement that spread through the restaurant as they were shown to a thankfully unobtrusive table in a corner of the room.

'How do you cope with all the attention?' Margaret asked as they were seated.

'What attention is that?' said Newt. 'Oh, I see. I hardly notice it. I just smile serenely and walk on. I think perhaps I might be a little intimidating. Champagne, I think.'

'Just a glass, I think,' said Margaret.

'Very wise. Now then, where shall we start? What about that boy of yours! What a little star we've found there. You must be so proud!'

And so they talked about Neil for a while, about what a talented musician and arranger he was, how Newt had hired him on recommendation from Ken Potts, and about Newt's delight when he'd discovered who Neil's mother was.

'That was another of Ken's master strokes, for sure,' said Newt. 'I would never have taken a chance on a kid fresh out of university, with no experience of the business. But then I trusted Ken completely. He never made a bad call. And the fact that Neil is such a good looking young chap didn't hamper his chances. I can now see where he gets it from!'

'Oh, you didn't come on to him, did you, Fruity?' said Margaret in a tone of mock reproach.

'Well... I may have let it be known that I admired his aesthetic qualities, shall we say. But there again, Ken came to the rescue. He told me in no uncertain terms not to mess with his protégé, and that was that. Dear Kenny. I miss him every day, the old bugger.'

Over dinner (neither of them had the fish and chips),

151

Margaret steered the conversation to the main purpose of their meeting, which was to discuss Newt's potential involvement in Margaret's charity initiative. He listened attentively as Margaret talked about Robert and his loss to MS so early in life, at one point taking Margaret's hands in his own and holding them tightly. She explained about her autobiography and the plan to have a high-profile book launch to which she hoped to attract people from the worlds of ballet and popular entertainment, to get media coverage, and ultimately to raise as much money as possible for further research into MS.

Margaret only had to look into Newt's doleful eyes as she spoke to see that she was pushing on an open door. He promised to get as many show business pals to attend the launch as he could, as well as making a very generous personal donation to the cause. She insisted on paying for dinner to thank Newt for his generosity, but he wouldn't hear of it.

As they were finishing coffee, Newt asked what had become of Margaret's best friend all those years ago, the young ballet dancer with whom he'd had a brief, passionate affair. 'I didn't like to say,' said Margaret. 'But, very sadly, he died in 1992. AIDS.'

The next stop on Margaret's campaign trail was Neil's quartet friend, Vince. This wasn't so much to enlist Vince in her fundraising activities (not yet, anyway) as to make him aware of what she was doing, to show that she empathised with his situation, and simply to get to know someone who had become an important part of her son's life a little better. They had met before, when the then fledgling quartet had rehearsed at Margaret's house, and she had, of course, been in Harrogate when the foursome gave their silver medal performance at the British quartet championships. What she had failed to realise until quite recently, however, was that Vince was himself an MS sufferer.

The easiest and most appropriate way to do this was to invite the quartet to rehearse once again at her home and for them to stay for dinner. Neil seemed happy enough with this idea, and certainly happier than he would have been not so long ago when hostilities between him and George were at their peak.

And neither did George object to Margaret's suggestion of having the quartet round, which proved to her that her husband was well and truly over any issues he once had, and the chances of any lingering awkwardness were slight at best. Things had certainly changed from the first time the quartet rehearsed at their place, when George had stormed off in a strop. This time, he told Margaret that he looked forward to hearing how they were coming along.

Margaret and George greeted Vince and Danny, who arrived together, then Henry. George had played golf with his old business colleague a couple of times recently, and it was clear from the vigour with which he shook Henry's hand that their friendship had been well and truly rekindled. Neil wasn't at home, and was the last to arrive, a situation that seemed familiar to Vince, Danny, and Henry, judging by the heckling he received when he joined the others in the conservatory.

Neil greeted them all, soaking up the taunts with good grace. His manner was especially lively, and Margaret sensed something of the kid at Christmas about her son. He gestured to Margaret with his eyes, opening them wide, and mouthing the word 'Well?' Then, ushering her to one side, he whispered. 'Ma! How did it go with Newt?'

'Fine, darling. Fine. I'll tell you all about it later. What's the matter?'

'Did he say anything about the soundtrack recording?'

'No. Why?'

'Okay, cool.'

That seemed to calm him down, and it was a less agitated Neil who now called them to order. 'Guys, guys. Listen. I've got some news. I was going to call you all individually, but as we were meeting here today, I thought it would be great to tell you all together.'

'Do you want a roll on the drums?' said Vince.

'No, listen. It's…we… Newt…he's decided…he's given us the recording gig! We're doing the song soundtrack. It's us! We've got it!'

All hell let loose, and Margaret and George backed away as the four friends mobbed each other. Neil pulled Vince up from his seat by both arms, and the others gathered round to form a bouncing huddle of the sort that would do justice to a winning goal scored in the fifth minute of extra time. George, to Margaret's surprise, put his arm around her and kissed her gently on the cheek.

When the mayhem subsided, Margaret and George congratulated the quartet, then left them to it as they chattered wildly about their news. Questions were quick-fire, and there seemed to be far more of them than answers. Margaret went to see to dinner; George retired to his study to read the FT and sneak a G&T or two.

Neil had come prepared with copies of the sheet music for all nine songs, three of which they had already learned for the studio demo session. Neil said that he had MP3 teach tracks for the lead, tenor and bass parts, which he would send to the others later that evening. He then showed them a copy of the production schedule for *A Cappella Fellas*, on which he'd ringed two dates.

Neil pointed to the second of the dates. 'We start recording here, week nine. It's now week three. And here, in week five, I'm scheduled to meet the four actors to brief them on the arrangements and give them some directions on quartet singing.'

'So, you get to meet the big stars!' said Vince.

'Well, I was hoping that we could all be at that meeting. I've suggested it to the team, and they agree that it would be great for these guys to hear a real live quartet. Can you all make it?'

'Definitely!' said Vince. 'This Rock 'n' Roll lifestyle just gets better and better!' Danny said he'd have to take the day off work, but that wild horses wouldn't stop him being there. Henry just nodded eagerly.

'That's a lot of learning to do,' said Danny. 'Taking into account the three songs we already know, we've got to learn a song a week from now on.'

'Maths genius,' said Vince.

'Tough, but achievable,' said Neil.

'Let's get started,' said Henry.

After dinner they sat around the large, elegant living room with its high-vaulted ceilings, rich wood-panelled walls, and deep, comfortable sofas, drinking coffee and chatting in groups. Neil and Danny continued an animated discussion about the song learning they had to do ahead of the recording sessions. Henry and George were reminiscing, and Margaret was asking Vince about his MS.

'This probably sounds stupid, but I try not to think about it,' said Vince. If I got up in the morning and MS was the first thing on my mind, then I wouldn't get through the day. I take the medication, try to follow doctors' orders, but then I just get on with things and enjoy myself. But I need help as well. Angie's a rock. And this lot, too. Danny takes my mind off things. We talk music 'til the cows come home. And Neil, well, he's been there before. He talks about Robert when he senses it might help. Not in a sentimental way, but just like *it's okay, I understand*. And he always keeps an eye out for me. He's a bit of a treasure. But don't tell him I said so!'

'That's very sweet of you to say,' said Margaret. 'If you don't mind me asking, what stage is your MS at?'

'Progressive,' said Vince. At this point he would normally throw in a flippant reference to Emerson Lake and Palmer or Wishbone Ash but decided against it. 'For the last two years.'

Vince's words sent chills down Margaret's spine as she thought of Robert...*gone within a year*...and sealed her resolve to push on with her charity plans.

In another corner of the room, George lowered his voice as he reminded Henry of the ten pound bet they'd had on the golf course not so long ago. 'On the matter of wishing that Neil would get himself a girlfriend...have you worked it out yet?'

'No,' said Henry.

George shook his head. 'Now then,' he said, getting to his feet and speaking to the room. 'I think it's about time we heard these chaps sing.'

Twenty-Six

The Famous Four

Todd Bannerman, perhaps best known for his portrayal of hard-hitting, hard-living New York characters – gangsters, crooked cops, righteous vigilantes – was also building a reputation for his stage work these days, with a string of Broadway and West End successes to his name. He was widely regarded as one of the most versatile, as well as genuinely likeable, actors around. In *A Cappella Fellas*, his character is struggling to cope with the loss of his wife in the 9/11 disaster.

John Fontaine cut his acting teeth in a series of U.S. daytime soaps before getting his big break in a prime-time series on NBC, a dystopian sci-fi epic, which was now a smash hit around the world. He and his long-standing girlfriend, Melanie-Jane Morgan, were considered one of the hottest couples in the business and the subject of much attention in the tabloids and gossip magazines. In *A Cappella Fellas*, Fontaine's character is a survivor of 9/11 whose family life is falling apart, and who is on the verge of a nervous breakdown.

Brad Frampton, the archetypal bad boy of the movie business, was as well known for his off-screen shenanigans as his on-screen work, though he was one of those actors who just had it, and if you could bottle whatever *it* was – a mixture of charisma, charm, sex appeal, and something hypnotically primeval – then Oscar winners would be ten a penny. Frampton was always sought after, always big box office, and always reliably unreliable. His character in *A Cappella Fellas* is confined to a wheelchair following his escape from the ruins of the twin towers and is battling drink and drug addiction. It didn't escape anybody's attention that Frampton was uncannily qualified for the role.

Joey Pellegrini (variously referred to as Thor, The Viking, and the Blonde Beast) was generally considered to be the heir to the action man throne previously occupied by the likes of Schwarzenegger, Stallone and Willis. Whenever a script required a character whose job it was to save the world single-handedly, Joey was usually there to fill the brief. His reputation as a ladies' man, his nice guy image, and his frequent appearances on late night chat shows, made him one of the most popular actors on the circuit. In a departure from his more familiar action roles, Pellegrini's character in *A Cappella Fellas* is the head of an architecture practice who finds it impossible to work after being caught up in the 9/11 disaster, and who seeks recompense through the justice system.

The four central characters, each of them damaged by their experiences, turn to singing as a form of therapy. They meet when they join an a cappella club, and the quartet go on to enter a national TV talent competition, the film telling the story of their journey as they fight to rebuild their lives.

Today, the four actors were meeting the arranger of the songs they would be performing in the film. They had already been sent music teach tracks with directions relating to the voice part they were required to learn and, while they would be miming to a recording when the singing scenes were being shot, it was important that the lip synchronisation should be exact. In addition, it was important for the actors to understand something of the principles of close harmony singing, and how a quartet presents itself, in order to appear convincing on film.

It was early afternoon at Pinewood Studios and they were gathering in a small cinema room. Neil's initial nervousness at being thrown into a room full of high-profile movie stars, at least one of whom was famously erratic and capable of causing trouble at the drop of a hat, was helped by the fact that he already knew Joey Pellegrini, and it was he who introduced the other actors. A cast PA was also on hand to facilitate proceedings. Bannerman and Fontaine were gracious and looked eager to listen and learn. Frampton seemed much less engaged, confused even. But at least he had turned up, which was gratifying. To conclude the introductions, Neil introduced Danny, Vince, and Henry, who then took seats at the back of the room.

Once the ice breaking was done with, Neil wasted no time in getting down to business. The plan was to find out how well the actors already knew the songs, then he would explain a little about four-part harmony and how the songs had been constructed, or arranged, and what sort of interpretation each song required. From The Edge would then demonstrate the barbershop singing style. They had three hours, and the PA was keeping time.

Whether one-upmanship was something widely practised in acting circles, Neil didn't know, but what quickly became evident was that Joey Pellegrini, having already stolen a march on his colleagues by tapping Neil for information at their first meeting, wasn't shy in demonstrating his new-found knowledge. He was the first to answer Neil's questions and offer his own theories on how best to tackle the job in hand, only some of which approximated to conventional wisdom in the world of harmony singing. So Neil found himself playing the sort of game he imagined primary school teachers are accustomed to: listen to your pupil's contribution, acknowledge any points deserving of merit, then suggest a better way of approaching the question in hand. He found himself using the phrase 'that's one way of looking at it' quite a lot at first; then, noticing the PA checking her watch for the third time, he decided that cutting to the chase was the thing to do.

Plugging his mobile phone into an external speaker, Neil played each song in turn and asked the four actors to sing along.

He didn't expect much by way of decent harmonies, and indeed he didn't get any, but encouragingly, over the course of a couple of hours, it became clear that all four of them at least had a good grasp of the words to all the songs. In his arrangements Neil had been careful to avoid too many melodic, rhythmic, or harmonic complexities, so that learning the words was most of what was required: the actors would be lip-syncing after all.

Todd Bannerman asked questions throughout – about the song meanings where they were unclear or ambiguous, about his character's emotions at the point in the film when a particular song would be performed, and about any specific inflections he might introduce to create a more convincing performance. He could sing, too. If Neil were giving marks out of ten, Bannerman would get nine-and-a-half.

As Neil had expected, Joey Pellegrini, with the benefit of extra tuition, and with a natural inquisitiveness and thirst to find the right approach to everything, was a pleasure to coach. He too had a voice. Eight out of ten.

John Fontaine was all energy, throwing himself into whatever Neil asked of them with unabashed vim. His body language also suggested that he had studied quartet singers in action (at least on YouTube, Neil suspected), which showed that he was keen to get things right from the start. The only thing that could be held against him was the worst singing voice Neil had heard since the camp guy on the last series of *X Factor* who was so bad that the auto-tune machine went on strike. Seven out of ten for effort.

And so to Brad Frampton. He was in the room, which was a start. He had also learned his song lines, more or less, which was worth a few marks. And his voice was okay. But he seemed to be going through the motions, seemed restless to be elsewhere, and though not exactly impolite, there was a sullenness about him that took some of the shine off an otherwise constructive and good-humoured session. Four-and-a-half out of ten.

In summary, if this were an episode of *The Great British Sing Off*, Todd Bannerman would be Star Singer, and leaving the competition this week (suitably long pause)... Brad Frampton.

With the remaining time they had together, Neil asked Vince, Danny, and Henry (who, like well-behaved pupils, had been quiet at the back of the class throughout) to join them to demonstrate the barbershop singing style. Using one of the songs from the film, the idea was to show how the four voice parts (lead, bass, baritone, and tenor) are layered and textured, and how they blend together to create a big, resonant sound.

Danny started by singing the first twelve bars of the melody to *This Way Lies Love*, then one by one they added the other voice parts until all four were singing, and they ran the whole song from beginning to end, finishing with a rousing crescendo and a final chord that they milked for about twenty-five seconds. Everyone in the room applauded loudly.

'Way to go!' shouted John Fontaine.

'Jeez, I got goose bumps, man,' yelled Joey Pellegrini.

'Awesome, dudes,' said Brad Frampton, to everyone's surprise. 'Now, who fancies a drink?'

Twenty-Seven

Mad Brad & Soho

The group, minus the cast PA, who took her leave immediately after the song coaching session, wandered slowly through the maze of studio buildings. The late afternoon sun, still bright overhead, and the freshness of the air that greeted them, came as welcome contrast to the snug, unventilated interior of the small cinema room, and within five minutes they were entering the extravagant interior of the grand Victorian mansion that housed Pinewood's Club Bar.

As the instigator of this little jaunt, Brad Frampton shouted up the drinks. Whisky soda for Todd Bannerman ('just the one, then I gotta shoot'), a half of John Smiths for John Fontaine ('I love your English bitters'), mineral water for Joey Pellegrini ('it's a little early for me'), a pint of London Pride for Henry, pints of lager for Vince and Danny, and a lemonade and lime for Neil. Frampton himself opted for a large Jack Daniels with Coke, no ice.

A voice from somewhere seemed eager to add to the drinks tally. 'Make mine a glass of champagne, darling,' said Veronica Rossi, a vision of svelte elegance appearing suddenly amongst them. She sashayed quickly around the assembled group, smiling sweetly as she went, before parking herself alongside Joey Pellegrini in a manoeuvre that reminded Vince of a programmed space probe making a soft landing on a passing asteroid.

The normally voluble Vince had, up to now, maintained a low profile, partly because he was out of his comfort zone by quite a margin (though his recent encounter in the Gents of the Dorchester Hotel meant that he wasn't entirely without celebrity connections), and partly because Neil had made him promise not to make a fool of himself. Now, making swift inroads into his lager, he was relaxing, and could see the potential for fun and games that his starry companions presented. And of all of them, he could see that Brad Frampton was most likely to deliver the goods. Already onto his second large JD and Coke, he was starting to loosen up, joining in more, and joking with the others. All things considered, it looked likely that Frampton was set to make an evening of it.

Vince looked around at the others. Danny and Henry were chatting, aside from the main group, and Vince got the impression that they weren't at ease. Who could blame them? It was barely credible that From The Edge were here in the company of people who, for all that they had the same human frailties as anyone else, were household names and faces, their work known to millions, their every move the subject of incessant scrutiny by a rapacious world media.

No wonder some of them went off the rails, like Frampton, Vince mused. Others, like Bannerman, were Teflon-coated: none of the crap that show business threw at them seemed to stick. They turn up, do the work, get paid magnificently, then go under the radar until the next time. Fontaine was something else again, one of those who courted the limelight (that girlfriend of his, Melanie-Jane whatnot, what a stunner) and seemed to ride the wave expertly. And as for Neil's new friend Joey Pellegrini, what could you say? All the blokes wanted to be his mate, all the women wanted to shag him. Just look at the way Veronica Rossi landed on him, as though helpless to resist his intense gravitational pull.

What would Angie make of this little lot, Vince wondered. She'd had a decent enough flirtation with the world of celebrity in her modelling days, then turned her back on it, and Vince reckoned she'd be intrigued. The *Finesse* red carpet do at the Dorchester had been a bit of fun, and she enjoyed getting glammed up and seeing the old faces, but when they got home that evening and she'd thrown off her heels to massage her aching feet, she talked about how superficial and sickly sweet everything had been. Yes, good fun, but also a good reminder of a world she didn't miss.

Vince considered Angie's words as he weighed up his options. Make his way home or hang around a while longer. Just then, Brad Frampton gestured in his direction. 'Another one of those, dude?'

'Rude not to,' said Vince.

Brad Frampton's recent detainment at Paddington Green police station, the consequence of an act of attempted lewdness outside the London Palladium whilst inebriated and in possession of a kebab, was the culmination of a long evening of liquid consumption that had started in Soho. And so it was, with dim but fond memory of that evening, that Brad Frampton, accompanied by his new friend with the walking stick, returned to the half square mile of London where many of the shadier elements of humanity were openly celebrated.

Brad and Vince were sitting at the bar in The Coach & Horses in Greek Street. Wearing a Yankies baseball cap, non-prescription glasses, and ubiquitous leather jacket and jeans, the movie star could pass for your average punter. Only his voice, rising through the gears now, was likely to blow his cover, and he was already attracting one or two curious glances.

'What I love is, in just a few blocks there's, like, fifty pubs, all of them stacked with *types*,' said Brad, knocking back a large brandy for openers. 'You got users, losers, pimps, gimps, guys on the make, out of work actors, sex workers, and more drag queens than downtown Manhattan and Beverley Hills put together. You walk into any pub and there's always some ancient dyed blonde hooker wearing leopard skin pants and lipstick the colour of your freakin' mail boxes. Then there's the resident smart ass on the corner stool talking crap all night long, getting every fucker to buy him drinks. You gotta love it, dude. Bar tender!'

'Soho's most famous corner stool smart ass used to sit over there,' said Vince.

'Who's that?'

'Jeffrey Bernard, a journalist and infamous drunk. Back in the eighties, he would sit over there by the toilets and hold court most days of the week from opening time onwards. There was a play about him, *Jeffery Bernard Is Unwell*, by Keith Waterhouse,' said Vince.

'Of course, man. That was some funny English shit. Not as funny as Monty Python, my all-time favourite, but funny shit.'

'Right. Anyway, Bernard became particularly unwell towards the end, leg amputated below the knee through diabetes, and you could often see him going up and down the streets of Soho in a wheelchair.'

'Like my character in *A Cappella Fellas*...an alcoholic in a wheelchair,' said Brad.

'Well, Bernard was an irreverent and very funny writer who happened to be an alcoholic and occasional wheelchair user. Though, as I say, most of the time he was sat on that stool over there getting pissed.'

'Shame he's gone. I could have gotten some great notes from that guy.'

'I know a bit about being in a wheelchair,' said Vince.

'Really?'

'Yup, I had a bad episode a few years back, and I had to use one for a couple of months. I've still got the thing. Sort of on stand-by, just in case. Until then, it's just my trusty stick,' said Vince.

'Jeez. You know, it'd be pretty cool to get hold of a wheelchair and try it out after a few more drinks...apply the method...get into character.'

Vince didn't know what to say.

After The Coach & Horses, Vince and Brad visited The French House, The Lyric Tavern, and The Blue Posts. And it was while in the latter establishment that Brad disappeared, returning a little time later in possession of a wheelchair.

'What the fuck? Where…how…' Vince spluttered.

'Little drop-in clinic over there,' said Brad, pointing in the direction of Soho Square. He hopped aboard and started wheeling himself with admirable purpose, people swerving and stepping off pavements to avoid him, Vince following behind with his walking stick. They looked a fine couple. 'Let's find a pub, dude,' said Brad.

After a few aborted attempts to enter some of the more crowded and inaccessible hostelries of the parish, they eventually managed to gain entry to a more spacious corner bar, one of the few that seemed to have given any thought to wheelchair access. And, after a little awkward manoeuvring, they found a table just big enough to accommodate them. Brad insisted on staying in character, and so it was Vince who went to the bar to get the drinks. When he returned, Brad was looking indignant.

'What's up?' said Vince, handing him a large JD and Coke.

'These jerks are reciting Monty Python sketches,' said Brad, with an angry finger stab in the direction of the table alongside theirs. 'Listen to it…*waffer thin mints…pining for the fjords*…fucking assholes, they're getting half the words wrong.' He snarled as he picked up his JD, a small blue vein pulsing slightly in his forehead.

'Blimey, it's not a crime, Brad. It's just a few blokes having fun. What's the problem?' said Vince.

Brad returned his glass to the table with a slam that caused JD and Coke to splosh over the rim. 'And did I just hear someone say *shoebox in t' middle o' t' road*? That's the last fucking straw!'

Brad placed his hands on the table in front of him and strained to raise himself from his seated position. The little blue vein stood out further and pulsed a little quicker, as his face turned puce. '*Fuck it!*' he shouted, falling back into his chair.

The Three Yorkshiremen sketch being played out at the adjacent table suddenly came to a halt, everyone now looking in silence at Brad. Suddenly, and violently, Brad swivelled the wheelchair, causing it to collide with the Monty Python table, knocking over a couple of empty glasses.

'Oi, steady, mate,' said one of the guys who had been reciting Python.

'Fuck off,' said Brad.

The offended party wiped his bearded chin, smoothed the front of his rugby shirt with both hands, and rose to his full height of six foot five. 'Would you like to apologise for that?'

'No,' said Brad.

'What the fuck are you playing at, Brad,' said Vince, watching on incredulously and suddenly scared. 'Get out of the chair, stop fooling around, and apologise to this guy.'

'What do you mean, get out of the chair? *How can I?*' said Brad, with a convincing display of anguish.

Pure madness. The guy was crazy.

'Look, mate,' said the rugby shirt guy. 'You're drunk and making a nuisance of yourself. If you weren't in that chair, I'd…'

'You'd do what? What would you fucking do?' said Brad, swivelling his chair around, dragging the rear wheels with such force that he shot backwards, smashing into a fruit machine, which came alive with an electronic fanfare, a blaze of lights and, to everyone's surprise, a torrent of pound coins.

'My winnings…my bastard winnings…' came a voice from another table, as a guy in a shabby grey raincoat leapt towards the machine and threw his arms around it. 'This here is the last of the old school slots, and I've been nursing her all evening – now get the fuck out of my road.' And with that, he started scooping the unexpected bounty into the side pockets of his coat.

That was it. Chaos. The manager appeared, flanked by two bouncers in uniform black, who reclaimed the cash, separated the combatants, and restored order. A minute later, Brad, Vince, the Monty Python crew, and the raincoat guy were outside on the pavement.

Brad rose from the wheelchair and offered his hand to the rugby shirt guy. 'Brad Frampton. Sorry about that, dude. I got a bit too deep into character there. Now, let me get you guys a drink. Lead the way, Vince!'

Twenty-Eight

The Thing About Danny

Danny joined Bowman-Lamy as a Senior Systems Analyst two years ago and he remembered the day of his second interview, the one that clinched it, like it was yesterday. Whereas in the first interview Vince had questioned him mostly on the basics (education, previous experience, aptitude, motivation for the role), the second interview was more of a personality assessment, which had worried him at the time. However, once Vince had asked him about his interests and the conversation turned to music, he quickly relaxed and was on solid ground: Vince's passion for music seemed to match his own.

When, two weeks into the job, he first went to the pub with Vince, they picked up where they'd left off in the interview room, comparing notes on their favourite albums and bands: The Kinks, The Beatles, The Beach Boys, Van Morrison, and many more. That evening, Danny saw the real Vince for the first time, as distinct from Vince the HR director: joker, drinking enthusiast, would-be ladies' man, would-be friend.

These days Vince worked only part-time at Bowman-Lamy, and today was one of his days in the office. It was lunchtime, and they were sitting with packed lunches at a wooden bench on an expanse of well-kept lawn at the rear of the building, where employees often gathered in the spring and summer, weather permitting. A tall bank of trees provided welcome shade from a hot sun that was unbothered by clouds, and separated them from a small, gently flowing tributary of the Thames. Not a bad spot to work.

Vince had just finished describing his evening in Soho with Brad Frampton, and Danny was shaking his head. 'Unbelievable. You couldn't make it up. I've seen you get into some situations in the two years I've known you, but that takes the biscuit,' said Danny, offering Vince a Jaffa Cake. 'Do Jaffa Cakes pass for biscuits?'

'What, it's been *two years*?' said Vince, holding up two fingers by way of unnecessary embellishment.

'Yup, two years,' said Danny.

'That's mad,' said Vince. 'I mean, it's not like either of us has had a particularly eventful couple of years, is it?'

'No, quite. Let me think...speaking personally, I've been to hell and back in my marriage, taken up singing, joined a barbershop quartet, won a silver medal, had a second child, and been back to marital hell again. As you say, uneventful, really,' said Danny.

'Losing Ken was the biggie for me,' said Vince.

'For all of us, goes without saying. If it wasn't for Ken...'

'Indeed. He brought the four of us together, made us connect and gel. But how well do you think we really know each other? I mean, outside of the quartet?'

'Well, I've seen you operate at close quarters, remember – when I stayed at your place, in particular. And let's be honest, it's not as if you hide much. Heart on the sleeve kind of guy,' said Danny.

'And for a while I thought you were the same...but now I'm not so sure.'

'What do you mean?' said Danny, removing the last Jaffa Cake from the box. 'I don't tell everyone the ins and outs of my entire private life, if that's what you mean. But I'm pretty open with you. I told you the whole story about Ben, and that's about as personal as it gets. I'm not sure I see your point.'

'I guess so. Maybe it's the fact that I don't know much about your background. I know you were born in Liverpool, but you never talk about your mum and dad, growing up, that sort of stuff.'

'I could say the same about you,' said Danny, folding his arms.

'Cobblers! I've told you all about my lot…how Mum met and married Bill after the cowardly twat who got Mum pregnant did a runner…how Bill became Dad. You know that they moved to Australia later in life, that I've got a sister Jo in Scotland… I could go on.'

'I don't talk about that stuff much.' Danny's expression darkened for a brief moment, but then his face softened again as he chased away his unease.

'Sorry, I didn't mean to…' said Vince.

'It's okay,' said Danny, unfolding his arms. 'Another time, maybe.'

Vince swatted away a persistent fly from his sandwich, waving his arms a little too enthusiastically. 'Sure, no big deal,' he said. 'Anyway, it seems Angie and Hannah have been seeing a fair bit of each other recently. They seem to be getting on famously. And Ange has been gushing about your kids.'

'Ah, that's cool,' said Danny. 'Yeah, Hannah has really taken a shine to Angie. Sort of looks up to her in a way. It's really helped Hannah.'

'Angie was wondering if you'd both like to come round for dinner some time. How's Saturday evening sound?'

'Sounds fine to me. I'll check with Hannah and see if we can get Dot to babysit. I'll let you know tomorrow.'

'Great. Ange makes a mean casserole,' said Vince. 'And her dumplings are outstanding.'

'Something smells delicious,' said Danny as he embraced Angie. 'Vince mentioned your casseroles were a bit special.'

'And I suppose he couldn't help throwing in the old dumplings gag for good measure?'

'He might have done,' said Danny with a twinkle, as he placed a bottle of red and a bottle of white on the kitchen work surface.

Hannah was fussing over Vince in another room, enquiring about his health, and the two of them now joined the others in the kitchen. Hannah threw her arms around Angie as if she was being reunited with a long-lost friend rather than one she'd seen only two weeks ago.

'You'll always find me in the kitchen at parties,' said Vince.

'Jona Lewie, 1980. Stiff Records. Got to number sixteen,' said Danny, quick as a flash.

'Bugger,' said Vince.

Angie and Hannah indulged in a bit of mutual eye rolling.

'The party hasn't quite started yet, music geeks,' said Angie. 'Why don't you go and lay the table, light some candles, open a couple of bottles, and get from under my feet while I finish off in here.'

'No probs,' said Vince, saluting to Angie as he steered Danny slowly into the dining room. 'C'mon Dan, I know my place.'

'Go join them,' said Angie, flicking an errant wisp of hair away from her eyes and back over her right ear. 'Relax, sit down and have a drink...we don't need to do the boy-girl divide thing. I'll be through in a bit.'

'Don't be daft,' said Hannah. 'What do I know about ancient chart hits, harmony singing, and general boy nonsense? What needs doing?'

'Ah, bless,' said Angie. 'Well, if you insist, there's smoked salmon roulade in the fridge that needs slicing and plating up, and you could cut some lemon wedges and snip a few bits of dill?' she said, pointing in various directions.

'Got it.'

'And there's some chocolate pots in there as well. They need topping with raspberries and cream.'

'Got it.'

Having laid the table, but neglecting to light any candles, Vince and Danny were drinking beer in the living room. As he had been when he'd stayed with Vince at his old flat, Danny was transfixed by the shelves of CDs and music biographies that lined one of the walls, floor to ceiling. He scanned the collection, starting top left, his head angled at an uncomfortable forty-five degrees so that he could read the titles on the spines. After a while he said, 'Where's your vinyl, then? You had loads of vintage stuff in your old flat.'

Vince emitted a 'hmmph' sound. 'That was one of the compromises, I'm afraid. On the basis that I'd converted all of it to digital anyway, Angie insisted on the vinyl going into storage.'

'A small price to pay,' said Danny, reasonably certain of Vince's response.

'Are you joking? I love my vinyl more than I can say. The touch, the feel, the warmth, the beauty, even the scratches. The artwork, the liner notes, the memories. Shit, I'm depressed now.'

'Nonsense! You're a very lucky guy if that was your only compromise moving in with Angie.'

'Oh, just get some more beers,' said Vince, waving a hand in the general direction of the kitchen where, by coincidence, Angie was telling Hannah about Vince's trauma when she had insisted he sacrifice his vinyl due to lack of space.

'And what did *you* sacrifice when you moved in together?' asked Hannah.

'Just my dignity and my sanity, bless him!' said Angie.

After dinner, the centrepiece of which was a rich and elegantly flavoured game casserole with baby carrots, petit pois, and dumplings that lived up to their earlier billing, Vince and Danny returned to the living room, while Angie and Hannah remained at the table, sipping coffee. 'It's a miniature version of the Victorian upper-class dinner party,' said Angie. 'Gentlemen retiring to the billiard room with brandy and cigars.'

'Leave them to it,' said Hannah, raising her coffee cup. 'Thank you.'

'You're welcome. It was only a casserole.'

'No, just…thank you. You don't know what your friendship means to me.'

Angie touched Hannah's free hand, leaving it there for a second. 'And I'm very happy to have you as a friend.'

Hannah hesitated for a moment, and carefully returned her cup to its saucer. 'You…you said you can't have children…'

'That's right, why?'

'I… I'm sorry, that's all.'

'Don't be. I've known for years, well before Vince and I got together. It's okay, you know. Hey, don't…'

Hannah dabbed her eyes with a napkin. 'I'm sorry, it's just that…'

Angie made a hushing sound. 'It's okay. You don't need to say anything.'

'But I do, I really do,' said Hannah.

'Go on then, my sweet.'

'It's just that…well, would you consider…being Godmother to Ellie? And Vince, Godfather, of course?'

Angie's eyes opened wide with surprise. 'What a lovely thought! I would be honoured. And I'm sure Vince will love the sound of being a Godfather!'

In the living room, over a third or fourth post-dinner beer, Vince chanced his arm at the subject that had been bugging him. '"Another time, maybe," you said the other day. Well, what about now?'

'Why do you need to know? Why do you care so much?' said Danny.

'What the hell? Because I do. You're my singing mate… I interviewed you and hired you for Bowman-Lamy…we've been through a lot of stuff together the last two years…why do you think? It's only natural.'

'Crowded House. Track two off the *Woodface* album, 1991,' said Danny.

'Yes, yes, very good, but c'mon, Dan…'

Danny sank deeper into his armchair, took a slug from his beer, and let out a long, slow breath. 'I think I know what's happening here. Did Angie mention something? Something that Hannah might have let slip over a few drinks?'

'Sort of,' said Vince. 'Something about a childhood therapist?'

'Oh, fuck it,' said Danny. 'Then here goes. My birth mother died when I was two, and it messed me up. I didn't speak again until I was five. I had loads of therapy. Dad got remarried a few years later, to May, but we were never close. The opposite of you with Bill. I called her Mum, and she wasn't a bad person, she just didn't seem to like kids. Sort of emotionally detached. Dad was great, but I think the distance between me and May really hurt him. Our best times were when we went to watch Everton together. Just him and me. Then he died when I was in my early teens. May stayed on in the house, and I went to live with an aunt. I had more therapy. It was mostly shit. But I had music, and I got through. That's it really.'

'Oh my God. I'm sorry, Dan. I shouldn't have—'

'No worries,' said Danny. 'I'm glad you did.'

Twenty-Nine

Learning Difficulties

When it came to learning songs, Henry was thorough. As soon as the sheet music and teach tracks were available he would start right away and make sure he was word and note perfect in the shortest possible time.

His method of working was to listen to the bass teach track four or five times while following the dots on the page. He knew one or two guys from Maidenhead A Cappella who could learn a song just by reading the dots, and hardly ever referred to the recordings. By contrast, he wasn't a good sight reader, but by following the pattern and flow of notes while listening to a recording, he could familiarise himself to the point where he could wean himself off the teach track and sing from the page. And while they didn't sing from the page when performing, it helped to have the sheet music for reference in the early stages of rehearsing a song, to make sure they were true to the arrangement. Later, once the words and dots were down pat, came the business of interpretation and artistry.

That was the theory. Except that now it seemed to have deserted him. When Neil sent each of them the sheet music and MP3 music files for the six remaining songs they needed to learn for the film soundtrack, he dived in straight away, spending several hours a day going over everything. Then, one morning, he woke up with the dreadful realisation that his head was in a complete jumble, with words and music from all the songs running in to one other, forming one big musical soup that might start oozing from his ears any time soon. And panic set in when he began to think of the enormity of what they were about to undertake: recording songs, nine of them in total, for a major motion picture that would be seen by millions.

After breakfast that morning, Henry felt the overwhelming urge to escape the suffocating confines of his flat and get out into the fresh air to see if he could clear his head. Except that clearing his head wasn't exactly what was called for; it was more a case of reassembling everything he'd learned into its right and proper place.

On a country walk, Henry would normally listen to songs he was learning by playing them on a loop on his mobile, using the high-quality earphones he'd bought especially for the job (the ones that came with the mobile phone were next to useless). However, that was the last thing he needed to do today.

There was only one walk that would do: his favourite one, from Marlow to Cookham, along the Thames. He'd walked it for years, in all seasons. A beautiful five-mile meander bookended by riverside town chic at one end and quintessential English village at the other. His usual way of negotiating this was to drive to Marlow, then walk to Cookham, and catch the train back. Down the years he'd done a lot of thinking along that stretch of river: when he needed to shake off the stress of a particularly difficult week in the City, or when he needed space and time away from Jenny. At other, more relaxed, times he'd strolled over to Cookham to visit George Taylor at his place, or to meet him at Winter Hill golf club, where George was a member.

Today, however, was all about getting rid of his song learning demons. On the initial stretch of the walk, he played with several theories as to what the problem might be. Age, early onset dementia, the male menopause, and ACFS all featured, the last one being an invention of his own: A Cappella Fatigue Syndrome. By the time he reached the river bridge at Bourne End he was at a complete loss for what the problem might be. At which point, an idea occurred to him. What if Neil was at home with his parents? Their place was within easy reach now…they could meet up. If anyone could help him, it was Neil.

Henry sat down on the riverbank and, with an odd sense of nervousness, searched for Neil's number. He found it in his phone's address book and pressed the green button. After four rings, Neil answered. He was at his parents' place, he was free, and he fancied a walk. What were the chances? They agreed to meet at a riverside pub called The Bounty.

The Bounty was no ordinary pub. A single-story shack rendered in black and white painted weatherboard, it looked more like something you'd find at a holiday camp in a fading seaside resort. Outside, a sign declared 'Muddy boots, dirty hounds & children welcome. Walkers may just use our loo'. Inside was an Aladdin's cave of random bric-a-brac: fishing nets and flags hung from the ceiling, and the walls were plastered with photos, posters, pennants, musical instruments, car number plates, and much besides. The bar was constructed to resemble the bow of a boat, an old jukebox occupied one corner of the main room, above which an elevated section housed an old bar billiards table. A random assemblage of tables and chairs filled the barroom, which featured a large window frontage that looked out upon the river; and lining every inch of the windowsills was a long orderly row of green Jagermeister bottles.

If the river view from the front of the building was impressive, the view from the rear was something else. The back room of the pub looked out across an unspoilt expanse of pasture that stretched out towards the impressive ridge of Winter Hill, the entire vista uninterrupted by anything manmade. And to add to the unusualness of the place, it was entirely cut off from direct road access, so that deliveries had to come by boat from across the river in Bourne End. Quite a place.

Henry sat at the only vacant spot, at the bow end of the bar, with his back to the window. He didn't see Neil approaching, and gave a start when he suddenly appeared at his side. 'You gave me a fright, there. Good to see you. What would you like?'

Henry explained his predicament and Neil listened.

'I can see three problems,' Neil said after a few minutes. 'First of all, you're thinking *Aagh! It's a big film!* You're thinking it's do or die, necks on the line, that kind of thing. Truth is, it's probably one of the easier gigs we'll ever do. We've competed in front of panels of judges and concert halls full of other a cappella singers. Now that's tough. We sang in front of four big film stars just the other day, for heaven's sake! And we've sung for people at parties and given impromptu performances any number of times. That's never spooked you, and that was singing live! For this, we'll be in a studio with nobody listening except the sound engineer. And we can do retakes.'

'I hadn't thought of that,' said Henry.

'Second, I think you're in a slightly more difficult position than the rest of us, so maybe that's playing on your mind?'

'What? Why do you say that?'

'Well, Vince is the fastest song learner I've ever known; it just comes so easily to him. Danny gets to sing the melody, so it's usually easier for him. And I...well, I obviously know the songs backwards.'

'Mmm,' said Henry. 'And what's the third thing?'

'Well, you're going about it all wrong. You've never been given so many songs to learn in so short a time, so you've panicked and started learning them all at once. From tomorrow, go back and start again, focusing on just one song and stick with it for two or three days. Only then move on to the second, and then the third, and so on. Before you know it, your head will clear and you'll be much more organised. At the end, go back and cycle through them again, and keep repeating, shortening the time on each song as you go. You'll have them nailed soon enough.'

'Bloody hell,' said Henry. 'That makes so much sense. I just wasn't seeing the wood for the trees. Have you ever thought of becoming a psychologist, or a life coach?'

'Hardly. It's music I know about, so I'll stick to that, thanks. But I was just thinking…there's a beautiful symmetry to this.'

'You've lost me,' said Henry.

'Well, Dad teaching you about the commodities business all those years ago, and now here I am, a generation later, teaching you how to learn songs. Kismet and all that.'

'And I'm grateful to you both,' said Henry. 'Shall we go for a stroll?'

From The Bounty, they continued along the towpath, under the Bourne End rail bridge, and on towards Cookham village. The early afternoon sun was beginning to push through the light cloud cover, and it was pleasantly warm with little breeze. The river traffic was steady, with the usual mix of cabin cruisers, brightly painted narrow boats, slipper launches, and rowing boats gently passing by. The grass in the open fields bordering the river had recently been mown, and the sweet herbaceous scent filled the air. A bell rang somewhere on the golf course, which occupied higher ground way over to their right, signalling to someone that it was safe to tee off.

'That reminds me,' said Henry. 'I must arrange another round of golf with your dad. He's still a very decent player, and I always enjoy reminiscing with him.'

'He's on the course two or three times a week. He loves it. Mid-morning start, boozy lunch, and back in time for *Countdown*. He doesn't like to miss Rachel Riley if he can help it,' said Neil. 'I don't think it's too harsh to say that Pa's love of golf lies mainly in the clubhouse afterwards. That and betting on the outcome.'

Henry thought back to the last wager he'd had with George. 'Listen. I've got something else to ask you.'

'You'll be fine. I told you, follow the method and you'll have nothing to worry about,' said Neil.

'No, no…that's all very clear, thank you. The thing is – and I hope this isn't betraying too much of a confidence, but – you know you and George are at peace these days?'

Neil looked at Henry with a mixture of curiosity and suspicion. 'Yeeess…'

'And that he's cool about your music, and the quartet, and Yellow Braces, and…and…well, about your being gay and everything?'

Neil arched his eyebrows. 'A-ha?'

'Well then, why did he tell me he still wishes you'd find a girlfriend, do you think?'

Neil allowed his facial muscles to soften and he let out a slight sigh. 'I've got to hand it to Pa. He really is seeing things differently these days, coming to terms with the way I am, how I live my life. But he still struggles with certain things. See, he always wanted grandchildren. Not so much for himself, but for Ma. And since Robert died, the subject has been off the table. Sounds to me like he might be projecting his wish onto number two son, hoping one day I'll have a kid, despite, well…the obvious.'

'You're way too young for all that, but you might want kids one day. It's not as if—'

'Yes, sure. Elton John, Rufus Wainwright, Ricky Martin… no shortage of precedents.'

'Quite.'

'And you might be right, but I suspect Pa hasn't thought that far. Some unreconstructed part of his brain still thinks that I'll hook up with a woman at some point. As if I would, bless him. What he doesn't know is that Ma and I have talked about this before, one time when we were…well, remembering Robert. And the grandparent thing isn't such a big deal for her. She did mention Pa's view on the matter, though. As a matter of interest, why did he mention it to you?'

Henry picked up a stray stick from the grass and hurled it into the air. 'We were just catching up. Playing golf, chatting about this and that.'

'I see. Golf. Did any money change hands?'

'I believe we did have a little wager,' said Henry.

Thirty

A Proposition

A pre-World War II London Underground advertisement for the island proclaimed it to be 'Britain's peaceful gulf stream Riviera, 1,000 acres of cave-honeycombed island where the gorse is always in flower'. And while these days the island's charms were referred to in less elaborate terms, the prospect of a peaceful British island retreat in the summer months was still of considerable appeal to many. The weather was the tricky thing. You never knew what you were going to get.

For the last fortnight, the weather on the island had been wet with little by way of sunshine, and temperatures had been unseasonably cool thanks largely to a relentless westerly wind. The rain was welcome, as the island's water reserves were running very low, but it didn't make for ideal holiday conditions for the scores of visitors who poured off the ferry three or four times a week.

The inclement weather meant that more visitors than usual spent time in the village – where they could shelter in the pub or the church as the next rain shower swept in – rather than roaming the more remote and exposed parts of the island. And that meant that whenever she was around, Cat had no shortage of people asking her questions about the island. Many were about the wildlife, such as whether the puffins were still in residence; others were distinctly odd (she was once asked, 'do you still get pirates?'), but it was all in a day's work. However, the subject about which most people asked was the weather, and over the last two weeks she couldn't count the number of times she'd been asked 'when's the rain going to stop?' or 'when's the sun coming out?' like she was the Met Office on legs.

But today, at last, the weather was changing for the better. Overnight, the wind dropped away to nothing, the last of the rain moved on, and the forecast promised at least a few days of dry, warm conditions with plenty of sunshine. Cat was already in good spirits, but the promise of a spell of proper summer weather lifted her spirits still further.

Since her breakfast with the professor, a burden had been lifted. The pressure she had been under to be a guinea pig as part of the professor's research, coupled with the more bizarre attention she had received from other quarters, had for a while made her lose sight of the reason she did what she did and question whether she enjoyed doing it any longer. She loved nature and she loved connecting the natural world to its past, and that was all there was to it. She was delighted that the artefacts she had found on the island were of such significance, and the academics could ponder and prognosticate all they liked, write any number of scientific papers, and convene on the subject to their hearts' content. For Cat, it was back to business as usual.

She had acted on Henry's simple advice to 'do what you feel's right for you,' and this sure did feel right. But what about Henry? What to do about Henry...

Ever since they met, on Henry's first visit to the island, it was clear to Cat, and she believed to Henry too, that there was something special between them. She sometimes wondered if it was a classic case of 'opposites attract', because on the face of it, or to the casual observer, they probably didn't appear to be an obvious match. And there was an age gap, though that hardly mattered. He once told her that when they met he found her energy and spirit magnetic, and she could say the same of him: his passion for music, the way he wore his heart on his sleeve, his honest desire to do the right thing.

At the time of his first visit, Henry was at a transition point in his life. He'd lost his job, and things at home were becoming difficult. He came to the island to take stock of his life and work out what next. Cat spoke to Henry just a couple of times on that first trip, but it was as if they had been friends for a long time. She could see in his eyes that he was searching for something. The night before he left that first time, she said to him, 'If your heart says fly, then fly. If your heart says sing, then sing,' and he often reminded her how that thought had helped him. Now he was the one giving her the same advice, but in different words.

They told each other that they were happy with the long-distance nature of their relationship. And yet, since around the time of the professor's first visit, Cat had begun to feel a little differently about their arrangement. She needed to talk to Henry.

On returning from his river walk with Neil, Henry couldn't wait to start learning the new songs afresh. His head was no longer a confused mess of notes, words and rhythms. Neil's analysis of what was wrong and how he could fix it had the effect of clearing that away, as though his brain had rebooted.

On second thoughts, he decided that starting in the morning would be best, when he was refreshed from a night's sleep. So what would he do with the evening? As he sat in the only comfortable chair in his small living room with a large malt whisky, Henry made a mental list of other jobs he could be getting on with. A new batch of house details had arrived from one of the town estate agents this morning. There might be something of interest there, but if they were anything like the last five sets of details he'd received, then maybe not. What was the state of his pension pot? He hadn't checked that for a while. Was the hot tap in the bathroom still dripping? He couldn't remember. How was the pound doing against the dollar? What's on TV? He hardly ever watched TV.

At last, Henry's thoughts inevitably turned to Cat and the island. What was she doing right now? Was she thinking of him? It was no good. He needed to talk to Cat.

'Hi, it's me. What's happening?'

'Cat…I'm fine. Anything wrong?'

'No, I'm just tired. In a nice way. It's been a lovely day, but super busy. Feeling the sun on my face for the first time in weeks… I can still feel it now. I'll sleep well tonight. How was your day?'

'Good, very good. You know we've got the studio recording coming up? Well, I've been getting myself into a right pickle learning the songs. So I went on a long walk by the river to clear my head, and I met up with Neil. He really helped me get things in perspective. So, all good.'

'*All* good?'

'Well, yes…'

'How's the house-hunting going? Seen anything you fancy?'

'No, nothing.'

'I miss you.'

'And I miss you. What's…'

'Have you noticed how our thoughts seem to synchronise? It's almost like we…'

'…know what each other's thinking? Go on then, say it.'

'You could move here…if you'd like.'

Thirty-One

The Campaign Continues

'These bloody things don't fit,' said George, straining to haul a pair of dress trousers over the considerable mass of his stomach. 'I swear I wore them to the Rotary gala do last year.'

'Yes, well…' said Margaret, her head cocked as she pressed the stud of a pearl earring into place. 'I've told you before you need to lose weight.'

'It's got to be a slow metabolism. I'm on the golf course three times a week at least. You can't say I don't exercise. Okay, I can't do the sort of contortions you get up to – legs round the back of your head and all that malarkey – but I put the yards in, Margaret.'

'It's called yoga, George. And on the matter of metabolism, that's a lot of rot. It's a simple case of consuming far more calories that you burn off playing golf.'

'You're the one who feeds me, Margaret. Good healthy fodder, too.'

'Yes, George. But I have no control over your consumption when you're at the golf club, or the Rotary club, or the bridge club, do I? Lord knows what you shovel into yourself, but I'd guess that steak and kidney pie and bread and butter pudding feature quite high on the list. A life-long addiction to school dinners, that's the problem. I know you too well. And don't get me started on the red wine. All I know is that by the time you get back from golf and plonk yourself down to ogle Rachel Riley, you look like you've eaten and drunk yourself to a standstill. It's like watching a python digesting a goat, George.'

'It's no good,' said George, straining one last time to fasten the waistband of his trousers. 'Time to abandon ship.'

'A day suit is perfectly fine, George. People don't wear black tie to the ballet any more. Not unless Royalty is in attendance, or some such.'

'Are you sure?' said George. 'One likes to look the part.'

'George, if by some miracle you were able to squeeze into those trousers, the only part you'd be playing would be that of a burst mattress,' said Margaret. 'Give me a hand with this necklace, would you?'

'Well, if a day suit passes muster at the Opera House these days, I fancy I'll wear that navy single-breasted number with my MCC members' tie. The old *egg and bacon!*'

'It's at the dry cleaners again,' said Margaret. 'Custard stain this time, I fancy. I could smell vanilla. Not that I've served you custard in years…incriminating evidence, I'd say.'

'Pah! Okay, okay. I'll admit I do work up an appetite over eighteen holes. Happy now?'

'I'm only thinking of your health, George. Just cut back a bit on the pies and puds and watch the red wine.'

'Hmmph. I'll see what I can do,' said George. 'Now, what's tonight all about?'

'Honestly, George, do you ever listen? *Romeo & Juliet,* new production. I've been reconnecting with a few old friends, getting them interested in the charity and the launch, and this is a little opportunity to socialise. Drinks before, and maybe a light bite to eat afterwards. And the idea is to make some new connections, spread the word, get some of the new crowd involved.'

'You were Juliet once or twice, I recall…'

'Three times. Once in Paris, once at ENB, and once at the Royal.'

'And damn good you were, too. I remember shedding a tear.'

'My God, George. Really? Which one, ENB or Royal?'

'Both.'

'Are you being serious? You've never so much as hinted at any of this in all these years. Are you pulling my leg?'

'Not a bit of it, Margot. That scene with the nurse...oh, and the one at the end on the bed...they had me going.'

'And you called me *Margot*. How many years is it since——'

'I don't know, but I just want you to know that beneath this bluff exterior, well...you get my drift,' said George, patting the left side of his chest twice with the palm of his right hand.

'And you're sure you're not drunk?'

'Not a bit of it.'

Margaret looked at George and saw something of his old self. The one she knew when they first met, when they were getting to know each other, when the kids were growing up. Before Robert died. There he was, standing before her with no trousers on, coming as close as he ever did these days to expressing his softer side.

'You're a rum old bugger, George. But you're *my* rum old bugger, and I love you for it,' said Margaret.

The Royal Opera House, having been the beneficiary of significant funding in recent years, mostly from lottery money, was arguably the cultural beacon for the performing arts in London. It was a magnificent building, though it tended to hide its architectural delights quite discreetly. Approaching from Covent Garden piazza, it was difficult to work out from the unassuming entrance that you were about to enter one of the world's great opera houses, as it was so tucked away. From the main Bow Street entrance, the building facade was more in line with the grandeur you might expect from one of the world's pre-eminent theatres, but still the full beauty of the building was somehow elusive. The whole structure seemed to deliberately tuck itself into a tight corner of WC2.

Inside, the grandeur became more evident as you walked through the hallways of the older parts of the building, as you climbed the broad, sweeping stairs to the Crush Bar, and certainly as you entered the inner sanctum of the auditorium itself. The red plush upholstery, the ornate gilt embellishments to walls and ceiling, and the tightly curved seating of the upper tiers created the illusion that the best opera houses do: of making a grand space seem very intimate. And to complete the picture, beyond the orchestra pit, the famous heavy red stage curtains, trimmed in gold and embroidered with *ER* in celebration of the theatre's Regal credentials.

There were eight in their party, the others consisting of three couples, the women all friends and ex-dance colleagues of Margaret's. To George's relief, most of them seemed charming enough, except for one of the partners who didn't say much, staying on the fringes of the group in case the subject of ordering more drinks came up. One or two of the women George recognised from years ago, and they seemed to remember him. Another of them seemed even more familiar, perhaps someone who popped up on TV from time to time. Leslie? Monica? Faces he wasn't too bad at, but names...how would he remember the names? He had an idea that one of them might be a Dame.

As the women congregated in a close group and chatted about the old days, George attempted small talk with the partners, but his mind drifted. He couldn't help observing the women and concluding that they could be nothing other than dancers. Even when they were a lot older, it was easy to recognise the physique: head held high, neck long and slender, the elegant line of the body, the unmistakable turn-out of the legs and feet.

Small talk wasn't George's strong suit. All very well exchanging thoughts on the weather as you passed a neighbour in the street, but when you find yourself in a small party of complete strangers, sticking to the weather doesn't quite cut it. Two of the partners had peeled away from the main group and seemed to be engaging around some aspect of the law, the bumptious tone of one of them suggesting that he was the senior of the two, professionally speaking, and was keen to press home his point. A QC, George fancied.

'Do you play golf?' asked the remaining partner. Thank heavens, thought George, just as he was contemplating an unnecessary trip to the Gents. A lively discussion about the upcoming Ryder Cup ensued, filling the time nicely until curtain up.

When the announcement came for the audience to take their seats, and they started to make their way from the bar to the auditorium, George made a point of catching Margaret's eye, and they walked together for a few moments at the rear of the group.

'How's it going with the girls?'

'Swimmingly, and they all seem keen to support the cause and spread the word!' said Margaret. 'I take it you're bearing up?'

'Oh sure, and I'm really looking forward to the performance. Can't wait for the *Dance of The Knights* bit…you know… *Da– dee da– dee da– dee da*. It's just that, well…you mentioned something about carrying on afterwards. A bite to eat?'

'That was the general plan, why?'

'It's just that I've been thinking about your advice from earlier: cutting back on the calories, and all that. Is there any chance we can…'

'No, George, that would be very impolite. And if you think I'm falling for that guff, you're very much mistaken. Hang in there, soldier.'

'If I must,' said George, as they took their seats in the Grand Tier. 'I'll do it for the cause.'

'Thank you, George,' said Margaret, as they settled down for Act One.

Thirty-Two

Just Like Ken

'It's not like in a musical, where the characters break out of normal dialogue and then start singing gratuitously. In any case, who would write a musical about 9/11? That would be just plain weird, wouldn't it?'

They were in Deanfield Studios again, for the first day of the soundtrack recording, and Neil was reminding them how the nine songs work within the story of *A Cappella Fellas*.

'So if it's not like a musical, why write original songs in the first place?' said Danny. 'Why not just get the rights to a bunch of stock a cappella arrangements and use those?'

'Ah, that's the clever bit. Newt insisted on original songs and original arrangements from the start. He wanted the music to be the thing that carries the film, not just be an incidental part of it. Okay, the 9/11 storyline is the major theme, but the music is also a central theme. The four guys come together because of the music, and they heal and move on because of the music.'

There was a pause as they all looked at one another for a moment, then Neil continued.

'And it's a risk, because it would have been easier to use established songs, ones that the audience already knows. With original songs, it's harder to win the audience over, because they're hearing them for the first time. But if an original song packs a punch and raises the emotional stakes at just the right point in the story, then it instantly resonates with the audience, and there's a magic moment created that you wouldn't get from a familiar song. That's the idea, anyway.

'And the other important thing is that, while all nine songs feature somewhere in the film, only a few will be sung in their entirety, at key points in the story: when they first sing together as a quartet, then the talent show audition, then the semi-finals, and then the final itself. And those are the songs that carry an important message that relates in some way to what the guys have been going through. That's why the nation takes to them in such a big way. Everyone knows their back story, everyone's in awe of what they've been through, and the songs they choose to sing at those key points reflect an important aspect of their story, an important point in their journey, and raise the emotional stakes for the audience.'

'Why didn't you explain how the songs work before now?' said Vince, looking puzzled. 'It might have helped us approach them in a different way.'

Neil looked momentarily up at the ceiling. 'You're joking, right? We've been through this before. All I was doing just now was adding a bit more context and colour. Hopefully you noticed that the arc of the story is described at the start of the music folder you've been learning from? And certainly, if you've read the detailed notes attached to each song score you should know exactly what each song is about. So I'm disappointed you have to ask that question, Vince. In any case, it makes no difference at all to the way you approach the songs, does it?'

'Why not?' said Vince.

'Because every single time you sing *any* song *ever* you should be committing to it one hundred per cent, selling the story to the fullest extent you can. Yes, each one has a different set of dynamics, different contours and texture, and we've been through that a thousand times. That's second nature by now. But the basic *approach* to delivering every song is always the same: live the story, feel the emotion, play the part the best you can. Because it will come across on the soundtrack every bit as much as if you were singing to a live audience. Hold back, and you'll be found out. So, let's give it everything we've got these next few days.'

'Wow, you sound just like Ken,' said Vince.

'Thank you,' said Neil. 'That's probably the biggest compliment anyone's ever given me.'

Thirty-Three

Scenes from *A Cappella Fellas*

SCENE 15: THE AUDITION

INT: SMALL TV STUDIO - DAYTIME

We see a panel of three judges behind a desk, TV cameras and a boom microphone. In the centre of the open floor in front of the desk is a prominent five-pointed star outlined in red. A Cappella Fellas enter, smiling nervously, and gather around the star.

    MAIN JUDGE
    Hi, so what's your name, and tell us a bit about yourselves.

    MATT
    We're A Cappella Fellas, and we got together a little while back after we found we had something in common.

    MAIN JUDGE
    And what was that?

    MATT
    We were all involved in 9/11.

    MAIN JUDGE
    What, you mean you were actually there? You all survived?

    MATT
    Well, I was, and so was Tom and Blake. Frank lost his wife.

Cut to each judge in turn, as they take in the moment. Then to each quartet member, settling on Blake, in a wheelchair.

    JUDGE 2
    Oh my Lord, that's quite something. Incredible. And,

Blake, do you mind me asking: are you in the chair because of injuries you suffered on that day?

BLAKE
Yes, Ma'am.

JUDGE 2
And how did you guys meet?

BLAKE
We were seeing the same therapist, and she's big into singing therapy, and knowing how much we all love music, she recommended to each of us that we join a choir. And that's where we met, at a choir in Queens.

JUDGE 3
And you just decided to form a quartet from there, just like that?

BLAKE
Pretty much. We hit it off, we love singing a cappella together, and because of what we had in common we thought, heck, why not. Let's give it a go.

MAIN JUDGE
That's an amazing story. I'm humbled. So, what are you going to sing today?

MATT
It's called 'Not Broken'.

MAIN JUDGE
Great. Well, the best of luck. Off you go.

Tom looks to stage left and a piano note sounds. They start singing, their voices not in tune. Close up of main judge wincing. He holds up his hand.

TOM
Sorry, can we start again? We've got this.

MAIN JUDGE
Take your time.

Tom nods again and the piano note sounds. They shuffle closer to Blake, Tom signals with a hand gesture, and they begin.

After first few bars, cut away to panel and each judge, one by one. Tense, unsure.

Cut to quartet and first big chord, then back to main judge, who smiles and looks across the panel.

As the words of the chorus 'We're not broken' are sung for the first time, close up of female judge, looking emotional. Main judge takes notice.

Back to quartet and remain until end of song. At crescendo, cut away to main judge who has a big grin, Judge 3 similar, female judge holding back tears but smiling too.

Cut to co-presenter and small audience in anteroom. Co-presenter mouths 'Wow' to camera.

Back to quartet, looking exhilarated and exhausted.

Cut to panel, judges standing and applauding.

FADE.

*

SCENE 45: THE GRAND FINALE

INT: LARGE TV THEATRE, LIVE AUDIENCE - EVENING

Open on show host. Applause. Cut to audience and back to host.

> HOST
> Welcome back to the grand finale of 'American Talent' and we're just moments away from finding out who your winner will be. We've had a record number of votes cast while we've been on air, and I can tell you that there are only ten percentage points separating all three finalists. That's the closest it's ever been in a grand finale. Thank you for calling in your millions, and the lines are now closed. And so, please welcome back onto the stage your finalists: Layla Martinez, Richie Payton, and A Cappella Fellas.

Pan to centre stage and large sliding doors as they open and finalists enter.

Close up of panel, judges applauding, then audience, then back to the stage where host greets finalists.

> HOST
> Ladies and gentlemen, your finalists.

Cut to audience, then panel, and back.

                    HOST
                    It's been an amazing finale, you all performed incredibly,
                    and the voting shows just how difficult it is to separate
                    all three acts. But there can be only one winner. So here
                    goes.

Theatre lights dim, spotlights on finalists.

                    HOST
                    In third place…

Long pause, various close-ups of finalists.

                    HOST
                    Richie Payton!

Applause. Cut to panel, audience, and back.

                    HOST
                    And so it's between Layla and A Cappella Fellas. After
                    twelve weeks, it's come down to this. The winner of this
                    year's 'American Talent' is…

Long pause, close-ups switching between final two acts.

                    HOST
                    Layla Martinez!

Lights up. Confetti shower. Cut between stage, panel and
audience several times.

FADE.

Part Three

The Road Home

Thirty-Four

Henry's Miscalculation

With the songs in the can, there was a sense of excitement in the air. And anticlimax.

'That was one of the best things we've ever done,' said Henry. 'When they played the tracks back at the end, I was gobsmacked at how good we sounded.'

'Yup, it's amazing the wizardry these sound engineers can perform. Even making the bass sound good. You've gotta hand it to Stuart,' said Vince.

'I'll ignore that,' said Henry. 'But what a buzz that was! Mind you, it feels a little like after the Lord Mayor's show right now.'

'I know what you mean. It feels like post-coital dysphoria,' said Vince. 'I've explained it to Danny before.'

Henry gave a seasoned sigh. 'Pray, do explain…'

'Well, you know, like after sex, when you feel a bit empty…sad even. See, when you orgasm, there's this explosion of hormones in the body…endorph thingies, oxy whatnots, and other stuff. Then, when the hormones drop, you sort of feel a bit low.'

Henry whistled. 'And you've been hiding your PhD in Human Biology for how long? You amaze me.'

'Just saying,' said Vince.

With their involvement in *A Cappella Fellas* almost at an end, the quartet were celebrating at one of their favourite restaurants, and while Henry and Vince were exchanging thoughts on the nature of the afterglow effect following their time in the recording studio, Neil and Danny were planning ahead.

'There's a lot to fit in between now and next May,' said Neil. 'We need a proper rehearsal regime, and we need to get some gigs booked so that we stay performance ready. And one or two other competitions would be great so we can see where we are against other quartets. Of course, first there's prelims in November, so it all starts now. We need to choose up to six songs to cover both prelims and the championships.'

'Wouldn't it make sense to pick six of the songs from the soundtrack?' said Danny.

'No. Not all of them are contestable,' said Neil. And in any case, *A Cappella Fellas* won't be released until next summer, after the championships, so I can't see us getting clearance to perform any of the songs in public before then. No, we're going to have to find some new songs.'

'We could dip into our back catalogue?' said Vince, dipping a crust of bread into a bowl of balsamic vinegar with one hand, while spearing a giant Cerignola olive with a cocktail stick with the other.

Neil marvelled at the dexterity of Vince's feeding technique. 'Yes, we could. But don't you fancy the challenge of new songs, possibly with arrangements no-one's heard before?'

'Of course, but I still don't see why we can't sing some of the film songs. Surely the copyright sits with the composer and the arranger, so that's Joel and you. What's the problem?' said Vince, topping up his wine glass.

'Well, no. You see, once a musical work is commissioned for a film, the producer of the film becomes the first owner of the copyright, unless there's a contract to the contrary between the authors and the producer of the film. And there isn't. So, technically, the copyright sits with Yellow Braces.'

'Which is Newton Burns. Surely he'll let us sing them! Just as a one-off? Who's going to find out, anyway? I doubt there'll be many movie copyright lawyers popping in to watch the British quartet championships in Harrogate next May,' said Vince, chasing the last olive around the bowl.

'That's not the point, Vince. Even if Newt was willing to let us sing some of the songs as a personal favour, the legal team would be down on him like a ton of bricks, I dare say.'

'Of course they would,' said Henry. 'Stands to reason. There'll be deals with record companies in the works, and spin-off deals covering use of the music on TV and radio, and so on. The legal people will have everything sewn up as tight as a drum. And the minute anyone gets wind of a YouTube video showing us four singing an as-yet-to-be-released song from the film…wallop, there'll be a heavy price to pay, I can assure you.'

'I hadn't thought of that,' said Vince, turning in Neil's direction. 'So, you'll be in for some tasty royalties downstream. Nice one, matey!'

'Assuming that's in his contract,' said Henry. 'But then we're straying into personal territory there. I'm sure Neil would rather keep the details of his remuneration to himself.'

'I'm not fussed,' said Neil. 'I was contracted and paid a fee by Yellow Braces to arrange Joel's songs and act as special advisor, and I'm still under contract until the end of production. But Joel and I both have a royalty component built into our contracts.'

'Nice little repeat earner,' said Vince, topping up Neil's glass. 'Better than the union rates we were paid to record the songs, huh? Well, I suppose the big talent gets the big bucks. Just don't forget your mates when we're on our uppers. That doesn't apply to Henry, obviously. He's minted.'

Henry shook his head and signalled for Vince to fill his glass as the main course started to arrive. 'Anyway, Neil, did I hear you doing some forward planning just then?'

'I was just saying to Danny that we'll have to get organised quickly if we're going to have a proper tilt at the British championships. It's only three months to prelims in November. We need to select songs, plan a rehearsal programme, and get some practice gigs lined up if possible.'

'Oh dear,' said Henry.

'What's up?' said Danny.

'Well, I find myself in something of an awkward spot. You see, I'm considering moving to the island to be with Cat. I was waiting for the right moment to tell you. But I've overlooked the fact that work towards prelims would be starting so soon. Oh, this is not good, I've really messed up here. What was it Churchill once said? "To build may have to be the slow and laborious task of years. To destroy can be the thoughtless act of a single day."' And, placing his knife and fork gently in the centre of his plate, Henry said 'excuse me' and left the table.

A hushed silence followed, as Vince, Neil, and Danny watched every step of Henry's walk towards the exit. Or was he just visiting the bathroom? They couldn't tell.

'A bit of a tumbleweed moment there,' said Vince at last.

'Well, as dramatic exits go, that one takes some beating,' said Danny.

'Should one of us go after him?' said Vince, resuming his main course.

'I wouldn't,' said Neil, pushing his plate to one side. 'I've lost my appetite all of a sudden.'

'Shame to waste it. Nice-looking bit of steak, that. Pass it over,' said Vince.

When Henry returned after fifteen minutes, he apologised for spoiling the party. 'What I can't understand is how I could have forgotten that the build-up to the championships would start so soon. I just hadn't thought things through. Not like me at all. I've not been having much luck finding a new place, and Cat suggested I could move to the island, as lately we've been, well… feeling—'

'Spare yourself, Henry,' said Neil. No need to explain. It's okay.'

'But it's not okay, is it? It throws a bloody big spanner in the works. What an idiot I am.'

'There are quartets in the States whose members live thousands of miles apart. They fly to rehearsals and performances as a matter of course,' said Neil. 'It really depends on how badly you want it…'

'Well, he clearly wants it very badly, that's why he's going to live with—' said Vince.

'You know what I mean, Vince…how badly Henry wants to take part in the next championships.'

'I absolutely do. Totally,' said Henry.

'Then we can work something out,' said Neil.

Thirty-Five

A Two for One Deal

As late summer Saturdays go, it was right up there with the best of them. After a spell of wet weather, several sunny days had followed, drying out the ground, making the grass and hedgerows even more luxuriant, and filling the clean air with sweet, subtle scents. It was a languid, come-hither kind of day, full of the promise of long hours filled with carefree relaxation.

'Barbecue or picnic?' said Angie.

'Picnic, hands down,' said Vince. 'I'm not sweating over a barbecue on a day like this. I don't see the appeal of cindered sausages and risky chicken myself, but no doubt caveman types will be wheeling their Webers out all over Britain as we speak. Not for me. Oh, hang on…isn't it the village fete today?'

'Yes, so it is,' said Angie. 'Okay, why don't we pop along to that and take a picnic we can eat in the meadow by the river afterwards. I fancy a big old salad with rocket and blue cheese, walnuts, beetroot, peppers, nice dressing, all the works. Then strawberries, and a few glasses of fizz. Just what the doctor ordered.'

'Sounds good to me,' said Vince. 'When was the last time you had a whole Saturday off, babe?'

'I can't remember, but I promise you this won't be the last one. I could get a real taste for this. Right, you dig out the hamper, the cold box, the blankets, and your folding chair, and I'll scuttle along to the shops and get the food and fizz.'

'And a few cold tinnies,' said Vince.

'Okay, if you must,' said Angie.

Just then, Vince's mobile phone rang. It was Danny. He had thought, or rather Hannah had suggested, that if they were free it would be great if Vince and Angie could come round for a barbecue. They had just bought a new Weber.

'Ah. We were just planning a trip to our village fete and then a picnic by the river,' said Vince. 'Hey, rather than messing up the new barbie, why don't you and Hannah bring the kids and we'll hit the fete. They've got rides, a water thing, and a dog show. Then we can pitch a spot by the river and chill with a few beers. The kids'll love it. We'll bring all the food and drink. Hang on, let me just—'

Vince shouted to Angie, who was making for the door.

'Babe... Danny, Angie, and the kids are coming over. Get picnic stuff for six...wait, that's probably five...plus whatever babies eat at picnics. And get loads more cold tinnies. Thanks, babe.'

'Bloody thing. I was sure I wouldn't win it. What am I going to do with it?' said Vince.

'Hang it on a wall?' said Danny with a smirk.

'You're joking. Look at the brushwork...look at the perspective. It's all out of whack. Amateurish.'

'Well, that's what you bid for. "Delightful village scene by local amateur artist" it said,' said Angie. 'You're an amateur artist yourself, so what's the problem?'

'I may be an amateur, but that's taking the word to new depths.'

'Then why did you bid for it, Vince?' asked Hannah.

'Well, I was doing my bit for the village. Half a million needed for the church restoration, so I thought I'd bid high to get things rolling.'

'But it was a silent auction,' said Danny. 'Nobody knows who bids what, so if you bid high, there was always a very good chance you'd win it. And you did.'

'Bloody thing, you wouldn't get a fiver for it,' said Vince, shaking his head.

'How much did you bid, if you don't mind me asking?' asked Hannah.

'Two hundred quid,' said Vince, cracking open another can of beer.

Danny and Angie fell about laughing, Danny throwing in a roll in the grass for good measure. Angie clinked glasses with Hannah, who couldn't help joining in the merriment at Vince's expense. 'Oh Vince, what are you like?' she said, doing her best to control the biggest fit of giggles she could remember in a long time.

'I think it's a lovely picture,' said Ben, approaching Vince's chair, a football tucked under his arm. Ellie crawled across the blanket to join her brother.

'Then it's worth the money after all,' said Vince. 'There you go, buddy. It's yours. Your Dad can hang it on your bedroom wall.'

'Thank you, Vince!' said Ben, with genuine delight. 'Play football with me, Vince.'

'Ah well, I'd love to, Ben, but my football days are over.'

'Over what?' said Ben.

'I mean... I can't kick the ball because my legs aren't strong enough.'

'You could do headers,' said Ben.

'Okay, let's try. You go over there a bit and throw it to me, and I'll head it back.'

Ben moved to where Vince had indicated, and Hannah picked up Ellie from the blanket.

'Okay, go,' said Vince, and Ben threw the ball underarm towards Vince, a little too high for him to head from his seated position. To compensate, Vince raised his arms to catch the ball, overstretching his upper body, and overturning his chair in the process. The next thing, Vince was lying on his back, arms and legs akimbo, doing a credible impression of a dying fly.

The adults again made merry at Vince's expense. Ben ran to his side. 'Sorry, Vince,' he said.

'That's all right, buddy. As I was saying, my football days are over. Now, if your Dad wouldn't mind helping me up, we can try that again.' And once restored to an upright position, Vince proceeded to head the ball back to Ben six times out of six, to applause from everyone...even Ellie.

'You're better at headers than Duncan Ferguson,' said Ben.

It remained pleasantly warm as the afternoon wore on, no-one especially caring about the time, everyone just content to enjoy the simple, undemanding pleasure of relaxing with good friends in a beautiful place. The smell of cooking drifted by, and a cork popped somewhere nearby. Ellie was asleep and Ben was playing safely with a group of children, their shrill voices cutting through the still air. As Vince opened his eyes, Angie spoke, breaking the comfortable silence that had descended on the group. 'Shall we?' she said.

'Shall we what?' said Vince.

'You know...'

'Oh, yes, yes. Sure. You tell them.'

'Typical,' said Angie. 'Well, Vince and I would like to set a date for our wedding. And we wondered if we could combine it with the christening service for Ellie. Getting married and becoming godparents at the same time would make it such a wonderful occasion.'

'Double bubble. Two for one deal,' said Vince.

Danny looked at Hannah, whose face lit up. 'That would be absolutely fantastic,' she said. 'How exciting!' And Hannah hugged Angie as though her life depended on it.

A week later, Hannah filled in the Edinburgh Postnatal Depression Scale questionnaire for the last time, again ignoring the standard multiple-choice answers in favour of:

1. I have been able to laugh and see the funny side of things

    Yes.

2. I have looked forward with enjoyment to things

    Hell, yes.

3. I have blamed myself unnecessarily when things went wrong

    I burnt a saucepan the other day, which I definitely blame myself for, but not much else I can think of.

4. I have been anxious or worried for no good reason

    I have been anxious or worried when there's good reason, not so much when there isn't.

5. I have felt scared or panicky for no very good reason

    Not really.

6. Things have been getting on top of me

    Yes, Danny.

7. I have been so unhappy that I have had difficulty sleeping

    I'm sleeping pretty well these days, particularly after Danny's been on top of me.

8. I have felt sad or miserable

    ☺

9. I have been so unhappy that I have been crying

    I cried watching ET with the kids recently. Does that count?

10. The thought of harming myself has occurred to me

    The thought of filling in this form ever again makes me want to harm myself, but apart from that, no. Laters xxx

Thirty-Six

Going To Be Busy

The island was nothing if not capricious – at least, where the elements were concerned. It had recently been at its glorious best, when clear blue skies and the sun's radiance turned the island into a glittering emerald by day, and clear starry skies and the moon's spectral glow turned it into the most impressive of observatories by night. Today, however, an immovable mantle of thick cloud had settled on the island, pouring persistent rain, and making everything grey and dull.

Cat was greeting a group of twenty-odd school children and their chaperones to guide them on an island walk and nature ramble. For now, the gaggle of seven and eight-year olds, all in identical bright red waterproof capes, were huddled together in the small dive hut-cum-information centre at the start of the jetty, shrieking with barely dampened excitement. The idea was to use the hut as a holding pen until the heavy rain eased off before marching the children up the steep beach road to the top of the island. But after twenty minutes of waiting, and with the kids getting restless, Cat decided to press on. She called the group to order and told them that the adventure was about to begin. Weather like this, she explained, was the best kind for imagining stormy nights when pirates would land their ships and scramble ashore to raid and loot whatever they could find. And today's first stop would be the ancient castle, beneath which was a cave once used to hide people and, quite possibly...treasure.

A cheer went up, and the jumble of red capes started to form a long crocodile, which Cat led into the rain and on up the sharply inclined, meandering road to the top of the island. 'A-haaaghh!' she shouted, in her best pirate voice. 'A-haaaghh!' came the reply, twenty-fold.

As they walked, Cat tried to think of other ways of keeping the kids interested in the challenging conditions. It would be tough, as most of what she had planned involved viewing the wildlife, which would be very difficult if the current miasma persisted. The ponies would be sheltering, the deer would be impossible to find, the rabbits would be deep in their burrows, and the wild goats and Soay sheep would be beyond range at the far north of the island – too far for the kids on a day like today.

As they walked, Cat also thought about seeing Henry later in the day. She hadn't seen him disembark, as she'd been so wrapped up with the school party, but she really looked forward to being with him again, and especially to making plans for his move to the island.

That thought crossed her mind as the troupe climbed the last steep section of track onto the island's plateau. Just then, the rain eased and the sky lightened, as five wild ponies trotted over the hill to greet them.

Cat's cottage was at one end of a row of four, and like all of the older buildings in the village, was made of solid granite. The accommodation was simple, with a small kitchen-dining room, a slightly larger living room with a wood-burning stove, a small bathroom, and one bedroom. The furniture was comfortable and of good quality, but had seen better days. Cat's personal possessions, including a large collection of rocks and fossils, an old brass microscope, a stuffed herring gull, and a bookcase full of textbooks on zoology, botany, ornithology, archaeology, and much more, gave the place a homely yet slightly scientific air.

Whenever Henry had visited previously, he had been charmed by the cottage, with its quirky contents, its wonderful views across open fields, and the stunning peacefulness of its setting. Now he knew he would start viewing it from a slightly more practical angle – at the possibility of it becoming his home. Staying for a week or two at a time was one thing; staying longer-term now struck him as something that had to be thought through. For one thing, it occurred to him that while his unimposing flat in Ascot could hardly be compared to this lovely cottage on this magnificent island, there was little difference between them in terms of living space. But that thought quickly passed. He wanted to be with Cat, and that's what mattered most.

They were finishing dinner, nibbling at cheese and sipping red wine, the yellow glow of candlelight illuminating their faces and throwing strange shadows around the room. Through the window, the last of a beautiful sunset was giving way to a closing darkness and the promise of a clear and starry night. Henry looked at Cat's face, which, from the moment he first saw it, he had found fascinating. Her eyes were an intense green and so inviting to look into, her skin was pale yet weather-worn, which suited her, and her mouth was wide, which made for the most generous of smiles. Looking at her that first time, he had seen something deep, a sort of life force. And now, with candlelight playing softly against her features, the effect was redoubled.

'When did you…we…start feeling differently, do you think?' said Henry, in his softest bass voice.

'Do we feel differently about things? About each other?' said Cat.

'No…yes…well, about living together?'

'It seemed a natural thing to suggest. You were looking for somewhere, finding nothing, and, well…this was always an option.'

'The long-distance arrangement does seem to suit us, though. Looking forward to the next island adventure, the heart growing fonder, the romance and the excitement of the return!' said Henry. 'It's like Robert Redford flying in to see Meryl Streep in *Out of Africa*.'

'So it suits *you* is what you mean,' said Cat, a gentle smile illuminated in the candlelight.

'Be fair. I've never known such a free spirit as you. It suits you too.'

'Yes…and no. Free spirit I may be. And I don't need anyone to make me whole, or validate who I am. I'm perfectly happy on my own. But when you find someone you…' said Cat, her voice trailing off as she looked into Henry's eyes across a flickering flame.

'I do love being here,' said Henry.

'Well, then. Okay, it's going to be different, and there's bound to be some readjustments to make…even a few challenges to begin with.'

'Yes, there will,' said Henry. 'I was wondering how to approach this…'

'Henry, what is it?'

'Well, I miscalculated something. I've agreed to move here at precisely the time when I need to be close to the guys. We've a lot of preparation ahead of prelims in November and then the championships next May…rehearsals, shows, other competitions, you know? I'm not sure I could base myself here and be there for all of that…and I can't let the fellas down.'

'Ah, I see,' said Cat, her smile fading in the candlelight. 'If your heart says fly, then fly. If your heart says sing, then sing…'

For Henry, it wasn't a matter of choosing one over the other, but the way Cat had said it made it sound like a choice had to be made – fly or sing, stay or go, Cat or the quartet. Really? When she'd given him that very advice when they first met, it had liberated him, given him purpose and direction, and the strength to deal with both the end of his professional career and the end of his marriage. Now, the same phrase seemed to be shackling him rather than liberating him. How could that be?

He had come close to asking Cat if that's what she meant but couldn't quite bring himself to. It was like tempting fate when you feared that fate was about to deal you the worst possible hand. Instead, he convinced himself that Cat couldn't possibly have been giving him an ultimatum. That wasn't in her nature. Was it? So, he had watched while her smile faded. 'It won't stop me coming over just as often as before,' he promised. 'And when the championships are over, perhaps that's the right time for me to make the move,' he'd said. But her smile didn't return.

'Henry? Are you with us?' came a voice, as though from the far end of a long corridor. He looked up to see Vince, Danny, and Neil staring at him. Vince gave him a little wave.

'Are you okay?' said Neil.

'What? Yes, sure... I was just—'

'Back on the island?'

'Sorry... I suppose I was,' said Henry. 'But carry on... I'm with you now.'

'I was just starting to outline some sort of programme for the next few months, but we'll come back to that,' said Neil. 'So, have you sorted out your move? What's happening? We need to work around you to some extent.'

Henry took a sip of cold coffee. 'Just assume I'll be there for everything. The move's on hold for the time being. Count me in for whatever you've got planned.'

'Hey, listen...if you do move, it's fine. We'll deal with it... don't—'

'It's okay,' said Henry. 'Do you mind putting the kettle on again?'

They were sitting in the splendid garden of Neil's family home. The large, perfectly flat lawn had been recently mown so that it resembled a professional sports field, and water sprinklers were gently juddering in the background.

'The hissing of summer lawns,' said Vince.

'Joni Mitchell, 1975,' said Danny.

'Too easy,' said Vince.

Neil returned with Henry's coffee and started explaining the initial plan he'd come up with. He suggested that two rehearsals a week would be optimal, but he suspected they'd struggle to manage more than one most weeks, even if Henry didn't have a long-distance commute to contend with. For prelims in November, Neil already had two songs in mind, and if they were all free on the second weekend of October, he suggested that it would be great to give them a run-out at the Irish barbershop convention in Cork.

'Oh, if we're looking a bit further ahead, you're all invited to my wedding in March,' Vince threw in casually. 'I dare say we'll do a spot of singing then.'

'And it's Ellie's christening at the same church on the same day,' said Danny.

Just then, Margaret appeared, carrying a tray of sandwiches. 'Planning are we? Then don't forget my book launch. I need you boys for that! It's not until April, but make sure you pop it in the diary!'

'Oh, and how could I forget,' said Neil. 'Before all of that, we've been invited to sing at the wrap party for *A Cappella Fellas* next month.

'I love rock 'n' roll,' said Vince.

'Arrows, 1975 again…but Joan Jett got to number one with it on the Billboard chart in '82,' said Danny.

They were going to be busy.

Thirty-Seven

The Wrap Party

'It looks marvellous,' said Newton Burns. 'Someone's done a great job. Hey, look…that area over there is decked out like the studio in the *American Talent* audition scene, complete with the judges' desk. How divine!'

Newt and Neil were walking around the interior of a spacious London gallery that had been hired for the wrap party to celebrate the end of production of *A Cappella Fellas*.

'Oh, and look at this,' said Neil, pausing in front of a dimly lit area, little more than a small alcove, on the wall of which was mounted a circular blue plaque embossed with white script. It read:

The production team, cast and crew of 'A Cappella Fellas' are proud to commemorate the lives lost in the tragic events of September 11, 2001. Our story speaks of the valor and indefatigable spirit of survivors and their families, and of the determination of the free world to prevail in the face of those who seek to destroy our way of life. From Darkness, Always Light.

Set into the floor beneath the plaque was a torch, similar to the ones held aloft during Olympic ceremonies, whose light illuminated the inscription, and caused shadows to gently dance on the walls of the alcove.

'That's a lovely touch,' said Newt. 'We've worked closely with support groups in New York, and they wanted something to remember us by. I'm told that this will be displayed discreetly somewhere close to Ground Zero. Very humbling thought…'

'And *From Darkness, Always Light* is a beautiful touch. It's one of my favourite songs from the film,' said Neil.

'Quite so. Quite so,' said Newt, gently steering his companion towards another part of the room.

Staff were beginning to appear, setting up tables, preparing the bar area, testing a sound system, adjusting lighting, and generally getting the space ready for the evening's event.

'Why did you want to be here so early?' asked Neil, as they sat down at an occasional table.

'Just habit,' said Newt. 'You might think the wrap party is the least of my concerns. A production coordinator has put all of this together and done a splendid job. But it's one of those things I'm incredibly fussy about. It's not me being overbearing or untrusting, it's just that I'm what you might call an "insecure perfectionist" – I think I might have got that from Ken! But I could ask you the same question. I didn't expect to see you or anyone else here this early.'

'Ah, well. I guess I'm a bit the same. As we'll be singing later on, I thought I'd reccy the place. The others should be here soon, as I want to do a run-through of the songs and get warmed up. I'm trying to work out where the best place to sing would be.'

'Are you serious, dear boy?' said Newt with a quizzical look. 'Yes, why?'

Newt stood up and beckoned Neil to come with him, as he moved towards the *American Talent* set. 'Exactly there's where you'll be singing,' he said, pointing to a large red star on the polished floor.

A small group, consisting of Mac McAuley, Joey Pellegrini, and Veronica Rossi, were engaged in what sounded like a fairly vigorous exchange of words. The four members of From The Edge were close by, engaged in their own discussion about their impending performance. Neil was doing his best to keep their attention, but as star after star drifted by, it was becoming increasingly difficult. Vince, in particular, had one ear bent in the direction of the voluble threesome nearby, and at least one eye set in the direction of Veronica Rossi's impressive décolletage. Neil came to the conclusion that there was little point trying to maintain discipline in the circumstances. He couldn't blame Vince, or any of them, for taking it all in – it certainly made for fascinating people-watching, with exalted celebrities mingling with production staff and crew, the whole thing pulled together into a very lavish production in itself, with fine food and drink aplenty, and no shortage of bustling bonhomie and sugar-encrusted displays of gratitude wherever you looked.

Vince watched as Mac McAuley shook his head and backed away from Joey and Veronica, making towards the bar. Vince's first instinct was to edge closer to the flamboyant Ms. Rossi, but upon hearing the acidity of the words she was directing at Joey Pellegrini, decided against it, and walked alongside Mac as he approached the bar. 'Nice do,' he opened.

'Say what, fella?' said Mac.

'Splendid event,' said Vince. 'May I buy you a drink?'

'That's very generous of you, seeing as it's a free bar.'

'Ah, good point. Yes. Still. You're Mac McAuley, aren't you?'

'That's the one. And you're one of Neil's singer friends, right?'

'Yes, right. I'm Vince. Nice to meet you. I'm sort of friends with Brad, as well. Is he here? I haven't seen him around.'

'Me neither. He's probably lying drunk somewhere. Say, are you the guy who got smashed with him in Soho? The wheelchair incident?'

'Well, yes.'

Mac shook his head.

'It seems like your two companions over there are getting rather excited,' said Vince, attempting a change of subject.

'It's all part of the deal, Vince,' said Mac, sipping at a small glass of white wine. 'I've been to a thousand wrap parties, and it's always the same. Affairs begin on set, and often end at the wrap party. Sometimes affairs start at the wrap party and end the next morning. Most times, people are scouting for their next project. The director is usually the most popular guy in the room. That's why I keep moving. There's only so many elevator pitches I can bear to listen to in one evening. Now, I must be off. Someone I'd rather not talk to is heading this way.' And with that, Mac disappeared into the throng.

Vince made his way back to his group in no particular hurry. Everywhere he looked there were shiny, happy people he wanted to engage with, particularly the stylish, often scantily dressed women. He'd got on famously with Brad (where was he?), and fared reasonably well with Mac, and though Veronica Rossi seemed beyond his reach, he scoured the room for more potential luvvy friends. He didn't reason why, it was just a bit of a lark. But then, very suddenly, his breathing faltered and for a moment he struggled to take in air. He stopped still and became conscious of his stick for the first time. He stared straight ahead, at the elegantly sculptured neck and upper back of some sparkling starlet, watching her shoulder blades articulate as she gesticulated to her companions. He gripped his stick tightly and thought of Angie. She was a cut above this lot, he thought.

Just then, a hand landed on Vince's upper back, and he turned to see Henry's benevolent, smiling face. 'Penny for them?' he said. 'Come on, time to perform.'

Newton Burns stepped up to the microphone, and the din in the room quietened as the assembly came to order. There had been a few speeches and presentations already during the evening, including the liberal giving of gifts. Everyone received gifts, it seemed. The crew received t-shirts and baseball caps printed with the movie branding and 'A Cappella Fellas Crew'. And most of the cast members were sporting new Rolex DateJusts, no doubt inscribed with a few *bon mots* to serve as a reminder of their time together. But this was the big speech from the head guy, and an expectant hush descended on the room.

'Ladies and gentlemen, allow me to say a few words, and I promise to keep it brief,' Newton Burns began. 'These occasions are very special to me…the coming together of all the wonderful people who have collaborated to create something unique. And I do mean *everyone* in this room. I do rather dislike the notion of separating out the so-called "creatives" from the technical people or the admin people, and so on. Because without each other, we're nothing…nothing gets done. I stand here in front of you all, and I am more proud of this project than of any other I've been involved with. Collectively, you've made an old man's dream a reality. Of course, we don't yet know how we'll do at the box office, but I have a pretty strong hunch we'll do okay. I can't explain exactly why, but suffice it to say an old pal called Ken has a lot to do with it. And that brings me to one of the highlights of the evening. It gives me the greatest of pleasures to introduce you to the gentlemen who were coached by my dear friend Ken, and who sang all the wonderful songs in *A Cappella Fellas*. Now, let me just wander over to my assigned place at the judges' desk, as I give you… Vince, Danny, Henry, and Neil!'

Applause erupted as the foursome came forward and gathered around the big red star on the stage floor. Henry blew pitch, and they started to sing a new song, written and arranged by Neil, that lampooned Newt, Mac, and several members of the cast. The response was immediate, and the room filled with howls of laughter. At the judges' desk, Newt sat alongside Mac, Lorna, and Joel, all of them laughing along too. At the end of the song, and as the noise subsided, Newt shouted, 'You've got four YESs, you horrible lot,' and Neil stepped forward.

'Thank you all, we're so glad you enjoyed that little bit of fun. It could have gone so badly wrong, couldn't it? So we'd just like to finish with one of our favourite songs from *A Cappella Fellas*. This is called—'

Just then, there was a scramble at the edge of the stage

area, as Todd Bannerman, John Fontaine, and Joey Pellegrini emerged from the crowd to join Neil and the others. 'Can we join in?' Joey shouted to the crowd, who responded with wild enthusiasm. 'What are we singing, guys?' Joey asked, turning towards Neil.

'Well, we weren't expecting this,' said Neil, opening his arms wide to welcome the newcomers. 'Can you guys remember *From Darkness, Always Light*? If not, just mime like you did in the film!' More laughter followed, and then someone in the crowd shouted 'Where's Brad?'

'Ah, man. He's not here,' said Joey.

'Who's not here, dude?' came another voice, as Brad Frampton hopped onto the stage.

'Shit,' Vince whispered to Neil. 'And he's sober too,' Neil whispered back.

The octet delivered a very powerful and moving rendition of *From Darkness, Always Light*, and there was barely a dry eye in the house. Only Neil could tell that not everything was quite right, as he had noticed that some of the more important tenor notes were missing, and that Vince was struggling badly for breath.

Thirty-Eight

An Irish Excursion

'How come we didn't get given a Rolex?' said Vince, staring intently at a display of expensive watches in a jeweller's window at Heathrow Terminal 2.

'I suppose the whole gift giving thing is a bit of a tradition, just cast and crew. A little thank you for all those directly involved,' said Henry. 'Why are you bothered? We got well paid, didn't we?'

'I'm not bothered, I'm just saying. I think that's the one the cast were all flaunting. Six and a half grand! Not such a little thank you!' Vince yawned loudly. 'Jeez, aren't airports a real drag? Do you fancy a pint?'

'It's ten-thirty in the morning,' said Henry, taking a seat.

'The usual rules don't apply in airports,' said Vince, joining his friend. 'I mean, see that place over there that looks a bit like a Wetherspoon's. It'll be chock full of people supposedly in there for breakfast, but we all know the real agenda, and that's getting a few down you before the big bird takes to the skies. Nothing more liberating that a couple of airport lagers at naughty o'clock.'

Henry turned to look at his friend, and studied his face closely. 'You know, Vince...in any other circumstances, I'd decline the offer,' he said. 'But on this occasion, I'll take you up on it.'

Minutes later they were nestling into a corner table, sipping pints and making short work of bacon sandwiches. 'That's better,' said Vince. 'The perfect antidote to airport boredom. Cheers. So, what did you mean by "in any other circumstances"?'

'Oh, nothing,' said Henry, casually scratching the top of his head.

'Bullshit,' said Vince, cramming the last of his bacon sandwich into his mouth and washing it down with lager. 'You may be a cagey bugger a lot of the time, but something's up. I can tell…'

'Vince, as you know, I'm not normally one to…'

Vince said nothing, but looked directly into Henry's eyes, raising his own eyebrows as he did so.

'Okay,' said Henry. 'Listen, no need to tell the others, but Cat and I had a long phone conversation last evening, and it didn't go well.'

When Danny heard that they would be singing at the Irish barbershop convention in Cork, he knew that fate was at work. He had not long opened up to Vince about his upbringing, something he never thought he'd do, when Neil pulled the Irish rabbit out of the hat. For years Danny had been putting something off, something he had pretended wasn't important, but now he knew different. Cork was the birthplace of Mary Teresa Murphy, his mother.

Mary was born and brought up in Cork before moving to Liverpool in her late teens, where she took a job as a waitress at the Adelphi Hotel. And it was there she met Danny's father. Beyond that, he knew very little. He had old photographs of Mary, but his father had spoken about her only rarely. While he was a kind and gentle man, he wasn't someone who could be pushed to do something he didn't want to do. And then there was May. So Danny grew up knowing next to nothing about Mary, and only the kindly face in those old photographs gave a clue to what she might have been like.

He made up his mind to travel a day ahead of the others, to visit the site of Mary's family home, as well as visiting the small monument to one of his favourite musicians, Rory Gallagher, just off Paul Street in the centre of the city. Arriving late morning, and with the weather dry and sunny, though cold, he decided to get his bearings by walking around the city centre for a couple of hours. He called in at the English Market, with its old-fashioned butchers and fishmongers, and was reminded of St. John's market in Liverpool when he was a youngster, with its sawdust floors and wooden stalls laden with fresh produce. He also paid a visit to St. Fin Barre's cathedral where, for all he knew, Mary could have been a regular visitor as a child.

And then, after a late lunch, he made his way to Rory Gallagher Place, where he spent a while examining the bronze sculpture in honour of the great blues man who grew up in the city. He approached the unassuming object, set on a plinth at about head height, which revealed what looked like flickering flames on one side and a guitar on the other. He circled the sculpture three times, viewing it at various angles, before noticing that what he had taken for flames were actually intertwined strands containing lyrics from Gallagher's album, *Jinxed* – the very one that Danny used to play on repeat when he was in his early teens. He scrutinised the lyrics closely, many of them difficult to read through layers of patination, looking for one lyric in particular. And he was about give up and move on when at last he spotted it: *I feel like a lost child, searching in the dark.*

Thirty minutes later, in a municipal car park that he was sure was the site of Mary's birthplace, long since bulldozed, Danny tied a small bunch of flowers to the base of a lamp post. Attached to the cellophane wrapping was a note that read: *No longer a lost child, searching in the dark. Love, Daniel x.*

And thirty minutes after that, he took a high stool at the bar of what looked like one of the city's oldest pubs, in need of a drink.

'What'll it be?' asked the barman.

'Guinn…no, sorry, I'll have a Murphy's.'

Danny waited while his stout was settling, reflecting on the

225

day's events, when he became aware of a commotion behind him. He looked around to see a group of maybe fifteen young men enter the barroom, voices raised, clearly in celebration of something or other. Perhaps a stag party – not what he needed right now. Just then, their ringleader approached the bar, brandishing an impressive two-handed silver trophy, which he placed as carefully as he was able on the bar, with the instruction 'Champions Cup, when you're ready, thanks.' As it turned out, that was a very polite way of asking the barman to fill the trophy with an unholy cocktail of stout, bitter, lager, and cider from along the bar, topped off with whiskey from the top shelf. Danny looked on with a mixture of disbelief and growing amusement, as the lads made merry, passing the trophy between them to drink from it in turns.

Then someone shouted what sounded like a war cry in Gaelic, and this was followed by three minutes of Queen's *We Are The Champions* at full volume. Danny was considering whether to stick around when he felt a tap on his upper arm. The next thing, the ringleader was thrusting the trophy towards him with an invitation to partake. 'You'll have a drink, now,' was less of an invitation than a friendly command, and as the entire group started up with repeated cries of 'Drink, drink, drink,' Danny went along with the game, and was roundly applauded for doing so, before the trophy was passed along to the next unsuspecting punter.

The pub was filling up even more now and somewhere behind him, Danny could hear a fiddle being tuned and a few lines of song being tried out. The place was about to get really rowdy and Danny sensed it was time to go. Draining the last of his stout, he climbed down from his bar stool and made his way to the Gents. Seconds later, an older guy appeared at the urinal beside him, with the words 'Great craic, great craic. Tell me, do you like a song yerself, by any chance?'

'Er, well, yes…yes, I do,' was all that Danny could think to say. Then the older guy left the toilet without washing his hands.

As Danny reappeared from the Gents, head down, making for the exit, the barroom fell quiet as the older guy gave a shout of 'Hush now, this fella's gonna give us a song!'

For a moment, Danny was rooted to the spot like an animal being backed into a corner by a predator – in this case, a large pack of very eager Irish predators. Fight or flight – what would it be? There was only one thing to do.

'Give me a moment,' he said at last, and searched his brain rapidly for a song – any song – that might do the trick. He cleared his throat, the room fell quiet again, and he gave them his best rendition of *My Wild Irish Rose*. And as the final note slipped past his lips, the entire room went bananas.

The following afternoon, the quartet gathered at their hotel and spent a couple of hours going over the contest songs for the next day. Danny was relaxed and in fine voice. Henry seemed a little subdued but was focused on the job. Neil took them through their paces, as usual, and it was quickly apparent that Vince was struggling.

At the wrap party, Neil had noticed that all wasn't well with Vince's voice, his breathing in particular. The others hadn't been as observant at the time. But now, there was no escaping it. Vince was finding it difficult to sing to the end of phrases, and was forcing breaths where they didn't belong. They had to stop and start several times to go over passages of songs that ordinarily they would have sailed through without a thought. Neil was worried. And now they all were. Vince could only apologise.

At ten minutes past three the following afternoon, the quartet were introduced onto the competition stage by the compère in familiar manner. 'Stewards, close the doors please. Ladies and gentlemen, contestants number nine, representing the British Association of Barbershop Singers… From The Edge!'

It wasn't their finest hour.

Thirty-Nine

Vince Gets Help

'Around thirty percent of people with MS have decreased respiratory function in the form of mild dyspnea during moderate physical activity,' said Dr. Sukand Singh, consultant neurologist with Berkshire Healthcare NHS Foundation Trust.

'Mild...what was that, sorry?' said Vince.

'Dyspnea...difficulty breathing or shortness of breath. But, looking at the pulmonary function test results, your scores are actually very good, so I'd say the strength of the muscles you use to breathe, the diaphragm and so on, is not the problem here.'

'I sing,' said Vince.

'No, I'm Singh,' said the consultant.

'Sorry?'

'My little joke,' said Dr. Singh. 'How much do you sing?'

'A lot. All the time.'

'Well, the evidence of the function tests suggests you'd do well to keep on singing. But that still leaves us with the question of what's causing this recent difficulty.'

Vince was sitting in a small, tidy consulting room in St. Luke's hospital, where he'd spent more time than he cared to remember in recent years. On the walls were the usual anatomical diagrams, safety notices, and an x-ray light box. On top of a small filing cabinet was a cut-away plastic model of a human head and abdomen. On the desk next to a computer monitor was a framed photo of a family group, almost certainly a wedding party, with women dressed in vibrantly-coloured silks and gold jewellery, the men looking proud in their turbans and yellow kurtas.

Vince hadn't seen Dr. Singh before, but he seemed to know his onions. He continued: 'So, would you say that you can't get enough air at times? That you can't breathe as deeply as you're used to?'

'Yes.'

'And would you say that it makes you anxious, as if you are trying to breathe with a blanket over your head or a heavy weight on your chest?'

'Sometimes, yes.'

'Do you have difficulties swallowing or clearing mucus from the nose or throat?'

'No, not at all.'

'Okay, good. Then, since your pulmonary function looks fine, that leads us down a couple of other paths.'

'Sounds like a detective collecting clues, narrowing down the field,' said Vince, paying closer attention.

'Quite. A bit like Columbo, you might say. Now then, I see here that you take medication to help with muscle pain and stiffness. They can sometimes cause breathing problems. When was the last time you didn't take the muscle relaxants?'

'A couple of years ago, but I might have forgotten to take them by accident once or twice,' said Vince.

'And what happens if you forget to take them?'

'I can barely walk, the pain and stiffness is too much.'

'I see.'

'Okay, that's one possible path. What's the other one?' said Vince, sitting closer to the edge of his chair.

'Well, breathing problems with MS may be the result of irregular sensory information involving abnormal pressure in the lungs, airflow, or the motion of the lungs and the chest wall. But I'm less inclined to believe it in this case. We can do further tests to make sure, but I think side-effects of medication is more likely…and certainly easier to prove.'

'Which means stopping the muscle relaxants?'

'At some point, yes. Temporarily, at least.'

'I wouldn't be able to get out of bed, never mind sing,' said Vince.

Vince didn't waste any time in telling the others about the consultation, and they were understanding and concerned, as always. Vince hated the fact that his condition was too often the cause of disruption to the quartet's progress. First it was mobility problems, and now this. Not being able to get around too well is one thing, but being unable to breathe properly is about the worst thing that could happen to a singer short of being rendered tone deaf overnight or losing your voice altogether.

However, with prelims just weeks away, there was little choice but to press on, keep practising, keep working on breath control, and be the best version of his singing self that he could be. Even if that was below his usual best.

Then, one evening, Vince received a call from Neil, which he assumed was a regular update regarding preparations for prelims. Instead, Neil said, 'Are you at home tomorrow? Ma wants to come and see you.'

He was, and she did. Margaret Taylor was the kind of person who lights up a room: a one-woman charm offensive. She was busy, energetic, organised, and caring. And when Margaret had something to tell you, chances are it was worth listening to.

It was a bright, late October morning, the kind of autumn day that can lift the spirits as well as any in high summer: a low sun in a pale blue sky, trees partly clad in bronze, yellow and red, and the air rich with the smells of turned earth and wood smoke. Vince took all of this in as he opened the door to welcome Margaret into his home. She cut a stylish and youthful figure for a woman close to seventy, and looked like a film star of a certain vintage in an elegant red three-quarter length coat with matching fedora and gloves.

Vince made Margaret feel at home, taking her things, and

seating her in the most comfortable armchair.

'Well, this is nice,' she said.

'Angie is out at the moment, so the refreshments are down to me, I'm afraid,' said Vince. 'What would you like?'

'Good grief, you sound just like George,' said Margaret. 'Surely your kitchen skills run to dipping a tea bag in some hot water, Vince?'

'What, oh sure. No, I didn't mean…it's just that Angie tends to…well, you know.'

'I dare say she dotes on you. And to some extent that's understandable, what with your MS. But I hope you don't take advantage of your lovely lady, Vince, MS or no MS.' Margaret added a wink for good measure.

'Tea and biscuits, then?'

'Lovely.'

Over tea, Margaret got straight to the point. 'I wanted to update you on my MS charity work for the book launch, and also talk to you a little about your own situation,' she said, picking up a ginger nut biscuit. 'Do you mind if I dunk?'

'No, no…dunk away. And an excellent choice, by the way. I saw you hovering over a Hobnob for a moment. You've got to be very careful with those.'

'Indeed. So, here's the thing with the charity. For ages, I've been looking at various MS charities to see which of them might be suitable beneficiaries of the money I hope to raise from the book. And they're all splendid, all very worthy. But then I had a thought: what if I set up my own MS foundation and keep it running after all the book business has finished? A longer-term project that I can devote myself to on an ongoing basis. That would enable me to contribute a lot more to the cause and would be much more rewarding. So, that's what I've done. I've established the Robert Taylor Foundation. And I want you to be involved in some capacity. What do you think about that?'

'I don't know quite what to say,' said Vince. 'What would it involve?'

'I don't know yet, but I need to get people on board to do a whole host of things – patrons, ambassadors, advisors, financial people, administrative people, and so on. Newton Burns has agreed to be an ambassador, bless him, and he's helping a lot with contacts. And I've got a number of people from the ballet world keen to be involved, as well as other professional people who are willing to work on a *pro bono* basis. It's still early days, and nothing's set in stone, but I'd like you to play a part in my little venture.'

'I'm still not sure—'

'Don't worry about that now. I'll keep you posted and let you know when I think you can help with something. That sound okay?'

'Okay.'

'Now, the other thing I want to talk to you about is your own health. Neil tells me you've had a bit of a setback. Pulmonary, yes?'

'Yes, a bit of difficulty breathing. I saw a consultant, and he—'

'Dr. Singh?

'Yes…'

'He's on my list of people to see. I'm meeting him next week for lunch. Sorry, please carry on.'

'Well, we discussed possible causes, and it might be something to do with my medication.'

'I'm sure Dr. Singh will steer you in the right direction. I've heard very good things about him. But I'd also like to offer you some advice of my own. Would you mind that, Vince?'

'No, please…'

Margaret proceeded to tell Vince about Robert, what she had learned from the experience of his illness, and what she knew now that she wishes she had known then. She had read and researched widely, and she was more convinced than ever that, while the right physical treatment and medication were very important, so was the right state of mind and spirit. For years she had practised yoga, meditation, and what had recently come to be known as mindfulness, and she knew absolutely that they worked. And her own professional training and years of experience as a ballet dancer had taught her a lot about posture and breath control.

'In a nutshell, I think I can help you,' she said. 'Will you work with me on this, Vince?'

Forty

Scherzo Number Two

Preparations for prelims were something of a mixed bag. Danny continued in fine form, his voice proving to be stronger every time the quartet sang together. He had found a new level of confidence from somewhere, and for a lead singer in particular, confidence was an invaluable commodity. To add to the credit side of the balance sheet, Neil was making good progress on one or two vocal issues of his own, including how to create a consistently resonant, forward-placed sound. On the debit side, Vince's breath control was still a worry. As for Henry, there were no big problems with his singing, but he seemed detached and distant a lot of the time, which didn't help matters.

Last time they competed at prelims, they were a new quartet, bubbling with raw energy and enthusiasm, and propelled by Ken's inspirational words and genius coaching methods. They were lacking in vocal technique and quality in key areas, but they were on a mission to improve, and fast. There were no high expectations, but desire burned inside them. They were in search of The Fifth Voice.

That was two years ago. In the intervening months, life had taken them all in different directions, and set them new challenges. But that was no excuse.

As Neil reflected on this, comparing then to now, the contrast seemed stark. And if he allowed himself to think negatively – not his natural inclination – then he might conclude that there was no way they could rediscover the ingredients that brought them the success they achieved in so short a time with Ken's guidance.

Ken. It all came back to Ken. Maybe he was the only difference that mattered. Neil wondered, could there be a way of recreating what Ken had done for them two years ago?

At first, Vince was sceptical about Margaret's offer. But then, what could he lose? Had she come across as eccentric, he would probably have steered clear. But she didn't. Everything she said seemed entirely plausible. Her experience with Robert's illness, her research, and the practical knowledge of physical and meditative techniques she'd acquired over many years, all rang true. She was pragmatic and purposeful, and Vince could see just why Neil was the way he was. Like mum, like son.

And so Vince embarked on a series of visits to Neil's family home to spend time with Margaret, working on specific exercises and practicing meditation, while all the time focusing on improving his breathing.

'Welcome to my sanctum,' Margaret said, the first time she led Vince to the room she used as her exercise and meditation space. 'This is where I come to relax and get away from George.'

The room definitely had a kind of zen vibe going on, Vince thought, though far from your classic hippie's den smelling of patchouli, with jumbo Rizlas lying around and a bong in the corner. The mood was mostly set by the lighting, which was low and warm. On a tall bookcase, arranged by shelf, were books on health (MS featured heavily), exercise (yoga, pilates), meditation, music (Tchaikovsky, Prokofiev, Rachmaninov), and ballet (Nureyev, Ballanchine, Forsythe). An ornate fireplace gave the appearance of a little shrine, with figurines, incense sticks, and tea light holders. On the floor were an oriental rug and a large rectangular rubber mat.

The first difficulty Vince could see was sitting, as the floor was the only place available to do so. Getting down onto the floor wasn't so much the problem – he could simply crash land

– but getting up again was. He didn't have the strength in his legs to lever himself up in the normal way, and had to haul himself by his arms with the aid of whatever heavy fixed objects were nearby. It didn't make for easy viewing, and when he'd been in that situation before he tended to give the appearance of a beached dolphin trying to thrash its way back to sea. He needn't have worried. Margaret apologised for the oversight and brought in a comfortable upright chair.

Sessions usually started with a hot drink (green tea wasn't all that bad) followed by some gentle stretching exercises. Then Margaret would adjust Vince's posture, remind him which muscles were important to utilise, and then take him through a sequence of exercises intended to control, and then prolong, his breathing. They would meditate with eyes closed, with the focus again on controlled breathing.

Except for the odd occasion, if Vince started a session with breathing problems, they were almost always alleviated by the end. And the difference it made to quartet rehearsals was noticeable. Neil was the first to say so.

And then Neil realised something blindingly obvious. His mother was helping Vince with his breathing because of the side-effects of MS, and it was having a positive effect. But breath control is absolutely central to everything singers do, and all singers can benefit from help in mastering breathing technique. *If Ma can help Vince, she can help all four of us.*

'So, do I get paid for this?' Margaret said, when Neil first sounded her out about the idea. 'Only joking, of course I'll help. It was only a matter of time before I suggested something along those lines myself. Working with Vince solo is one thing, but I need to see how he gets on when he's in quartet – when the adrenalin is flowing, and the demands on his breathing are greater.'

And so it was agreed that, whenever possible, they would rehearse at Neil's place, at times to fit in with Margaret's schedule.

Neil kept working on the puzzle…*could there be a way of recreating what Ken had done for them two years ago?*

He thought back to the times they had rehearsed at Ken and Bella's place. It was a rambling old farmhouse set in a couple of acres of woodland in the Buckinghamshire countryside. His music room was magnificent, with polished wooden floors, high ceilings, and crystal chandeliers. A Steinway grand piano was just one of many musical instruments in the room.

On one occasion, he played Chopin's *Scherzo Number Two in B-flat minor, Opus Thirty-One* for them, and it had reduced Neil to tears. Ken said that, while he had learned the piece over forty years ago, it took him twenty years to get it right. He was demonstrating the importance of relentless practice, and it put fire in their bellies. Later that evening, they sang for Ken like they'd never sung before. He would never forget Ken's words afterwards:

'*Did you sense it?*'

'Sense what?' Neil had asked.

'*Why, The Fifth Voice, dear boy. You've found The Fifth Voice.*'

If only they could rediscover that profound sense of inspiration. Ken was gone, but would it be possible…would Bella allow them to rehearse, just once, in Ken's music room?

'There you all are… Ken's boys! How lovely to see you. Come in, come in.'

Bella ushered them into the large hallway, the walls of which were covered in picture frames containing old family photographs and a selection of Bella's watercolours. She led them to a warm, cosy living room, sat them all down, and asked them what they'd like to drink. 'Margaritas, for old time's sake?' she said.

'Ah, I remember your famous cocktails,' said Vince. 'The best Margaritas I've ever had!'

'But Ken always had a banana daiquiri, of course,' said Danny.

'It's so kind of you, Bella, but it's a little early, and we don't want to put you to any more trouble,' said Neil. 'We're so grateful you allowed us—'

'Oh, hush now. How could I refuse Ken's boys? I'm only too happy to help. So, will you have tea or coffee, then?'

They chatted with Bella for a while, catching up on this and that. She was as vivacious as ever, her bright blue eyes still twinkled and her white hair, fashioned in an asymmetric bob, gave her a youthful look. She was happy to reminisce about Ken, and they all remembered him with deep affection. Only one subject was off limits, as if by some unspoken agreement, and that was the subject of Ken's letters.

'So, let me show you to the music room,' Bella said at last. 'That's where the magic happened, as they say…'

They entered the room with a sense of reverence. Some of the many instruments Ken had possessed were no longer on display, but the Steinway still took pride of place. And around the walls, reminders of Ken's lifetime in music were still there, including the famous photograph of Ken singing in a barbershop quartet with Newton Burns on the BBC's *The Good Old Days* in the early '70s.

'Make yourselves at home, and sing to your heart's content,' said Bella. 'I'm just through there if you need anything.'

'Could I ask a favour?' said Neil.

'Yes, dear?'

'Would it be okay if I played Ken's piano a little? He once played Chopin for us, and it inspired us so much. It would be an honour to play his beautiful Steinway.'

'Was it *Scherzo Number Two in B-flat minor, Opus Thirty-One*?' asked Bella.

'Yes, yes it was,' said Neil.

'His favourite piece. I have a video of Ken playing it if you'd like to see it.'

Each year at the preliminary contest of the British quartet championships, around forty quartets compete to be among the sixteen who will take part in the final stages of the contest.

From The Edge were scheduled to perform at 2.30pm. They allowed plenty of time for the drive to Birmingham, and arrived at the Conservatoire with an hour and a half to spare.

'From this point on, we're in the zone,' said Neil. 'You know the routine. And we're doing it Ken's way.'

They changed into their stage clothes. They sipped lots of water and ate bananas for energy. They did some gentle stretches, ran some vocal warm-up exercises, and then sang through their contest songs, all the time mindful of their breathing.

Minutes before they were due on stage, they formed a huddle. Neil spoke.

'This is it. We're ready. Breathe slowly, together. Let the nerves go. Remember Ken's last words to us. *I know you will succeed, because you have found The Fifth Voice.* Let's go, guys.'

Neil led them on to the stage.

Vince's breathing held up.

They qualified for the British quartet championships.

Forty-One

Getting Down To Work

If Margaret's work with Vince was paying off, the nature of his condition was such that you never knew what might happen next. He tried stopping certain medications, but what he gained on the pulmonary swings he lost on the mobility roundabout. *I wouldn't be able to get out of bed, never mind sing* proved uncannily accurate. But mind over matter seemed to be the thing that Vince could turn to if all else failed. He was a determined bugger when he was up against it. So, he resumed the medication, focused more than ever on breathing therapy, and carried on. He also decided to do something about Henry.

For the most part, Henry remained subdued, and Vince was sad to see that his role as the elder statesman of the group seemed somehow diminished as a result. Henry was committed to every rehearsal, and applied himself to whatever they were working on, but his old sparkle wasn't there. And it had been a while since he'd decorated his usual eloquence by dipping into his vast store of Churchillian quotes.

As only Vince knew what was eating away at Henry, he told him that he was there for him if he needed to talk. He thought the chances of Henry opening up any further than he'd done at Heathrow were zero to slim, but he was wrong.

They were in a coffee shop following a morning rehearsal and, to Vince's surprise, Henry's sluice gates were wide open within minutes.

'I've spent my life being mister proper…mister achiever… mister loyal,' he said. 'I was in for the long haul with Jenny. We built a life together, and I did my best to make it as good as it could be. But guess what? It wasn't good enough. She wasn't interested in *us*, only herself. And she looked elsewhere. Not that she had any intention of telling me, of course. It was a classic case of gullible bloke being turned over by a self-absorbed schemer who knows a decent meal ticket when she sees one.'

Vince really wasn't expecting this.

'Then I find Cat. Wow, what a difference: a woman who actually shows an interest and cares. We had things in common, but a lot of it was about the differences. Me the City boy with all the material trappings, Cat the island girl who couldn't care less about those things: a free spirit, a breath of fresh air. We learned from each other. I was fascinated by her work on the island, and her ideas about everything. And she was interested in my music, and what I had to say about the world. We were able to help one another. It felt good, it just sort of worked. And I thought the long-distance thing was part of what made it work, the romance of it all. It turns out I was wrong. I even offered to move over there when the time was right.'

'You still could,' said Vince.

'Not for a good while, not until we've…'

'It's your choice.'

'Not any longer it isn't. It's over.'

'How do you know for sure?'

'She said as much.'

'*As much?* I don't think it's over,' said Vince.

The following weeks were all about getting down to work. They had got through prelims, but they were a long way off where they needed to be in terms of quality of singing and performance.

Neil continued to look for ways of motivating the guys, of keeping things fresh: learning new songs, more challenging songs, working with coaches from Maidenhead A Cappella and elsewhere, and performing as guests on shows around the south east whenever there was an opportunity.

They all worked on personal goals. Danny continued to test himself by singing solo at open mic nights. For Vince, it was all about breathing, and he set himself incremental targets for how long he could post a note and hold it. Neil kept working on his forward placement and resonance. And Henry concentrated on taking the weight out of his voice at the bottom end and singing with a lighter tone.

Together they worked not just in quartet, but also in duets, to make sure that their voices were closely matched in vowel integrity and tonal quality. They worked tirelessly on their contest songs: on the ballad, to find the best way to deliver the story of the song with conviction, and on the up-tune to nail the harmonic rhythm and complex counterpoint. And much more.

They all dug deep in their own ways, despite whatever else was going on in their lives. Which included the small matter of a joint wedding and christening.

Forty-Two

The Double Celebration

'Shall we go somewhere with male strippers, that kind of thing?' said Hannah.

'What a dreadful thought,' said Angie.

'Think of it as karma,' said Hannah. 'All those years being ogled by men, now here's your chance to turn the tables...role reversal!'

'I've no desire to see some oiled-up gym bunny with acne flopping it around like a two year-old. You know what I mean? That thing little boys do...playing with it, flaunting it at every opportunity. I don't want some twenty year-old steroidal nitwit doing the same right in front of my face.'

'Okay, how about we round up a load of girls, dress up like tarts, and go on a massive pub crawl with a four foot inflatable willy?'

'No, I'm not having that either. Here's a radical idea: how about we go for a lovely meal, something special like a Michelin star place, just the three of us?'

'Three?'

'You, me, and the inflatable willy.'

'Brilliant. So, that's the christening party sorted. Now, what about the hen do?'

It took several minutes of giggling before they were able to say another word. At last, Hannah calmed down sufficiently to ask: 'Do you think the boys are having as much fun planning a stag do?'

*

Vince was looking tired and thoughtful. Tired because they had just finished a marathon rehearsal session, thoughtful because of his impending nuptials and everything that entailed.

They were scattered around the conservatory at Neil's house, making the place look untidy. Danny and Neil were sprawled across a large floral print sofa. Henry was lying on his back on the floor, holding his raised knees and twisting awkwardly from side to side. 'Back's playing up,' he said, not that anyone required an explanation.

By contrast, Vince was sitting bolt upright in a rattan chair, the fingers of both hands pressed together with the index fingers touching his mouth, in a gesture reminiscent of Sherlock Holmes in one of his more ponderous moods. He was contemplating what appeared to be a two-pipe problem at least.

Having filled the room with the sounds of vocal drills, many repetitions of their contest songs, and no shortage of lively chat for the last three hours, they were content to enjoy relative quiet for a while. Outside, the large, flat garden lawn glinted silver as the winter sunlight slanted across its frosty surface. A blue tit feeding upside down from a seed dispenser was being chased away by a nuthatch, sending seeds scattering in all directions. A black cat hopped onto the top of a wooden fence from next door, beginning to show interest.

The conservatory was warm and cosy, and eyes were closing when Vince broke the silence. 'I can't choose a best man,' he said.

Eyes opened slowly, and they looked around at one another. It wasn't a statement for which there was an obvious or immediate reply. Henry, who had stopped gyrating and was now curled up on the floor, made a gently inquisitive noise. 'Mmmmm?' The others closed their eyes again, waiting for Vince to elaborate.

'I mean, you're all excellent candidates in your own ways.'

'Once an HR manager, always an HR manager,' said Danny in a slow drawl. 'Would you like us to submit our CVs?

Mine's two years' old, it probably needs updating...'

'Nice one, matey,' said Vince. 'But, seriously, how can I choose between the three of you?'

'You're assuming we're all interested in the position,' said Neil softly.

'Well, if you're not, that would narrow the field, so thank you for that contribution,' said Vince. 'But, listen, here's the thing. I would like you all to be my best man...best men. Is that possible?'

'The Church of England is fairly flexible on most things these days,' said Henry from the comfort of his foetal position. 'Most things get the nod so long as the financials are commensurate.'

'Really? Well, I'll have a word with the vicar in that case. That's that one sorted. Now, what are we going to do about a stag party?'

There was a general stirring of bodies, yawning, and stretching of limbs.

'Did you just say *stag party*?' said Neil. 'Seriously?'

'Well, I'm not thinking of the full-on variety,' said Vince. 'No tarring and feathering and being chained to lamp posts... just a nice meal, a few drinks, and a visit to The Honey Pot in Maidenhead to finish off the evening.'

Neil took aim with a cushion and caught Vince full in the face.

The hen and stag evenings came and went without undue incident, preparations for the wedding and christening went into full swing, and before they knew it the big day had arrived.

Guests were arriving at Holy Trinity church, Cookham, which was just around the corner from the Stanley Spencer gallery Neil and Vince had visited almost a year earlier. Spencer had made a big impression on Vince, and as Holy Trinity featured in his paintings, he had a special affinity for the building and its beautiful riverside setting. Angie had set her heart on a church wedding, and though they were not residents of the parish, they were able to secure a dispensation to be married in the venerable Norman church that had served the village community since the twelfth century.

An overnight frost and thickish fog had cleared, the air was crisp, and a lazy sun was showing signs of peaking through a light covering of cloud. The running order was wedding first, christening second. Vince had suggested to Danny that it should be the other way round, on the basis that he was part of the headline act, and headliners always close the show. Common sense had prevailed when Angie and Hannah took charge of the arrangements.

Danny and Hannah were talking to a couple of Hannah's old equestrian friends in the churchyard, while Ben played peek-a-boo with Ellie, jumping out from behind gravestones. Ellie was straining to escape her buggy and was becoming impatient. Hannah's mum Dorothy came to the rescue, lifting her out and walking her by the hand to where Ben was playing.

Neil, Margaret, and George were nearby, talking about Newton Burns, who was on business in America and unable to be there. Vince and Henry were inside the church with Vince's sister, Jo, and Angie's mother, Shelley. Trish, Angie's friend from her modelling days, was also there with boyfriend Tim. The pews were filling up nicely, and now the vicar, standing at the church entrance, invited everyone to come inside and be seated.

Vince took up his position in the front pew, with Danny to his immediate right, then Neil, then Henry, all in a row.

A signal was given, the church organ piped up, and Angie and her father began their slow procession towards the altar. Henry checked his right-hand jacket pocket for the small box he'd placed there earlier. At the appropriate point in the service, it was his job to pass it to Neil, whose job was to pass it to Danny, whose job was to open the box, take out Angie's wedding ring, and pass it to Vince. And when the moment came, the best man relay routine went without a hitch. Or, to put it another way, *with* a hitch: Angie and Vince were pronounced husband and wife.

None of the guests were quite sure how the transition from wedding to christening would work, and nor did the principal players, come to that. It was a case of smiles and congratulations all round as Angie and Vince marched slowly back up the aisle before taking up position at the baptismal font at the rear of the church. They were joined by Hannah, Danny, Ellie, and Ben, with the vicar on hand to shuffle them around a bit, and take his own place for the start of Act Two. A few of the congregation came forward to get a better view of proceedings, but most stayed in their pews, swivelling round to face the action.

It was all very relaxed, as one service slipped into the next, Angie and Vince making way for Hannah, Danny, and the children. The vicar said a few words about the novelty of the occasion and made a joke about not being paid overtime. Hannah bent down to whisper in Ellie's ear, and she nodded, allowing Hannah to pick her up and hold her in her arms. The vicar changed gears, switching from match to hatch mode, and started on the business of welcoming Ellie into the family of the church. She seemed to know it was her time to shine, as she grinned throughout, raising murmurs of affectionate approval from the congregation. Not even the head-wetting seemed to bother her, and she behaved with the aplomb of one who knows it is her destiny to be centre stage.

'She's showing off again,' said Ben, to the amusement of everyone.

The reception was held in the function room of a local pub, with around thirty people in attendance. Angie and Vince had insisted on it being a relaxed affair, dispensing with some of the more formal points of wedding reception etiquette, including the number and sequence of the speeches. Angie's father, Alan, gave a short but heartfelt discourse on paternal pride, and Angie said a few words about her own pride and joy at the occasion. Hannah congratulated the newlyweds, and thanked everyone for putting up with not one, but two services. When it came to the official best man's speech, Danny, Neil, and Henry all stood up.

'Unaccustomed…' said Danny.

'…as I am…' said Neil.

'…to public speaking…' said Henry.

There was a mixture of laughs and groans from the guests, and then Danny and Henry sat down, giving the floor to Neil, who gave a warm and humorous speech on behalf of all three of them.

Finally it was Vince's turn. He rose to his feet and stared around the room with a look of menace. His cheeks seemed swollen, as if padded from the inside.

'Some people call me The Groom,' he said, and then paused for a full five seconds.

'But from now on, I will be known as… The Godfather!'

His Marlon Brando impression was spot on, and the guests responded appreciatively. Then, removing the pieces of bread roll he had concealed inside his mouth, Vince switched his attention to Angie, and confessed to being just a little nervous at the prospect of being serious for a moment. He spoke of his love for his wife, and of the challenges they had faced together. There were more jokes, some a little near the knuckle, and after three minutes of material that was so well rehearsed that it seemed improvised, he concluded:

'I can't tell you all how lucky and proud I am to have this wonderful, beautiful woman alongside me every step of the way.'

Forty-Three

The Book Launch

Margaret was close to panic, and as someone to whom panic was as alien as a condom to a Catholic priest, that was saying something. Final preparations for the book launch were in full swing, and she fretted as a small army of organisers and helpers busied themselves around her.

Was the room suitable? It looked odd-shaped, too many areas where the line of sight might be obstructed. She'd imagined a simple open space in which everything was in plain view. An ideal location, she had been assured, one of the most popular venues for literary events in London. She supposed the PR people knew what they were doing, but that didn't stop her worrying. *Calm down, Margaret, this is so unlike you.*

At last, she decided to avail herself of a side room that didn't appear to be in use, where she could sit in relative quiet and breathe deeply. *Practice what you teach, Margaret.*

The room was largely empty, except for a pile of cardboard boxes, a few empty catering trays stacked on a long trestle table, and a couple of plastic chairs. She closed the door behind her and pulled up a chair so that it faced an external window looking out over grey London rooftops. She closed her eyes, closed her ears to the muffled sounds of people busy in the main room, and took a series of slow deep breaths until she was calmer and more in control. In her mind, she ran through a list of things that needed to be in place for the launch, and couldn't think of any detail that hadn't been attended to.

Just then came a gentle knock at the door, which opened slowly.

'Hello, Mags?'

Margaret opened her eyes as the huge friendly face of Newton Burns appeared before her. 'Someone told me you were in here. Just checking to see you're all right,' he said.

In another room in the same building, From The Edge were in the middle of warming up when Vince started hiccupping. They paused to allow him to gather himself, but after ten minutes there was no respite.

Vince went through some of the exercises Margaret had taught him, but every time he was about to signal the all clear, the hiccups started again. 'Shit,' he said, remembering something Dr. Singh had mentioned. 'The consultant said something about hiccups. You know, an MS thing.'

'Stay calm,' said Danny. 'You'll be—'

'I'm going to find Ma,' said Neil. 'She might be able to help.'

Margaret was on the scene minutes later, happy to help, and relieved that she could take her mind off the launch preparations and attend to something else. She left Newton Burns bemused to learn that a severe case of hiccups required her immediate attention. 'It's a long story,' she said.

The room was buzzing as the evening was about to begin. The focal point was a small, brightly lit stage area with a back projection showing the cover of Margaret's autobiography, *A Dancer Domesticated*, alongside the logo of the newly established Robert Taylor Foundation. In the centre was a lectern topped with a microphone, and to one side a table stacked with copies of the book and promotional materials. Friends, family, agents, publishers, actors, dancers, reporters, and publicity people filled the room, chatting excitedly, as waiting staff snaked their way adeptly through the crowd offering drinks and finger food.

The lighting in the room dimmed a fraction, and the unmistakable figure of Newton Burns approached the lectern to lively applause.

'Good evening, ladies and gentlemen, and a warm welcome to the launch of a very special book, the autobiography of a remarkable lady I first met over forty years ago when she came to London to dance with the Royal Ballet. Prior to that, Mags had made it all the way to *première danseuse* with the Paris Opera Ballet at the age of just twenty-one...unprecedented for a young English dancer at the time. After a season as guest artist with the Royal Ballet she then moved to English National Ballet, where she spent the rest of her dancing career. In her time, she danced the great roles: Juliet, Odette-Odile, Beauty, and many more. She even worked with Nureyev, would you believe?

'As you can tell, I'm not exactly sparing your blushes, Mags. This, ladies and gentlemen, is a woman whose arabesque was world-renowned, the envy of the ballet world. And I wouldn't mind betting she's still got it − hey, Mags? But seriously, and I'm almost done with the cringing introduction, this is a woman whose life *after* ballet is every bit as remarkable. She might call it ordinary, but I choose to call it remarkable. To this day, she still runs ballet classes in her village, she's a stalwart of the WI, and she does all sorts of charity work that goes unnoticed to you and me. Which brings me to the Robert Taylor Foundation, the charity established by Margaret herself to help fund further research into MS, and it's very much the driving force of this evening's event. At which point, I will introduce the lady herself to tell you about *A Dancer Domesticated* and the Robert Taylor Foundation. So, please welcome...the rather marvellous Margaret Taylor.'

Margaret walked towards the lectern amidst rapturous applause, embraced Newt, then composed herself.

'Thank you so much. I don't know what to say after that introduction...he does lay it on thick, doesn't he? But thank you, Newt, for your generous words, and to all of you for being here this evening. It means more to me than I can say.

'All of that dancing stuff was a long time ago, you know…it almost seems like another life. After I finished dancing I settled down, married dear George, and had two wonderful sons, Robert and Neil. Neil's here this evening – there he is over there – and I couldn't be more proud of him. With his vocal harmony group he's doing some great things at the moment…and I'll come back to that in a moment. But my elder son, Robert, died almost five years ago, at the age of thirty-two. He had MS. And I would give up every accolade, every achievement in my career as a dancer, to have him back. That goes without saying. Any mother would say the same.

'I was persuaded some time ago that it would be a good idea to write an autobiography. I couldn't see who would be interested – and that's not just me being modest. By then, my dancing days were so far in the past, and I'd done so much else since, that I had to scratch my head and think…*really*? You see, I'd become… domesticated, as the title of the book suggests. But there seemed to be an appetite for my story, so I set to work. And what seemed to me to be a vanity exercise to begin with only took on a sense of real importance when I asked the question "what good can come of this?…who else can benefit?" And the answer wasn't that difficult to find. It became clear that I should write the book in Robert's memory, with whatever money it raised going towards further research into MS. You see, Robert was someone who helped others. He was a surgeon, and he routinely helped to make people better, even save their lives. So it seemed right.

'And then one day I discovered that one of the guys in Neil's vocal harmony group, his good friend Vince, is himself an MS sufferer. At which point, I became even more committed to the cause, even more driven to help in the fight against this dreadful illness. Vince, like Robert, like many thousands of people in this country, find themselves in a daily battle just to get through. And so, because of the connection, I thought it would be a good idea to invite Neil, Vince, and the boys to entertain you a little later on – a bit of light relief when all the serious stuff is out of the way.

'But for now, I'd like to read a couple of passages from the book. You didn't think you'd get away without a reading, did you? Let me start with this one. The year is 1961, the place is Paris, I'm nineteen, I've just started rehearsing the part of Clara in The Nutcracker, and into my life comes Dmitri…'

Margaret gave a huge sigh of relief as the last of the guests drifted away into the London night. It had gone well. Her throat was a little sore, and her right hand ached slightly from signing many more books than she imagined she would, but she was content. Her agent was pleased, as apparently was the publisher, and the PR people had come good. There would be publicity aplenty, and the profile of the Robert Taylor Foundation would be raised to new levels.

She was sipping champagne with George, Newt, Neil, Vince, Danny, and Henry, and all in all, she was happy. Vince was less so. For the last ten minutes he had been conducting a post mortem of their performance in his head, and at last he spoke.

'I hiccupped while Neil was doing his introduction, and then again at the end of the first song. People must have thought I was drunk.'

'Nonsense,' said Newt. 'I was all eyes and ears, and I didn't notice anything.'

'Me neither,' said George. 'You did a fine job, my boy. You were all tremendous.'

'I can honestly say that's the best I've heard the four of you sing. No word of a lie,' said Margaret. 'The evening was a big success, and you boys were the icing on the cake. Everyone I spoke to said how fantastic you were.'

'It's not just the hiccups,' said Vince. 'I wasn't breathing properly towards the end of the second song. I ran out of breath on that long held note towards the end.'

Neil was sitting back, listening with a big grin on his face.

'What's amusing you?' said Vince.

Neil sat forward. 'The way we sang tonight was right up there. A-grade. And the fact that you're nit-picking at that level means we're close to the top of our game. It was a small detail, just one note. Nobody will have noticed. And that shows how far we've come. We're nearly there, chaps.'

Forty-Four

The Big One

Neil's reassurance that they were close to the top of their game was what they needed as they made the final push towards Harrogate and the British quartet championships. It gave them an important measure of progress and the sense that they were beginning to peak at just the right time. They all took satisfaction from their performance at Margaret's book launch, except for Vince.

Neil was a hard taskmaster and wasn't one to throw praise around lightly, so if he said they were hitting top form, then it was true. But the whole breathing thing was bugging Vince badly. Occasional bouts of hiccups were a nuisance, but they didn't matter once he was singing, as the very act of singing made them go away. It was his reduced ability to apply the subtleties of controlled breathing mid-song that were annoying him, and that showed up particularly when the tenor had the melody. His biggest annoyance, however, was that his ability to sustain long held notes was still not what it was, and there were a couple of places in their contest songs where that mattered. And he wasn't having it. Something like that could cost them all-important points.

So Vince decided to stop taking the muscle relaxants that he knew were at the root of the problem. Yes, it would cause difficulties in other areas, but he had to do it for the sake of the others. And the others didn't need to know.

Almost three weeks later, Vince's legs were stiff and painful, walking was hard work, and he tired very easily. But he was nailing those long held notes.

It was the eve of the British quartet championships, and memories were flooding back. On the same day at roughly the same time two years ago, they were sitting a few hundred yards away in Harrogate's Valley Gardens admiring the colourful spring flowers in glorious sunshine. Today they were dodging heavy rain showers and were ensconced at a window table in Bettys Café Tea Rooms. Not that a window table conferred any advantage, as the windows were steamed up due to the large number of people in the shop, all of whom had apparently decided that the only sure way to fight off the gloom of a rainy Yorkshire morning was to gorge on tea and Fat Rascal scones.

'This time two years ago I was single,' said Vince.

'This time two years ago we'd just found out that Hannah was pregnant with Ellie,' said Danny.

'This time two years ago, I'd just started with Yellow Braces,' said Neil.

Henry excused himself and left the table.

It was late afternoon, and they were in Neil's hotel room for a final full rehearsal ahead of the competition. The plan was to spend an hour and a half running the songs and focusing on the final touches to finesse their performance. Before they started, Neil said that he had received several good luck messages, and was reading a few of them aloud.

'Bella sends her love: "To Ken's boys, it was wonderful to see you, and from what I heard, you're sounding fantastic. I know you'll do Ken proud. Love, Bella."

'Here's one from James Pinter: "The best of luck, lads, and don't bother coming back to Maidenhead A Cappella unless you've got something shiny to show us."

'A text from Newt: "Gentlemen, I am distraught that I won't be in Harrogate with you, but I have pressing business with *A Cappella Fellas* to attend to. If your recent performance in London is anything to go by, I'm sure you'll do wonderfully well. And remember, Ken's up there willing you on. Love, Newt."

'Well, well! A message from our old friend Cliff "Tonsils" Thompson. He says, "Knock 'em dead, and I'll be hollerin' for ya from across the pond, Best wishes, Cliff." Oh, and he's attached a photo. You'll love this…he's wearing the same t-shirt as last time we saw him, the one that says "*Life's A Pitch*", with tartan shorts and knee-length white socks. Mind you, he looks like he's lost a bit of weight.' Neil passed his phone around.

Vince checked his own phone. 'I don't believe it. Brad Frampton. He says, "To my Soho buddy, have a blast – love to the guys, Brad." Well, who would have thought…'

'Has anyone else from *A Cappella Fellas* sent a message?' said Danny.

Neil shuffled in his chair a little. 'Yes, I received something from Joey Pellegrini,' he said hesitantly.

'Well, come on, read it out,' said Vince.

'I…well, it doesn't read very…you see, it's a little…'

'Out with it, Neil. This sounds interesting,' Vince insisted.

'I think I ought to explain the context before I…'

Vince gave Neil one of his no-nonsense stares.

Neil called up the message and cleared his throat. '"Dear Aerobic Guy, I'll always remember the fun we had singing, and that day in the gym. Wishing you and the boys lots of luck, Muscle Guy."'

Vince, who had been feeling uncomfortably stiff and lethargic, felt the sudden, invigorating rush of hilarity take hold. 'What the fuck?!' was all he could spit out before giving in to hysterics, with Danny, and even Henry, incapable of resisting.

It took Neil a little while to explain, once order had been restored.

*

Angie, Hannah, Ben, and Ellie drove up to Harrogate together, setting off very early on Saturday morning. The kids watched DVDs in the back seats, Ben sang Danny's name in the style of a football chant, and Ellie filled the cabin with a noxious odour that forced a premature pit stop. As a treat, they went to Burger King. Back in the car, they played *Eye Spy*, sang songs, and Ben and Ellie eventually fell asleep.

Margaret and George travelled to Yorkshire a couple of days in advance to visit an old friend of Margaret's in Pontefract.

They all met up at the international conference centre in Harrogate on Saturday morning, where the British barbershop community had once again come together in impressive numbers. The thousand-seat auditorium was brim full of singers and their supporters from around the country. Everywhere you went, singers stood around in quartets or larger groups, singing, practising, and doing what they loved best.

From The Edge were due on stage at 11.30am, so there was little time for further rehearsal beforehand. Neil was in full-on inspirational mode, assuring them that they were ready. Danny was calm and confident. Henry was subdued but focused. Vince was in pain and his legs were as heavy as lead, but he said nothing.

In their dressing room, they got ready and checked that their stage gear was neat and tidy. Henry placed the small granite stone flecked with grey, white and orange crystalline patterns in the pocket of his dress trousers.

They checked their phones one final time and shared a couple of late good luck messages that had arrived. As Henry was about to switch off his phone, it buzzed in his hand. The message read: 'Let your heart sing and fly back soon.'

Henry walked over to Vince, who had been watching him, and smiled. 'The era of procrastination, of half measures, of soothing and baffling expedients, of delays, is coming to a close,' he said softly.

'Good to have you back, Winnie,' said Vince. 'You should

give that speech right now. It couldn't be more appropriate to the moment.'

'No, I think not,' said Henry. 'Neil's the only man for that particular job.'

Minutes later, they gathered in a close circle and put their arms around each other's shoulders. As usual, they waited for Neil to speak the familiar words.

'This is it. We're ready. Breathe slowly, together. Let the nerves go. Remember Ken's last words to us. *I know you will succeed, because you have found The Fifth Voice*. Let's go, guys.'

Neil led them to the stage, where they delivered the performance of their lives.

As they exited the stage and reached the wings, Vince collapsed. As they gathered around him, loosening his collar, offering him water, and checking his breathing, he looked up at each of them in turn, his face drained of colour. 'I'm just off to see Ken,' he said, before his eyes closed.

Angie, Danny, Hannah, Neil, and Henry stood in silence at the bedside. Vince was at rest, his face a mask of peacefulness, his hands together across his chest.

'I'm just off to see Ken' turned out to be an overly dramatic pronouncement. Vince had collapsed of exhaustion, but his vital signs were all good. He needed to sleep for a long time, but he was fine.

Neil reached into a pocket and took out a long purple ribbon, attached to which was a gold medal. He draped it across Vince's hands like a rosary, so that it would be the first thing he saw when he woke up.

Forty-Five

The Final Letter

Gentlemen,

Me again, but I promise this is my final message.

As you know, my previous letter was delivered contingent upon certain circumstances, and as I'm sure you've guessed, those circumstances were that you didn't win the British quartet championships at your first attempt and that you were not singing together again by the end of the year. So, if you're reading this, then thank you for fulfilling my wish and sincerest congratulations on becoming British Quartet Champions. Wear those gold medals with pride.

Congratulations also on playing your part in 'A Cappella Fellas', the project closest to my dearest friend Newt's heart. You will have spotted the obvious parallel between the quartet in the film and your good selves: A Cappella Fellas just miss out on winning a national competition at their first attempt, but then we had to allow for the possibility of a sequel! I'm sure you won't have to look too closely to spot a few more parallels.

More than anything, you've harnessed the full power of The Fifth Voice, which was always my sincerest wish. Your singing success is testament to that, but so is the way you came through difficulties in your lives, winning against the odds. So please allow me a few final words to each of you.

Neil, as baritones do, you held the quartet together. Your supreme talent and your passion were the glue.

Henry, as the bass, you were the foundation of the quartet, steady and strong. Like granite, you could say.

Danny, as the lead, your job was to tell the story. I have a feeling your own story was largely locked away, but when you sang, what beauty you released!

Vince, in so many ways you were the driving force, battling against adversity with roguish humour. As the tenor, your job was to sprinkle the stardust. And oh, how you did it!

Travel well, and keep a song in your hearts.

Ken

P.S. You may or may not know this, but I never did win a Gold medal myself.

Read what happened before:

The Fifth Voice by Paul Connolly

The lives of four singers are far from harmonious. Danny's marriage is on the rocks, while Vince is struggling with a debilitating illness. Henry is having a mid-life crisis, and Neil is at war with his father. But when they sing together none of that matters. Because something magical happens.

On a mission to compete against the best quartet singers in Britain, they turn to veteran entertainer, Ken, who inspires them to discover a curious vocal technique called The Fifth Voice.

Over the course of a year and several adventures, they make discoveries about the power of music and friendship that help each of them shape the rest of their lives. And when they eventually find The Fifth Voice, they discover a prize much greater than the one they imagined.

Lightning Source UK Ltd.
Milton Keynes UK
UKHW041916200519
343004UK00001B/105/P

9 781781 328675